KATE MAYFIELD

Kate Mayfield consults to corporate clients, including Fortune 500 companies in the USA and Europe, where she is called upon to help their employees present a successful first impression. Her extensive experience in the worlds of self-development, entertainment and fashion, combined with having lived and worked in London, New York and Los Angeles, gives her a unique take on personal presentation.

A graduate of New York's American Academy of Dramatic Arts, Kate also received a theatre scholarship award from Western Kentucky University. She has taught the Pilates method and has trained extensively in other body awareness and movement education systems, including the Feldenkrais method and the Linklater method of freeing the natural voice.

Kate has appeared on national television in the States and numerous radio programs in the UK and USA where she discusses the topic of personal style. She is the co-author of *10 Steps to Fashion Freedom: Discover Your Personal Style from the Inside Out* and is a contributing writer to several magazines and websites.

MALCOLM LEVENE

Malcolm Levene has been teaching the art and science of personal presentation for more than twenty years. He has run several successful retail ventures and works with numerous corporations, where he offers his high level motivational training.

His corporate clients include several Fortune 500 companies and his private clients include celebrities and public figures.

Malcolm is quoted by the media on both sides of the Atlantic regarding identity, image and business style, and how it affects our level of confidence and our effectiveness in business.

He has created the *Get Real* multi-media training programme as a response to the ever-increasing distance between many modern day workers and their customers. He is a passionate advocate of 'authenticity' as a key to success in life.

Malcolm has been voted 'The Best of British Men' and the New Yorker dubbed him 'The Freud of Fashion'. He is the co-author of *10 Steps to Fashion Freedom: Discover Your Personal Style from the Inside Out.*

Ellie Hart Goes To Work

◆

A modern girl's guide to having it all

◆

Kate Mayfield
and
Malcolm Levene

Vermilion
LONDON

1 3 5 7 9 10 8 6 4 2

First published in the United Kingdom in 2004 by Vermilion,
an imprint of Ebury Press
Random House UK Ltd.
Random House
20 Vauxhall Bridge Road
London SW1V 2SA

Random House Australia (Pty) Limited
20 Alfred Street, Milsons Point, Sydney,
New South Wales 2061, Australia

Random House New Zealand Limited
18 Poland Road, Glenfield,
Auckland 10, New Zealand

Random House (Pty) Limited
Endulini, 5A Jubilee Road, Parktown 2193, South Africa

Random House UK Limited Reg. No. 954009
www.randomhouse.co.uk

Papers used by Vermilion are natural, recyclable products
made from wood grown in sustainable forests.

A CIP catalogue record is available for this book from the British Library.

ISBN: 0091898498

Printed and bound in Great Britain by
Cox and Wyman Ltd, Reading, Berkshire

For Kathy J. and Barry Mayfield

'We tend to neglect the place from which the best ideas come, namely that part of ourselves that dreams. The unconscious is our best collaborator.'

Mike Nichols

Acknowledgements

When asked if she would like to take a look at something a little different, Eileen Campbell didn't just say yes. She approached our manuscript with enthusiasm and an open mind and ushered the project with care and professionalism. Many, many thanks to Eileen for liking Ellie enough to find her a home.

Thanks due to Pat Lomax for her intelligent guidance and encouragement.

We are grateful to our publisher, Fiona MacIntyre, for her vision, magnanimous support and professionalism.

Even when we were separated by the Atlantic, the talented team at Vermilion made their positive and supportive presence felt. Amanda Hemmings, our skilful and sympathetic editor at Vermilion, with whom it has been nothing short of a dream to work, is a strong, laser-beaming light. Julia Kellaway, assistant editor, has somehow reached the summit of people who just never get ruffled. We are grateful that Helen Pisano, our kind and sensitive copy-editor, was meticulous and paid more attention to the details than we ever could.

A big thank you to Diana Riley and the other members of her marketing team, Polly Broadhurst and Dawn Burnett, for their energy, guidance and particularly for their perspective. A special thank you to Emma Lawson at Midas PR.

David and Alec of Two Associates have designed the brilliant cover. Credit and kudos go to them for endowing Ellie Hart with a face, a figure and some god-awful front cover clothes – as it should be. Thank you to them and to Philip Lord, the internal designer of the book, for their patience with all of our requests and the way they have interpreted them.

Special thanks also due to Dr George Little, whose gardening expertise inspired an entire chapter. To Jim Kakalik, the savviest of computer mavens, we now owe a lifetime of indentured servitude. Gus

Campbell we thank for his tenacious support, among other things we cannot mention.

Reverend Paul Turp of Shoreditch Church and Headmaster Mr Alasdair Friend were both very kind to two strangers. They helped us enormously by patiently and generously plying us with very relevant information.

Michael Leapman's lovely book, *The Ingenious Mr Fairchild*, was a source of inspiration and knowledge and we thank him for writing it.

Several friends, associates and family members have been kind enough to read and comment upon the manuscript at different stages. Thank you so much for taking time away from your busy lives to help.

Finally, we are indebted to our clients who, through the years, have gifted us with golden fodder.

Contents

Contents

Prologue

'Oh, no it can't be. It cannot possibly be that moment. Must I move my body out of this cosy bed?'

The alarm kept saying 'yes' as Ellie Hart of Chorleywood, Hertfordshire said 'no'. For one luscious moment she nestled down below her warm fluffy duvet, the very same duvet she had agonised over before spending all that money, but was ever so glad she did. As she remained in that state somewhere between wakefulness and sleep she thought she was about to remember a dream. The soft muted image of a face appeared in her mind but she could not make it out. Was it someone she knew? Was it a man, a woman?

Just as Ellie was about to doze off again, that peaceful moment suddenly became sheer terror. Somewhere in her groggy head she remembered that she was due at Heathrow in exactly two hours, which would have been fine except that Ellie had not even begun to pack her suitcase.

Wardrobes were flung open, clothes flew up in the air and around the room, and a leather bag fell on her head as she reached for her suitcase. 'Really must reorganise this cupboard,' she said, exasperated. Her computer accessories, those little gadgets that she endowed with personalities of their own because they always seemed to be hiding, were eventually located and thrown into a bag. Another panicky moment – where were the pages of the reports she had printed out? Her hands groped around on the floor – no ... yes, found! Thank goodness.

Ellie ran her hands through her soft brown hair, trying to remember her packing list. And then another sinking feeling came over her – she couldn't remember if she had called the mini-cab company last night. She had completely forgotten to ask her assistant to do it. But maybe her assistant had remembered to do it anyway. She peeked out of the window just in case, to see if the car was waiting for her. The street was dark and silent. 'Bloody hell!'

Ellie ran to the phone and dialled Preston's number. It rang, and rang, and rang. Finally his machine picked up. 'Preston, it's me. Preston, are you there?' Hmm. 'Why isn't he answering?' She made a mental note to find out where her boyfriend was at this hour. Next. She hated to do it but she had no choice.

A sleepy voice answered the phone. 'Wrigley,' Ellie said. 'I absolutely must get to Heathrow. I'm going to New York today.'

'Good morning, Ellie. Have you any idea what time it is?'

'I know, I know and I am so sorry, but I forgot to call a mini-cab and, and, well, Preston isn't answering his phone.' Ellie spilled out her anxiety in one breath.

'Ellie, Ellie, Ellie,' Wrigley tsk-tsked her name in a weary but patient voice.

'Please, Wriggers, please come and get me.'

'I'll be there in 15 minutes. Oh, um, Ellie?'

'Yes, Wrigley?'

'I believe that will make it 5.15 am.' Wrigley reminded her of the inconvenience of the hour.

'Sorry, sorry, Wriggers.'

Ellie rushed to get dressed – something she was used to doing. She couldn't find the suit in which she normally travelled. 'Probably at the cleaners,' she muttered. She could have closed her eyes and reached for any hanger for all she cared at this point. 'Whatever! These will have to do.' She pulled out a black jacket, a slightly wrinkled white blouse and grabbed a pair of jeans.

She knew better than to keep a friend waiting at quarter past five in the morning, so Ellie stood outside shivering in the dark with her bags, ready to hop in the car. Just as she was thinking that she could possibly kill for a hot cup of tea, Wrigley drove up in his lovingly cared-for '67 Morris Minor Traveller. The old Woody suited him perfectly; its vanilla-coloured body and shiny wooden trim made her smile even under the greyest of skies. She had christened it 'The Forager' because he spent so much time in it searching for the finest produce available for his restaurant.

You might not expect even your best friend to hop out and help you with your bags, but he did. And as she slid into the front seat he handed her a steaming cup of tea. Ellie almost cried at Wrigley's kindness and from the pure release of tension from the morning.

'Thanks for making the tea, Wrigley, but you're raving, you know,' she said, 'and you look it with your hair sticking up on end like that.' Wrigley's dark wavy hair had a mind of its own this morning. Unshaven and practically undressed – he had pulled his favourite old cashmere jumper over his pyjama bottoms, and topped the ensemble off with a leather duffle coat – somehow, he still managed to look recklessly handsome.

'But I adore you for being insane enough to do this for me.'

'Yes, well. Just don't spill your tea on my leather seat.' He smiled at her as he adjusted his horn-rimmed glasses. 'What happened, how did I end up being a part of your morning?'

'Oh, I worked late last night and instead of going home to pack, I ended up at the local wine bar with a few of my team members.'

'You're not serious.'

'Indeed I am, and why not? I've decided that I simply must try to get on better with them.'

'Did you think that going out the night before you flew off to New York was good timing? Especially since you're going to be making such an important presentation.'

'You remembered.'

'But of course. What has the divine Ms Hart been constantly worried about for I don't know how long? Has she spoken of nothing except the big presentation in New York?'

Ellie was silent as she sipped her tea.

'Well, are you ready?' asked Wrigley.

'I hope so. I just … I don't know … I *think* I am. I'd better be! But these last few meetings have been very tough. I've never done anything like this before. I'm due to see McMurty after this trip – can't wait for that. I'll be lucky to walk away from that meeting without an ear-bashing.' Ellie drew a breath. 'I don't want to think about it right now. Did I tell you that Preston didn't answer his phone this morning?'

'Yes, Ellie you did,' Wrigley said in a slightly strained tone.

'What do you think?' Ellie asked.

'What do *you* think?'

'I don't want to think about that either. By the way, I tried to call you last night. You didn't answer your mobile, were you doing something very important?'

'Oh yes, I was doing very important stuff last night.'

'Do tell.'

The car was winding its way into Heathrow now; the journey was smooth and perfectly timed. Wrigley pulled up to the kerb, looked her in the eye and with a straight face replied, 'I was playing mah-jongg with your mother.'

'Pardon? You were what?' she shrieked.

'All right, which part is so incomprehensible to you, Ellie?'

'I know you adore mah-jongg Wriggers, but really, my mother? Why?'

'I *like* your mother.'

'You amaze me. I don't understand you, but you do amaze me. Thank you for this morning. We'll discuss this problem you're having with older women when I get back. Oh my God, here I go, Wriggers, wish me luck.'

As she was walking away, she abruptly turned again and ran back to the car. 'Damn it, Wriggers, I forgot. This was your morning to have a lie-in, wasn't it?'

'Um, yes, Ellie, it was. Doesn't matter, I haven't really had a proper night's sleep all week.'

'Oh Wriggers, beat me.'

'Just having you on. Don't even give it a thought, run along now, you'll be late.'

Wrigley watched her go. Somehow she had managed to turn this morning of crisis into a fun little jaunt. But he was concerned. He knew that she could not continue to be so disorganised and still meet the demands of her job; especially with the plans she had for her future. He'd heard her call herself 'Miss Wing It' too often. He had known Ellie almost all of her life. He had been impressed by her ability to live on the edge and still exude charm. But the current truth was that he knew he wasn't helping her by indulging her in her escapades. 'Where exactly was that line between enabling her in her flakiness and supporting her when she needed a friend?' he wondered. The more time he spent with her, the more he cared about her future. That thought was a little disarming too.

Ellie's flight to New York had just taken off and already she was exhausted. Even the comforts of Business Class could not cushion her against the weariness she was experiencing from the demands of the last month. As manager of her eight-person team, it seemed that everyone wanted something from her and she just couldn't seem to get everything done. Ellie let her mind roam through her personal checklist of people and things that daily competed for her attention. 'My mother's birthday is soon, the Women's Conference ... must phone ...' Her eyes closed and she drifted off before the seat belt sign had been turned off.

A face appeared before her. It was hard to see at first but as it moved closer towards her she could see that it was that of an older male. She didn't recognise him at all and he reminded her of no one she had ever seen before. It was as if his face were floating before her patiently, allowing her to study it. She noticed that even though he appeared to be in his sixties or seventies, she couldn't really guess his age. His skin was glowing and healthy-looking. The lines around his cheeks were deep but the skin folded around them gently and naturally.

His jowl was firm and his throat faded away into a peaceful nothingness.

While Ellie studied his face she was compelled at last to look into his eyes, and it was there that she felt herself rest. His eyes were mischievously alive and bright, and at the same time their depth was infinite. Their colour was an almost unnatural, intensely dark blue, sprinkled with grey flecks. Aside from the physical beauty of the man's eyes it was the feeling they evoked in Ellie that moved her, for they looked at her as if they knew her well.

His hair, a brilliant white, was pulled back from his face, although she could not see its end. His overall demeanour was warm and inviting, yet there was also something alarmingly fierce about the way his eyebrows arched. His lips were full and relaxed and the fact that he was neither smiling nor frowning contributed to an air of rather dignified mysteriousness.

Ellie felt a slight nudging, a persistent tug on her arm. 'Ms Hart … Ms Hart … We're about to land, Ms Hart.' Startled, she woke up to find the flight attendant standing over her. 'Oh, are we there? Have I been asleep the whole time?' The flight attendant assured her she hadn't moved a muscle the entire flight.

Ellie's journey, however, was just beginning.

Ellie Wakes Up

Ellie had just enough time to check into the hotel, freshen up and change her clothes before she caught a taxi to the office. As she took her navy blue suit out of the bag she noticed that it had actually seen better days. She zipped up her trousers with a little bit more of a struggle than usual. 'Oh no, what's happened here?' Ellie had been a consistent size ten since she left university. But it was too late to worry about that now, she had to hurry; she absolutely could not be late.

She turned her pale green eyes to the mirror. Frowning at her reflection she said, 'I look a bit beige.' With no time for fiddling with foundation, she hurriedly brushed a little powder onto her fair complexion. She dabbed a little extra on her pert nose where a trail of almost faded freckles remained from her childhood. Then Ellie rummaged through her bag to find her one and only lipstick, which was in a particularly naff pinky colour. As she slid the pink stick across her lips, she began to feel overwhelmed with a nervousness that ran through her entire body. Her mouth was so tense that her well-defined lips, which often revealed her pretty smile, almost disappeared.

This moment had suddenly become real for her. This afternoon she would be presenting a first-of-its-kind initiative for the company. Ellie had been working on this proposal for over a year, in addition to her normal duties. Several members of the New York office were, in effect, her group of guinea pigs.

She gathered her things and made her way out of the hotel. Stepping out into a cold autumn day, Ellie gave herself a pep talk. 'You can do this. After all, remember where you started. How many times did McMurty's face turn red until I was finally able to take a meeting with my own staff? Now I can even have lunch with him without wanting to keep my face covered with my napkin.' The thought gave her comfort. But now she was on her way to sell her idea to a group of people who made her go wobbly at the knees. She was out of her comfort zone.

Traffic was chock-a-block already and heading downtown at 3.30 pm on a Wednesday in Manhattan would not be fun. Ellie always felt a little intimidated whenever she was in Manhattan. Her company's New York branch was so posh and its offices were filled with employees who seemed to be more competitive and, well ... sharper than those to whom she was accustomed. It always took her a little time to adjust to the more outgoing and open behaviour of the Americans. It was all a bit too in-your-face for her, but at the same time she had to admit it was exciting. 'Oh no, daydreaming again. Traffic looks horrid, decision time.'

Ellie decided to make a run for it. Computer bag, handbag and Fortnum and Mason's shopping bag in tow, she hopped out of the taxi and became one of many in a sea of rush-hour people dashing to their destinations. She rounded the corner and saw the company building ahead of her, she could even see the bank of lifts through the huge glass doors. 'Almost there,' she muttered. But she skidded on the worn heels of her black suede ankle boots when she noticed the security guards. She had forgotten about the new security precautions. She was happy to succumb to the search but could only think, 'Oh bloody hell, I need to get up there right now!'

She hadn't time to straighten her blouse collar, which now stood slightly askew, or smooth down her hair, which mimicked her collar, or even to say hello properly to that nice man at reception. Nevertheless, standing before the conference room door, Ellie managed to find the presence of mind to take one deep breath before she entered. Just as she was about to open the door it flew open and there stood Jasper McMurty.

'Jasper!'

'Good afternoon, Ellie. Flight all right?'

'Yes, thanks.'

'Don't start without me, I'll be right back.'

With that Ellie stood watching her boss stride past her and out of the door with no explanation of why he was there.

'What was I thinking – of course he would be here.' This was too important to miss. Here she was, one of his prime protégées, embarking upon the most important step in her career in the company. But why had he surprised her like this? Suddenly, as the hour approached, her stomach felt as if it had dropped to her feet and her palms became warm and sweaty. Annoyingly, she also needed a quick trip to the loo. McMurty's presence did nothing to calm her nerves, which were reaching the height of misery, and she still had not even entered the conference room!

Ellie opened the door at exactly 4 pm. All heads turned to watch her entrance. She slowly made her way around the room, saying hello, feeling in a way as if she were floating through a small body of water, being carried away by the waves. Tyler Elliott seemed to swing his way towards her, literally leaving a testosterone breeze in the air as he passed by her nodding hello. He was known in the London office as 'Ty the Guy'. Hmm ... what's different about him? she thought. Can't quite put my finger on it ... looks a bit odd.

In the corner by the floor-to-ceiling windows, which proudly displayed the light of Manhattan, stood Daphne Marchant. Daphne slowly turned towards Ellie and in a split second they had sized each other up. Ellie thought Daphne appeared to be cool, calm and collected – as usual. 'She looks fantastic,' Ellie said to herself. 'Surely not the Daphne I knew in London.' Immediately Ellie felt a pang of insecurity and self-consciousness. Daphne had always made her feel like the country bumpkin.

Who would make the first gesture towards a greeting? Ellie geared up and purposefully walked over to Daphne with her hand held out. Daphne chose that moment to take off her expensive jacket and drape it over the chair. This seemingly natural act caused Ellie to stand with her hand held out for just a few seconds too long, resulting in an awkward moment in which Ellie stood waiting until Daphne was ready. Touché, Daphne, Ellie thought.

Ellie, however, was becoming accustomed to Daphne's calculated manoeuvres and was actually uncharacteristically prepared for such an event. She allowed Daphne this petty victory and waited patiently for Daphne to respond to her. When they finally shook hands Ellie's unoccupied hand brought forth the Fortnum's bag.

'This is for you, Daphne. I thought you might need another supply.'

'Why Ellie, you sly fox. How did you ever manage to get this through Customs?'

'It's just tea, Daphne.'

'Cheers, Ellie.'

'Pleasure, Daphne.'

Right, Ellie thought, let me get on with this then.

While everyone waited for McMurty to return, Ellie took advantage of the extra time to pass out the reports she had prepared. She studied the group as they began to take their seats. Key members of several departments had been invited to her presentation. As Ellie moved into place, McMurty quietly returned and sat close to the back of the room – but not as far back as Daphne. She might as well be on Long Island, Ellie thought.

'Good afternoon again, everyone. Thank you for your time today and for making yourselves available so that we could all be here together,' Ellie had begun. 'As you know, I am here today to introduce the idea of creating a new department within the company.' Immediately she heard a sigh. She swallowed, paused and picked it up again: 'This new department, while an adjunct to our Training and Development Department, has a unique purpose. I firmly believe that the creation of a Diversity Department will enable our firm to excel, expand and to lead by example.'

Silence. McMurty wasn't half right; this was a tough audience. She felt a little shaky as she tried to find her natural pace. McMurty's presence had thrown her a bit and she didn't know whether or not she should make eye contact with him. Was her voice clear and strong enough? Could they tell that she could feel her heart thumping? However, as soon as she approached the section of her material to which she was most connected, she became appropriately animated and spoke passionately and intelligently. With her morale and confidence a bit boosted, she entered into the interactive phase.

Not surprisingly, the first question came from Daphne. 'Budget, Ellie?'

Ellie shot a quick glance at McMurty. 'Yes, I know that each of you will be interested in discussing the budget for this proposal, but the sole purpose of this afternoon's meeting is to acknowledge the need for, and to garner support for, this project.'

Tyler, who had looked particularly sullen all afternoon, suddenly livened up. 'I don't have time for this. If you can't present a budget for something as important as a new department, then I can't be expected to offer you any comments or support.'

'Tyler, I will absolutely present a budget, but not this afternoon and not tomorrow. I believe it is more important that there be an understanding of the underlying principles of this proposal.'

'That's where you're wrong, Ellie. You know what the bottom line is here. Don't tell me that now is not the time to discuss what this is going to mean financially.'

Stunned, Ellie watched him as he stood up, collected his things, threw his jacket over his shoulder and walked out of the room.

'Tyler,' Ellie called after him. But it was too late. He was gone. 'What the ...?' she almost said aloud. Judging by his bland expression,

Ellie didn't even think Tyler had been paying attention. Caught completely off guard and visibly shaken, she looked at McMurty, who folded his arms and looked at her without expression. She was on her own.

Ellie looked down at her notes but did not really see them. The silence in the room was almost unbearable. What do I do now, what do I say now? she thought, grasping for a way to continue. McMurty had warned her that it was imperative for her to be prepared for something like this. He predicted that she would be challenged to reveal her budget at the first meeting. He had advised her to 'just sell the concept, keep them focused on why this is so important. Do not be drawn into an emotional discussion about costs.'

Breaking the silence, Daphne leaned forward with both elbows on the conference table, her hands clasped under her chin. 'Well, not exactly elegantly delivered, but Tyler does have a point, Ellie.' Daphne, now with the room's attention, continued, 'To be frank with you, Ellie, I'm just not sure that I understand why we need a whole new department for something that we embrace anyway – don't we?' Daphne looked around the room for support.

As heads nodded, Ellie said to herself, 'You wankers, haven't I just spent the past two bloody hours telling you why?' She did not want to end the meeting like this, but it was growing late and they all had an early start tomorrow. It was very important for her to leave the room on a positive note, but the nods of agreement Daphne received from the group unnerved her.

Finally, Ellie summoned her nerve and calmed herself enough to speak. 'I'd like you all to please look around you.' Ellie's voice faltered slightly for a moment, but she slowly and deliberately looked around the room. 'Look at the person seated next to you and the person across from you. Take a good look at all of the people in this room. How much diversity do you see?' Now, finally, she had the room's attention.

'I think it is obvious that we have great deal of work to do,' she said. 'My point is not that we, as a company, are intentionally keeping our doors only half open. My point is this: we must commit to providing an environment of respect, in which diverse teams harness the benefits of a wide range of skills, experiences and approaches. We cannot afford *not* to do it. Do you want us to be in front, a leader? Or, do you want us to be left behind?' Ellie made eye contact with Daphne and finally McMurty.

'This is a perfect time,' she stressed, 'to attract the best talent, no matter who they are, or where they come from.'

That was it, it was the best she could do for now. She had saved face, but she didn't know if she had saved her project. It was a beginning and it was tough, but it was over for now and it was time to get the hell out of there.

As the group began to file out of the office, Ellie was left on her own to gather her papers and pack up her computer.

'I hope I wasn't too rough on you, Ellie.'

Startled, Ellie turned to see Tyler standing in the doorway. She turned away from him and continued to pack her things. 'Still here?' she asked.

'Yeah, I had some work to catch up on. Look, Ellie, it wasn't personal or anything. Just wanted to give you something to think about.'

'Hmm, cheers, Ty, thanks a lot,' Ellie said with more than a hint of tiredness in her voice.

'You know what they say over here don't you, if you can't take the heat ...?'

Ellie looked up at him and met him eye to eye. She saw something in his manner and body language that suggested he was enjoying this and that there was indeed some little thrill he was getting out of this whole encounter. She had seen this particular type of behaviour before; it seemed to her to be reserved for the male species.

Too tired to care and lacking the magic to pull anything out of her hat, she could only respond with, 'Oh just sod off, Ty.'

Ellie walked back to the hotel in the hope that the cold evening air would help clear her mind. She felt too upset to join the others at the restaurant and opted for a passable room-service dinner and half-heartedly turned on the news. Her mind replayed the afternoon as the images of the world's problems whooshed before her. Ellie felt alone, very alone. It was too late to call anyone in London. She checked her messages, hoping to hear from Preston, but alas, no such message existed. There was, however, a message from Wrigley inviting her to call him at the restaurant whenever she finished her meeting, no matter what time it was.

Good old Wriggers, she thought. 'That's just what I need.' She dialled the number and waited.

'Good evening. Wrigley's On the Square.'

'Hello, Jean-Louis?'

'*Oui*, this is Jean-Louis, is that Ellie?'

'Yes, I'm in New York. You're there late tonight. Is Wrigley still there?'

'*Oui*, we're having the most *fantastique* time! Hold please.'

'Ellie, how did it go? How are you?' Wrigley shouted over the music.

'Shattered, ' Ellie said. 'I think I really made a mess of it.'

'Rubbish, Ellie. What happened?'

'Too tired to tell you now, but it was incredibly hard.'

'Come on now, listen here, it's just the first step. It's going to be all right. You might not have been perfect, but I'm sure you didn't mess it up. We talked about this and you knew it would be hard. Finish up there in the morning with a bang. All right then?'

'Will do, Wriggers,' she said, trying her best to sound convincing. 'By the way, whatever are you doing there at this hour?'

'Private party tonight, it was good fun Ellie. Jean-Louis's duck confit was very moreish. We're still clearing up.'

She smiled at the thought of his staff cleaning up to the tunes of Nickel Creek, the current music mascot for after hours at Wrigley's restaurant. She thought about how she enjoyed stopping by after work, chatting with them and soaking up the jovial and warm atmosphere they created.

'I'm knackered and you must be too, Wrigs. I'll call you tomorrow.'

'Good night then, Ellie and don't worry. Everything will be fine.'

'Mm, all right then.' She put the phone down thoughtfully. What a day.

After a warm bath and a comforting cup of hot chocolate Ellie fell into a dreamless sleep.

The next morning's meeting was gruelling. Tyler's reason for showing up remained a mystery to her because his participation was close to non-existent. Daphne fired questions at her as if she were funding the project herself, and McMurty sat in a corner, almost hidden from her view. Ellie had originally planned a show of hands, a kind of 'vote for support' as a way of wrapping up her presentation. Something told her not to take a count, to end in a different way, but she ignored the impulse. She was afraid to veer away from her plan. And so when the count was taken and not one hand was raised in support of her project, she regretted that she had not listened to herself. Diversity was not alive and well – even as an idea.

Ellie took a deep breath in and said, 'Right then. Looks like I have my work cut out for me and that I will be seeing you all again sooner than I had expected.' She hoped she sounded convincing. She managed to gracefully thank each of them for their time and participation. Again, she was left alone in the room. What am I doing here? she thought. Why have I put myself through this? Ellie sat for a moment, her spirit crushed with an unexpected sense of failure. 'Well,' she said with a lump in her throat, 'I've got a flight to catch.'

Ellie tried to stay awake on the plane so that she would sleep through the night when she arrived home. Her mind tossed the two days' events around as she began to let the effect of the meetings sink in. Her expectations of coming back to the London office feeling well-pleased with her success seemed childish and embarrassing now. She thought about the bright pink blush that the entire group must have seen on her face. A blush caused from anger and being caught off guard. Ellie sank down into her seat and dreaded the days ahead. Had she made the biggest mistake in her career by pursuing this project?

Maybe she was wrong. Maybe her company was just not ready to diversify its clientele or its employees. But she had done the research, and the research had proven to her that many financial institutions such as theirs had already performed amazingly well after they had implemented diversity programmes. Then she remembered an interview she had conducted with the head of diversity from a very traditional and well-established accounting firm. He told her that it had not been easy, that he had actually failed at his first attempt to sell the idea to the company. Oh, these thoughts were making her head hurt!

By the time she arrived back in Chorleywood she had surpassed the point of exhaustion and wanted nothing more than to crawl into her own bed. And that she did. 'Bliss!' was the exclamation as her feet felt the sheets and her head sank onto the pillow. Her mind had entered a peaceful state of floating calm when a figure appeared before her. There he was again. The man whose face she had seen before had reappeared; only this time she could see the entire length of his body.

Oh my God, she thought. He looks like he just stepped out of the Victoria and Albert Museum!

His thick white wavy hair was shoulder-length and neatly held back with a rather handsome, large black velvet bow. He wore a fawn-coloured frock coat, which fell just below his knees, with matching knee breeches made out of a fine wool worsted. A double row of tiny brass buttons ran down the front of the coat to his waist. The man was tall and slender and the coat's curving lines revealed an ecru waistcoat that flattered his particularly long torso. The waistcoat was just slightly shorter than the frock coat and was embroidered all over with tiny sprigs of flowers in vermilion, malachite green and burnt orange.

A fine muslin shirt produced a cravat loosely knotted in the front, which fell in a soft bunch at his chest. Peeking out from his coat sleeves were the shirt's oversized cuffs, trimmed in Dutch lace. He wore stockings and soft, crumpling leather black boots with square toes. One of his long elegant hands carried a black three-cornered hat and the other hand grasped a pair of very soft buckskin gloves and an ebony walking cane with a dull silver crook-necked handle engraved with filigree on the end.

The man looked perfectly at ease standing in a garden where beautiful colours surrounded him. Brilliant reds and oranges and the vibrant hues of deep, deep lavender and blue were cradled in a mass of sage-coloured ferns and muted mosses. The colours began to take the forms of gigantic flowers and they swayed slightly in a breeze.

The man seemed to almost glide across her field of vision. Ellie was mesmerised.

What is going on? This is just too bizarre, Ellie thought.

He slowly turned towards Ellie.

'Who are you?' she managed to ask.

'Why, good afternoon. I'm Mr Fairchild.' He spoke in a leisurely manner and his voice was sonorous, his clear enunciation impressive.

'Yes, of course you are. And whatever are you doing?'

'Oh, I'm just doing a little gardening.'

'Okay then, Mr Fairchild, carry on.' Amused, Ellie rolled her eyes and shook her head.

She watched him stroll through the garden in silence and every once in a while he would easily bend and pull away a weed. As he walked, she watched the garden become more overgrown and the bright colours began to fade.

'Umm Mr Fairchild. To whom does this garden belong?'

'It belongs to you of course!'

The flowers, which just a few moments ago were large and succulent, had become small and some of them were dying. The longer he walked the more colour was drained from the scenery. More weeds began to choke the ground as his odd boots trod upon them. Ellie began to feel uncomfortable.

'Mr Fairchild, please, stop walking.'

He turned and looked at her. Once again she felt herself fall into his deep blue eyes. He looked into her eyes for what seemed an eternity but she did not turn away. She held his gaze even though she felt fearful and uncertain.

'All right then, you must be ready.' He broke the long silence.

'Ready? Ready for what?'

'Well, my dear, the only reason I could possibly be here tending your garden is if you are ready to learn how to tend it yourself.'

Ellie did not know what on earth – or beyond for that matter – this strange man was talking about. She hadn't a clue.

'Awareness, Eloise. Awareness,' Mr Fairchild whispered. 'Your awareness is wanting in sharpness, sorely represented by the colours of your garden. In some areas you are bright and largely gifted and in others you are dull and grey. The disparity is quite enormous, my dear.'

'Hang on, hang on. Just a minute, please.' Ellie thrust one hand on her hip and the other across her eyes as if to blot out the vision of this very unusual man. 'I just need a second here to adjust. You've just read my mind, called me by the name only my mum uses, and have insinuated that I have a dull grey awareness or some such thing.'

He chuckled. 'Open your eyes, Ellie. Look at your garden. It is you. What do you see?'

Of course Ellie had never really bothered with gardening, so she had to concentrate to see the garden in any detail. Her eyes were drawn to a single ray of sun by the wall of the house. It was warm and bright and fell upon a small row of rose bushes. The roses were in full bloom, voluptuous in colour and volume. The red roses were the deepest red she had ever seen. Next to the red roses another bush of white roses stood in contrast to the vibrant energy of the red ones, their milky white petals looked soft and velvety. So pure and calm, she thought. And there, as if to balance the two, a small yellow bush was just beginning to flower with a rich buttery flare of yellow and a small elegant shape.

Mr Fairchild encouraged her. 'Good, good. You can see what is flourishing. The roses are agreeably beautiful, are they not? But now, look again, what is meant to be adorned in the same manner?'

'Um, come again?'

Patiently he replied, 'What in your garden is not pleasing to you, what needs improving?'

Ellie looked, but the garden seemed blurry again to her.

A little frustrated, she said, 'Don't all gardens look pretty much the same, just bits of green and some colour?'

'Open your eyes, Ellie. Look.'

Ellie pointed to a rose bush under an apple tree. 'Well, maybe this isn't right. This rose bush doesn't have much going for it and seems a bit out of place.'

'Good, what should you do with it, Ellie?'

'I think I would move it,' said Ellie, 'because maybe ...'

She paused. A most strange feeling came over her, a feeling that the sick plant was trying to tell her something.

'... I, I think it might want to be moved to the sun.'

'Excellent. Excellent, Eloise. You have seen what is working and productive in your garden, and also what is not. And just as importantly, you instinctively knew what to do to improve it.' Mr Fairchild sounded very satisfied.

As Ellie surveyed her garden she heard Mr Fairchild's voice:

'Acknowledge the need for change.'

She glanced about and saw that she was standing alone in the weeds. She looked around for Mr Fairchild but he was nowhere to be seen. 'Mr Fairchild,' she called. 'Mr Fairchild, where are you?' But there was no answer, only a sudden and very noticeable silence. 'Mr Fairchild? Are you winding me up? I don't know what this means.'

'Awareness, Ellie,' was his invisible reply. 'Open your eyes.' Just his voice hung in the air. In the distance, Ellie heard a final 'Acknowledge the need for change, Ellie. Open your eyes.'

Ellie opened her eyes and bolted upright from the bed. 'What the bloody hell was that noise?' Her alarm clock was talking to her, telling her that it was going to rain all day and the temperature would be slightly colder than usual. 'It was a dream,' she said out loud as she dragged herself to the bathroom. 'A dream.'

Ellie never saw the single red petal lying on her pillow.

Dream 1 Lesson

Acknowledge the need for change.

Ellie Can't See the Forest for the Trees

Just as Ellie was about to bite into a piece of hot buttered toast the phone rang.

'Hello,' she said with her toast in mid-air.

'Ellie, what are you doing home?'

'Well, if it isn't the ever-elusive Preston.' Ellie wondered what he was up to. 'Why did you call me if you thought I wouldn't be here?'

'I just wanted to leave you a message. Why aren't you at the office?'

'Bit of a lie-in today. I'm going in later. I tried to reach you. I've just returned from New York.' Ellie had a sinking feeling that Preston had forgotten all about her trip and her presentation.

'Right … of course, how did it go?' Preston asked absently.

'Not very well, Preston. It was –'

But he interrupted her. 'Oh that's too bad. Ellie, listen, darling, the reason I called is to tell you that I'm afraid I'm not going to make your mother's birthday dinner on Saturday.'

'But Preston, this has been planned for weeks.'

'I know, I know and I'm terribly sorry, but something has come up. I really have to run now, Ellie. I'll give you a ring later.'

With that he was gone.

Ellie took her tea and toast to the kitchen window. It was a rare weekday morning that she was able to spend time at home. Her mother had helped her to buy the turn-of-the-century, small mid-terrace cottage and she truly loved it. She stared out onto her small patch of rear garden. 'Garden!' she exclaimed. Her dream came rushing back to her. 'What was it that strange man said? Open my eyes, awareness? Yes, yes, but there was something else.' Ellie grabbed a pen and paper and wrote down the message that now burned brightly in her mind: 'Acknowledge the need for change.'

Ellie tried to concentrate on the New York meeting for a minute. 'What could I have done differently?' she wondered. But her phone call with Preston pressed upon her, and without warning a lump formed in her throat and hot, angry tears made their way down her cheeks. She had been so caught up in her work that she had easily ignored the downhill turn their relationship had taken in the past few months. She blinked back more tears and looked again at the note she had written. The need for change in her life? She blew her nose. 'Not half!'

Ellie looked out at her garden, the clouds darkened to a smoky grey, and it began to rain. She shook her head from side to side; she couldn't believe that everything seemed to be such a struggle right now. 'What a lovely morning off,' she said as she blew her nose. 'I have an absent, dodgy boyfriend. I have quite possibly ruined my career. And I'm only thirty-two. What a stupid ass I am. Brilliant.'

She had no time left to indulge in further thoughts. It was time for Ellie Hart to go to work.

◆

Tilda, Ellie's assistant, was waiting for her when she stepped out of the lift. Tilda's appearance was bursting with colour today. Her light ginger curls were piled high on her head. She wore a ruby red tight-fitting sweater set and a clingy red and white square-patterned skirt. Ellie's rather drab brown suit was in such contrast to Tilda's loud statement that for a brief moment Ellie felt somewhat diminished.

They walked to Ellie's office as Tilda bombarded her with an update.

'Your three o'clock with McMurty has been changed to three-thirty. That pushes the team meeting back to four-thirty ... or whenever. I hope it's four-thirty because you know I have to leave at five-thirty today.'

'Absolutely not,' said Ellie.

'But Ellie, I told you about today's appointment last week. You agreed to it.'

'Tilda, I'm really not interested in your appointment. You must be here for this afternoon's meeting.'

Tilda fumed but said nothing.

'Anything else?' Ellie asked.

'Your mum called.'

Ellie winced; she had forgotten to call her before she left for New York.

'Twice,' Tilda added.

Ellie sighed. 'Right then, let voicemail take my calls and give me 30.'

Tilda hovered. 'How was New York, Ellie?'

Ellie ignored the question. 'We have a lot of work to do. I wouldn't have asked you to stay tonight if it weren't important, Tilda.'

Ellie closed the door to her office. She needed time to prepare for her meeting with Jasper. Trouble was, thirty minutes wasn't going to be enough time. Thirty days wasn't enough time to prepare to face him. She had to admit she was feeling like a complete idiot.

She picked up the feedback reports from the New York meeting. Ellie had delayed looking at them until the last moment. Just as she picked up Tyler's comments there was a knock at her door. Tilda quickly approached her desk.

'Look, Ellie, I know you're busy but something's come up with one of our internal clients.'

'Which one, Tilda?'

'It's Archie, he's speaking to one of his clients today and he needs some important information pronto.' Tilda drew a breath. 'I really think I can handle it, Ellie, I get on quite well with Archie.'

'That's all right, I'll take care of it.'

'But Ellie, really, I know what to do.'

'Tell him I'll pop by on my way to Jasper's.'

Ellie gathered her things for her meeting with McMurty. She breezed past Tilda, leaving her standing at the door. Tilda, exasperated, leaned back against the doorframe and rolled her clear blue eyes to the ceiling. Ellie had promised to give her more responsibility months ago and still Ellie could not hand over the reins on anything more important than Tilda's usual duties. The wheels were turning in a new direction in Tilda's mind. She didn't know how much longer she could continue to work for Ellie.

McMurty's assistant ushered Ellie into his office. Her nervousness made her a little early for the meeting — for a change. But soon McMurty entered, an Asprey's bag in one hand and a suit bag swung over his other shoulder. He never hid his acquisitions, or tried to scurry them quickly into a corner. Instead, McMurty's message was always consistently clear: 'You don't have to parade your success, but neither should you hide it. It is there for you to enjoy and celebrate.' Ellie noted that, as usual, Jasper was immaculately turned out in one of his made-to-measure suits, perfectly pressed shirt, and what the back office would call an award-winning tie.

He went straight to the phone and took a call, but waved to Ellie and pointed to the conference table. Ellie sat with her back to McMurty, too nervous to hear the gist of his conversation. He put down the phone, walked over to a chair not terribly near her and paused a moment before he spoke to her.

'Hello, Ellie, how are you?'

'Very well, thank you, Jasper.'

'Let's get to it then.' McMurty leaned back comfortably in his chair. His body language said to an unobserving Ellie, 'Relax, because I am.'

Ellie forced herself to make eye contact with him.

'I'm still behind you on this project, Ellie.'

Surprised, she responded without thinking; 'What? Do you mean I can still go forward? That's great. That's great, 'cause you know, Jasper I was really worried. Cheers!'

McMurty sat up in his chair and took a moment to look Ellie in the eye. He didn't say it, but could only think that her response was meant for clinking glasses of lager instead of a polished reply from an executive. However, he had something much more immediate to speak to Ellie about.

'Ellie, you're going to have to convince some very important people that you are capable of successfully handling this project. Talent alone will not get you to the place you need to go with this.' McMurty paused to let his words sink in. He continued, 'How would you characterise your performance in New York?'

Ellie's throat felt very dry and she could barely swallow. This is it, she thought. He's going to give it to me now. She tried to sit taller in her chair and finally said, 'Look, Jasper, I felt that there were a number of people in the room who were just not on my side – I could have been offering carts of bananas to starving monkeys and they wouldn't have been behind me. It was very difficult.'

'All right then, Ellie, at what point did you think you got their attention – or did you?'

Trying to keep herself together she replied, 'Well, which bit are you referring to?'

Jasper just looked at her, intelligently bewildered. 'Just take a minute and think back.'

'Do you mean the bit about what Diversity means to me and why I feel so strongly about it?'

'Yes, but you didn't walk into the room like you felt strongly about anything, Ellie. I know it is not your job to be a professional presenter. You may have to do this only a handful of times in your whole career, and I know how difficult it is to pull off. But when you want something very badly, you have to stretch yourself a bit farther than you ever thought you could or should.'

McMurty walked over to Ellie, pulled a chair closer to her and sat.

'Do you understand what I'm saying here, Ellie?'

Ellie looked at Jasper and quietly responded with an authenticity and a presence of mind that had been absent from her demeanour for the last few days. 'Yes, I understand you. I know I need to make some changes, Jasper, and I know that I need to start now.'

McMurty had been waiting for a sign from Ellie that indicated that she knew she had some serious work to do.

'Right,' he said. 'Now we can move on. Let me give you some specifics. You were almost late for your own meeting. Being on time is not good enough. You were, in essence, hosting this event, which means you should have been in the room before your colleagues arrived. You didn't give yourself enough time to make sure the room was in order or even to gather your thoughts. I shouldn't have to tell you that. And, as you know from the feedback, image-wise you were not up to snuff.'

'Really? Do you mean that someone actually commented on my appearance?'

'It's in the feedback, Ellie.'

'Jasper, I haven't read the feedback yet.'

'Then I suggest you do so pretty quickly.' He continued, 'Several people commented on your appearance, Ellie. You need to set a better example, to be a better role model. It is your responsibility, as a business professional, to do so. That's what I mean by going a bit farther. It is absolutely essential you now make the effort.'

McMurty did not skip a beat. 'I know that you know exactly why introducing Diversity to our company is important. And I also know that you are the one who can do it best – but Ellie, no one else knows that. The main reason they don't know it is because you didn't sell it. Do you know why you didn't sell it?'

'Selling?' she almost said out loud. 'What does he mean, why is he talking about selling? I'm not a salesperson.' Ellie felt like crawling under the table, just the thought of selling anything made her feel uncomfortable. She slowly shook her head from side to side, hoping 'no' was an acceptable answer.

Jasper answered for her; 'Because you didn't sell yourself. There wasn't a person in the room that afternoon who doesn't believe that a Diversity division in our company is inevitable – even Tyler. They needed to be convinced that you were the right person to head it. And that's what I mean by selling, Ellie. You worried too much about the content of your presentation. It's apparent that you've done your homework. You just didn't inspire those people. You didn't behave like a leader. You didn't instill the kind of trust and confidence that it is going to take to lead this project.'

Ellie paused before responding, 'Sounds like I really messed this one up, Jasper.'

'Close.'

'Thank you for giving me another chance.'

McMurty rose. 'This isn't a chance. Treat this as an opportunity to show your metal. Go sort yourself out, Ellie.'

Ellie left McMurty's office and headed straight for the loo. She needed a moment alone before she faced her team. Thank goodness the loo was unoccupied. 'What the frig am I doing? What have I got myself into here?' She threw her hands up in dismay. 'I can't do it. I don't think I can bloody well do this. Sod it!' Ellie's stream of expletives continued as she paced the ladies' loo.

She looked at her watch. 'Four bloody thirty.' It was time for her next meeting already. Ellie looked in the mirror. 'Oh, I look awful.'

She rummaged through her bag looking for a lipstick, compact, anything at this point, but frustratingly found nothing. She turned on the tap and cupped her hands to catch the water. She lifted her hands, now full of water, and once again looked into the mirror. Angrily, she threw the water at her reflection. Astonished by her temper, Ellie rushed to grab a loo roll and frantically began to wipe down the mirror. The paper shredded and stuck to her fingers and hands. The pressure of the week seemed to have overtaken her and she burst out laughing and then crying and then laughing. 'This is ridiculous, I really must get out of this loo,' she said aloud with a quick glance at the door, hoping no one would enter at this particular moment. Ellie washed her hands, brushed herself off and tried to pull herself together. With another deep breath she left the ladies' and returned to the real world.

Ellie rushed by Tilda's desk. 'Keep your hair on, Tilda, you might just make that appointment.'

All eight members of Ellie's team were present. Their regular end-of-week-review meeting was in full swing when Ellie made a decision. 'After you fill me in on the highlights of the two days I was away, and anything else you feel is relevant, I think you should all go home. It's been a busy week for everybody and we all deserve an early evening.' Everyone looked relieved, especially Tilda. Sometimes Ellie's meetings could go on and on and, after all, it was Friday.

Her day finally at an end, Ellie returned to her office. But instead of preparing to go back to Chorleywood, she sat at her desk staring at the feedback sheets from her meetings in New York. Her mind was swimming with the week's challenges. She thought of Mr Fairchild and his patient smile comforted her.

'My mum!' Ellie suddenly remembered to call her and quickly picked up the phone. 'Hello, Mum.'

'Eloise, where have you been? I've been trying to reach you all day.'

'Oh, yes, Mum, I know, I'm sorry, I've had a bloody awful week. Listen, I apologise for not phoning you before now.' Quickly changing the subject; 'The good news is that we'll have a lovely time tomorrow night, Wriggers is giving us the private room.'

'Oh that *is* lovely, darling, Wrigley is such a treasure.'

'Yes he is. By the way, Mum, Preston sends his apologies. He won't be able to join us.'

'Why on earth not?'

'Umm, well, to be quite honest, I really don't know, he said something came up.'

'Well, what a surprise,' she said wryly.

'Please don't start, Mum.'

'It doesn't matter a bit, darling, we'll have a wonderful time anyway.'

'All right then, see you tomorrow. Bye.'

'Bye-bye, darling.'

Relieved that her mother was in good form, Ellie was ready to settle down to work.

'All right then, Mr Fairchild, you couldn't have been more accurate. I need to sort some things out.' She paused. 'This is entirely too weird, I actually remember him.' Ellie turned to her computer and began to make notes. She was determined to take a good look at what she needed to change. She began by first reviewing her meeting with Jasper. Then, as hard as it was to do, she picked up the feedback reports and settled in for a long read.

It was pretty painful to read her colleagues' criticisms, but as she weighed the information against Jasper's comments she knew that many of the remarks rang true. Now that her emotions had subsided and that she knew the project was still alive, all she really wanted to do was to prove to herself that she had the right stuff.

Although Ellie had lost track of time, her stomach was telling her that she had not eaten since breakfast. She walked through the empty office to the kitchen, where she found a packet of chocolate biscuits. As she waited for the hot water to boil she felt something inside of her that was, well ... different. Nibbling on a biscuit, part of her wished that everything could remain the same. She had coasted along now for a few years quite comfortably. But perhaps she had been coasting with blinkers on – no, definitely with blinkers on! These past few days had shaken her up and now, even though she knew that change was inevitable, it still made her feel a bit queasy.

Ellie made her way back to her desk and settled down once again with her tea and biscuits. She sat staring at her notes. Certain words and phrases jumped out at her. *'Not prepared, scattered, confidence issue, could have communicated more effectively, not ready yet, handled confrontation poorly, not ready to lead yet, looked a mess.'*

She let out a huge sigh. 'Oh well, just great. I can't believe this. If this is what they really think of me … Did I do anything right? Maybe I should get a full body and brain transplant.'

Weariness overcame her as she put her head down on her desk and cradled it in her arms. Still looking up at her computer she said out loud, 'I don't know where to start. Can I really do this?' Without meaning to, Ellie dozed off in her office.

Quite suddenly she heard a very annoying sound. It was a gritty, digging sound, a short, sharp and shallow persistent contact with the earth. There, in all of his glory, was Mr Fairchild, kneeling on a padded cloth with a digging fork in one hand and a rather foul-looking collection of weeds in the other.

Ellie didn't know whether to be pleased or exasperated to see the old man again. She watched him as he paused to pat his brow with a linen handkerchief that he had tucked in the sleeve of his smock. She noted that he was now in what must definitely be his work clothes. His knee britches were sturdier and thicker. Gone were his fancy coat and blouse. Over his pumice-coloured smock he wore a long, dark burgundy Hessian cloth apron that tied in a stiff, neat bow in the back.

Without turning or looking up at her, Mr Fairchild could sense that Ellie had arrived once again.

'Welcome, Eloise, how nice to see you again.'

Wary, Ellie stepped closer.

'Please, do sit down. This nice smooth rock makes a lovely seat.' Mr Fairchild dusted off the large stone with his handkerchief.

'Thank you,' Ellie replied and slowly sat down, once more glancing around her.

'You seem a little tired, my dear. Are you quite all right?'

Ellie heard her voice speak to the imaginary gardener in spite of herself. 'Well, I suppose I am a bit exhausted.'

'Exhausted? My, that sounds alarming. Well, we don't want you exhausted, that won't do.'

'It's been a rough week, Mr Fairchild.'

'Oh?'

'I don't think you would understand.'

Mr Fairchild's wonderful blue eyes sparkled as a soft smile spread across his face. 'I might understand, why don't we give it a try?'

Ellie eased into her version of the most recent events. She soon found it a huge relief to have a sympathetic ear, for Mr Fairchild was a patient and attentive listener. He slowly continued his work as Ellie began to pick up the pace and finally, when all was said, confessed and expressed, she ended with a very pertinent question:

'I know I need to improve and I know there are things I need to change, but really, Mr Fairchild, isn't there anything, anything at all that is good about all of the work I have done?'

Mr Fairchild gently laid down his tools and stood up for a moment to stretch his back.

'Could I possibly interest you in a stroll?'

Ellie was about to say, 'Sure', but there was something about the man's formal invitation that stopped her.

'That would be lovely,' she replied instead.

Mr Fairchild answered her question as they walked: 'Of course there are many good things about the work you have done. Surely you must realise that your employer has faith in you to allow you to continue thus far. It is very fortuitous that Mr McMurty is your immediate superior. He is a good man. In the world that you inhabit he is someone to be appreciated.'

'I suppose he must think that my contribution is valuable, otherwise, knowing Jasper, I'd be fired,' Ellie reasoned.

'Oh yes, this is true, however, what is most important is for *you* to acknowledge all the positive work you have done. When we reach the point where change is inevitable, it does not erase that which we have achieved. A beautiful garden, that is, a well-cared-for garden, is eventually balanced – all elements working together in harmony. Look again at your garden, Ellie. There are lovely areas and some that need care and attention. That will forever be the case. There is always something to attend to.'

They continued to walk slowly through the garden as Mr Fairchild continued, 'Here, look at your apple tree.' He pointed his walking stick at the beautiful old tree. 'This tree is well established now. It is such a wonderful asset. It provides shade, it creates food and it requires only the smallest attention. There are parts of you, Eloise, that are similar to the tree.'

'You know, Mr Fairchild, I'm not really with you on the metaphors. Could you bring it back down to earth for me?'

With patience Mr Fairchild responded, 'Eloise, your garden has natural assets – so do you. Your garden is in need of attention – so are you.'

'You mean I may have an apple tree, but then there are all of those weeds you were messing about with.'

Mr Fairchild chuckled. 'That is correct and I must get back to them if I am to be of any assistance at all to you.'

Puzzled by his remark, Ellie watched him as he knelt down again and continued working. 'What do you mean?' she asked.

'Surely you can understand how troublesome weeds can be if not dealt with efficiently?'

Ellie nodded her head, acknowledging that she understood. She felt the impulse to help him but he was doing such a wonderful job himself that she was hesitant to interrupt.

'Mr Fairchild, I must tell you that the last time we were, umm, together, I suppose you could say, I really took on board what you said to me about acknowledging the need to change. Do you know what's strange about it? Since then almost everyone around me has painfully reminded me of your words.'

Mr Fairchild smiled to himself and remained silent.

Ellie continued, 'The trouble is, Mr Fairchild, I don't know where to start!'

'Does everything seem to be overwhelming you right now?'

'Not half.'

'Do you know what happens in a garden when it is overwhelmed?'

'Um, sorry, no.'

'It means there are distractions, unwanted goings-on that need to be eliminated.'

'Bloody hell! Are you talking about those weeds?'

'Good heavens, Eloise, please refrain from such language.'

'Sorry.'

'Yes, I am talking about weeds. Weeds are opportunists in the art of invasion. They steal water and nutrients from other plants. It is important to identify the invasive weeds that will choke and kill any growth. It is preferable to clear the areas for new planting before they have a chance to establish themselves. Much easier that way.'

Ellie was beginning to hear the message. 'So, the next step then is to weed out the distractions?'

'Good, Ellie. That's right. You must identify and avoid distractions that keep you from attaining your goals.'

Thoughtfully, Ellie knelt to the ground. 'Do you have an extra weed taker-outer, Mr Fairchild?'

'Please, be my guest,' he replied as he handed her a very old-looking hand fork. 'Observe. My intense delight is to grab them by the root!'

They worked silently, side by side. At times Mr Fairchild saved a number of herbs and a row of wild mint as Ellie learned to identify invasive weeds. He showed her how a beautifully flowering, unassuming weed nearly choked the life right out of the soil. For some odd reason, Preston flashed into Ellie's mind as she and Mr Fairchild sat surrounded by a growing pile of distractions.

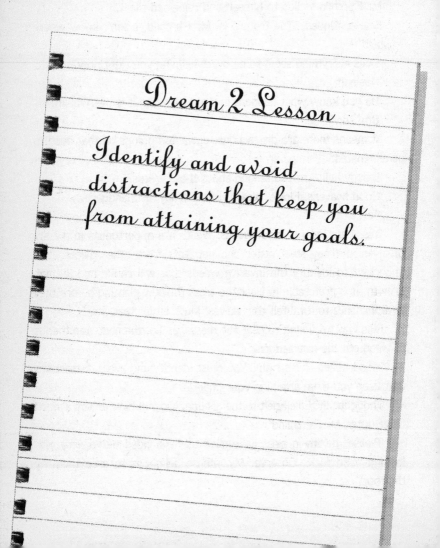

Dream 2 Lesson

Identify and avoid distractions that keep you from attaining your goals.

Ouch, That Hurts!

The night guard was very worried. There seemed to be an employee locked in her office who looked like she might have passed out. He had been tapping on the glass window for minutes now with no response. The guard went to the door and pounded on it with his fist.

Startled, Ellie jumped out of her seat, 'What the ... Where am I?' Disoriented, she looked around to get her bearings and finally realised she was in her office. She quickly opened the door, which sent the guard reeling backwards.

'Oh Charles, I'm sorry.'

'Ms Hart, are you all right?' he asked rubbing his forehead.

'Yes, I am, but are you?'

'Oh I'm fine, miss. It's nine o'clock, aren't you workin' a bit later than usual?'

'Is it that late? I fell asleep. Let me just grab my stuff and I'll be off.'

'Should I see you out then?'

'No, Charles, I'll be fine. Thank you.'

There were very few people standing on the platform as Ellie waited for the ten o'clock train to Chorleywood. She was still a little shaken by her dream and the experience with the guard. I must have been in a really deep sleep, she thought. The train arrived on time and as she settled in for the ride she thought to herself, I don't know what's going on with me. Maybe I'm going mad. The dreams were very real to her and she remembered the first one as vividly as her most recent one.

Her thoughts were interrupted by the sound of her cell phone. Maybe it's Preston, she thought. But it wasn't Preston – it was never Preston these days. It was Wrigley.

'Wriggers, don't tell me, I was supposed to call you.'

'Never mind, Ellie, I knew I'd have to call you. Everything all right?'

'No. Absolutely not, but what's new.'

'I can barely hear you, Ellie. I just wanted to ask you if it's all right to invite my Aunt Poppy for dinner.'

'You mean your "Agony Aunt" aunt?'

'The very one. She plays mah-jongg with your mum, and I thought your mum might like her to be there.'

'That sounds fun, Wriggers. I forgot to tell you …'

'You're breaking up, Ellie.'

'Can you hear me? Preston won't …'

But they were cut off just as the train arrived in Chorleywood. When Ellie finally arrived home, she made hurried preparations for bed. Before she closed her eyes she prayed aloud a little wish; 'Please, Mr Fairchild, not tonight, I'm very tired.' He must have been listening for she slept soundly through the night.

The next day flew by as Ellie tried to take care of her 'to do' list. Saturdays were always filled with chores and catching up on things that she didn't have time for during the week. 'How in the world do women with children get anything done?' she said to herself. And immediately the thought made her spirits sink. She felt something grab her in the pit of her stomach. For Ellie would have loved the opportunity to find out how women with children got things done.

Although she had enjoyed these last few years living alone, it wasn't how she wanted to see her future. During the first of the two years she had been dating Preston, she had seen the potential for a relationship with him that might have led to something more serious. Now, the outlook for Preston-ever-after was bleak. Something's brewing here, she thought. Something that made her feel a little strange and a little sad.

Before she knew it, it was time to get dressed and head for London. She needed to leave early so that she could reach the shops before they closed. She had managed to track down a mah-jongg set that had been made in China in 1923. It was waiting for her at one of her favourite antique shops. The thrill that it would give her mother pleased her.

'Let's see,' she said as she opened her wardrobe. 'At least I don't have to worry about what I'm going to wear.' She reached for her reliable old black dinner dress, as she called it. It was the same dress she wore to almost every special occasion. As she stepped into it she could tell right away that something wasn't giving. That 'something' was the material! She tried to zip the back zipper but it just wasn't moving.

'I don't believe this!' Ellie was astounded. 'I always wear this dress, it was fine the last time I wore it. Which was ... a few months ago actually.'

Once again, Ellie was in a race with time. Slightly panicked, she almost fell into her wardrobe trying to find something to wear. She came across a skirt she had never worn. It was a long, full riding skirt in dark cherry red suede. As soon as she had brought it home she thought she must have been mad to even think about buying it, let alone wearing it. She thought it was a bit showy for her. But tonight she was desperate.

She tried it on and, lucky for her, it looked like it might work. It was a little too tight in the waist but she could get by. She rummaged around looking for her favourite black jumper. She didn't own a lot of clothing items that she really loved and the black mock turtleneck was an exception. It was a fine silk rib design that actually flattered Ellie's figure.

Then she remembered that Tilda had given her a belt last Christmas that she had stuck in the back of her wardrobe. It was wide, made of soft black leather with a large silver buckle in a curved oval design, somewhat like an elongated heart. Tilda had told her it would look good on her, especially if she wore it loosely below her waist. Ellie hadn't a clue about such things but thought it was worth a try anyway. She couldn't tuck her jumper inside her skirt due to the lack of manoeuvring room, and little did she know that it would have looked quite naff to do so. The jumper was neither thick nor heavy and the length was short enough to fall neatly in soft folds on the outside of the red suede skirt. She placed the belt over her jumper a few inches below her waist. 'Not too bad,' she said, 'a bit different, but not bad.'

Indeed, it was actually very different for Ellie. Forced, as she was, to take claim to her wardrobe's contents, she had discovered a new outfit. A skirt whose line and colour flattered her and a belt that lent a little shape and a tiny bit of sparkle to her burgeoning image: an image of which she was entirely and almost completely unaware.

She took a little more care than usual with her makeup and found a complementary colour of lipstick hidden at the bottom of a rather old makeup bag to top it all off. 'Too bad I didn't have time to do something to my hair. Maybe I'll just try to put it up. It always works for Joanna Lumley.' It took her a few tries and it certainly bore no resemblance to Ms Lumley's up-do, but finally she was finished and ready to go.

Ellie never quite managed to leave the house without a cloud of rush behind her. She grabbed her raincoat and umbrella, jumped into her seven-year-old Volvo and drove to the station.

She took a taxi from Marylebone Station to Holland Park. It was just beginning to drizzle and the air was already chilly. On an intimate little side street near Holland Park, a neat row of shops sat door to door. Ellie stopped at the door with the blue wood frame. She peeked through the glass window upon which was painted in discreet black letters, 'Evans & Sons'. She lightly tapped on the glass and waved at Mr Evans, the elder, who was expecting her.

Dai Evans opened the door and warmly welcomed Ellie. Mr Evans had been a friend of Ellie's family ever since she could remember. Many years ago, while on holiday in Wales, Ellie's father had discovered Mr Evans's former shop in Cardiff. He made the move to London over twenty years ago and brought with him a very thick Welsh accent. Ellie had spent hours as a child rummaging through boxes under his tables and sitting proudly on top of Mr Evans's desk while her parents made their purchases.

'Here it is. Here it is. I am very excited for your mother. She will be so pleased.'

Mr Evans proudly displayed the mah-jongg set, which was in its original rosewood box. He slowly opened the box and beamed at its contents. Even though Ellie knew nothing about the game, she could see that the set itself was beautiful.

'It looks as though it's in very good nick for its age, Mr Evans.'

'It's a complete set, of course,' said Mr Evans. 'Everything in order and just look at the colours on those tiles.'

'Mr Evans, you're so kind to ...' As she spoke something caught her eye. She looked more closely into the display case upon which the mah-jongg box sat.

A gold, band ring in a wonderful pale lemon yellow colour held Ellie's gaze. It had the most intricately engraved floral pattern on it, but very sparingly, hardly to be seen. 'What an odd thing,' Ellie said.

'Yes,' said Mr Evans, who had been watching her, 'it is an odd thing. Do you know what that is?'

'A ring of some sort, obviously, but it is just so ... I feel like I've seen it somewhere before.'

'It's called a posy ring.' Mr Evans brought the ring out of the case and held it to the light. 'This one, which you have so tastefully admired, is rare. Its content of gold is 90 per cent. It hails from the seventeenth century.'

Ellie suddenly felt very strange. 'Did you say seventeenth century?'

'Yes, it has been examined by the British Museum. It was found during the building of a new road in Dover.'

'Gosh, what a history.'

'Ah, yes, but here's the interesting bit. Come closer to the light – I want to show you something.'

Mr Evans reached into his pocket and produced a small jeweller's magnifying glass which he gave to Ellie.

'Have yourself a little look at the inside of the ring.'

Amused, Ellie looked inside the gold band where there was an inscription of some kind. It was actually well preserved and fairly easy to read. But it was the words that made her take a quick breath.

Dearest Thy Hath Woon My Hart

'I don't believe it! Look at the way "heart" is spelled. That is "heart", isn't it?'

Mr Evans laughed. 'I believe the translation would be "Dearest You Have Won My Heart" and yes, it is a bit unusual to find your surname in a seventeenth-century wedding ring.'

'It's awfully large though, isn't it, Mr Evans?'

'Another unique feature – it was made for a man. However, sometimes the groom put his ring on the bride's thumb, so it might have been meant for a woman.'

'It's really very lovely,' she mused wistfully. 'Well, I really must dash. Mum will kill me if I'm late.'

'It's raining old ladies and sticks. Please wait here and I'll find a black cab.' Mr Evans grabbed a huge black umbrella.

'Oh no, please, I'm fine.'

'Wouldn't hear of it, I'll be right back.' The chivalric Mr Evans grabbed an umbrella and headed for a busier street.

Ellie placed the rosewood box in a bag she had brought with her. As she carefully packed it, she secretly thought the gift would somehow appease her guilt. Ellie had not spent as much time with her mother lately as she would have liked, what with being preoccupied with work and distracted by Preston, or the absence of Preston. Wait a minute, did I just say distracted? Did I really say distracted? But surely Mr Fairchild hadn't meant … She glanced again at the ring, and finally it dawned on her. Running away from dealing with her relationship with Preston had been her goal in life for the last few weeks. But now there was nothing else to think about as she waited for the taxi. Not so long ago, she would have seriously considered buying the ring for Preston. At this moment, standing in Mr Evans's antique shop, she knew it was not meant to be.

She heard a tapping on the door and, startled out of her thoughts, she saw Mr Evans waiting for her.

'Thank you so much, Mr Evans.'

'Please do send my best to your mother.'

'Will do,' She turned to the driver. 'Wrigley's On the Square, Kensington, please.'

Ellie felt a bit numb as she was driven through the streets of London. There were no tears; instead, a feeling of emptiness and a desire to just get through the evening.

When she entered the restaurant the bustling atmosphere brought her back to life, at least a little. The fireplace was roaring, the music was low but cheerful and the exquisite smell of great food nearly knocked her over. She waved at Jean-Louis, who was scurrying around gracefully with a tray full of something. He motioned her to the side door that led to the private room.

She was in for a surprise when she opened the door to the private dining room. Someone, probably none other than Wrigley himself, had decorated the room with what seemed like hundreds of candles. The double doors that led to the garden patio were wide open, but the heat from the fireplace, although smaller than the one in the main dining room, kept the room warm. The sound of the pouring rain only added to the cosseted feeling. The glowing light, which came from all directions in the room, settled on the splendid table that was before her.

'Wriggers, look what you've done! This is beautiful, isn't it, Mum?'

'I told Wrigley that he went to far too much trouble just for our little group.' Georgina Hart, a pretty, petite woman stood up to greet her daughter.

'Nonsense.' Wrigley's Aunt Poppy stood up too. 'He loves entertaining in this room almost as much as the other one.' A large, buxom woman, Poppy approached Ellie with her arms opened wide and gave her a big hug.

'Spot on, Aunt Poppy, and Jean-Louis helped with the preparations. We've been waiting for you, Ellie, ready for a glass of bubbly?' Wrigley stood ready to pop the cork.

'Ellie, your hair looks lovely up like that. You look different tonight,' Ellie's mother said. Her kind eyes and smile completely banished the thought of there being anyone else in the room who could possibly be Ellie's mum.

'You know, Georgie, you're right,' said Poppy. 'Ellie, what have you done to yourself?'

Not used to compliments on her appearance, Ellie blushed and tried to laugh it off. 'Oh, just a rather large dose of stress and anxiety, I suppose.' She quickly changed the subject: 'Well, Wriggers, don't just stand there, pop and pour.'

Wrigley had been staring at Ellie – he too noticed that she seemed to have taken a little extra care tonight, or maybe it was the candlelight; whatever it was, he couldn't take his eyes off her.

'Right,' Wrigley said, 'now you're all aware that it's Saturday night and that Jean-Louis and I will have to pop in and out, so let's toast the birthday girl now and carry on, shall we?'

Wrigley and Jean-Louis took great care to make the evening perfect. The food was divine, which went without saying, and the room felt magical. The little party took a break from over-indulgence before dessert. Poppy entertained them with a repertoire of excerpts of a few of her readers' letters. At times her weekly advice column attracted a host of colourful characters.

'Dear Poppy,

My beloved Ambrose tells me daily that he desperately needs his nails clipped. I cannot possibly help him, even though I would love to, and am at a loss because he doesn't seem to be able to take no for an answer. I simply don't know what to do. How can I explain to him that once and for all I am powerless? Please help!

Yours,
Badgered

PS Oops! Forgot to tell you that Ambrose is my dearly departed Retriever.'

Ellie, thinking of her own dream visitor, did not laugh as heartily as the others. She took a moment to look around her. She thought of Preston and felt a pang when she wondered if he really would have fitted in after all. She supposed he might have found the evening boring or silly.

'Mum, I'm sorry that Preston had to cancel tonight. And Wrigley, I tried to tell you that he cancelled but we were cut off,' Ellie said.

At the mention of Preston, a unison of ears perked up. Ellie's mother looked at Wrigley and he at her. Together an unplanned, 'Pity,' was said aloud.

'All right, you two, no need to be cheeky.' Ellie tried to not let her voice waver.

'Where is the Right Honourable Preston Wilcox tonight, Ellie?' Wrigley asked.

'Pay no attention to them, Ellie, they're being abysmally rude,' Poppy said.

'But they don't understand ...'

'Don't understand what?' her mother asked.

'I don't think this is the time to talk about it, Mum.'

'Talk about what, dear?'

'I've decided to break it off with Preston!' Ellie blurted out.

She moved her chair back from the table, abruptly excused herself and couldn't leave the room quickly enough.

After Ellie ran out, Wrigley and Georgie looked at each other, both surprised by the news, but still, they could not disguise their delight. Wrigley raised his fists in victory and said intensely but not too loudly, 'YES!'

'Wrigley, have you no consideration for Ellie's feelings?' Poppy asked.

'Of course I do. What you don't know, Aunt Poppy, is that Preston is a chinless wonder, a prat, who never deserved ten minutes with Ellie, let alone almost two years.'

Poppy looked at her nephew for a few moments. 'Ah, I see,' she finally said. This evening had proven to be quite enlightening for her. She wondered if Ellie had any idea how deeply Wrigley cared for her.

Ellie ran into the corridor and rushed past Jean-Louis.

'Jean-Louis. Where's the key to the private loo? I don't want to go to the ladies'.'

'*Mon amie*, everything is all right?'

'Please, Jean-Louis, where is it?'

'*Oui, oui,* follow me.'

When she had closed the door behind her, she stood with her back up against it. I didn't mean to do that, she thought, I've just ruined everyone's evening. She barely had time to catch her breath before company joined her.

The first to come to the loo door was Wrigley.

'Ellie, I'm so sorry, I didn't know. Please open the door.'

'I'll be out in a minute.'

'Come on, Ellie, open up. Here comes Georgie, she didn't mean to upset you.'

'Don't be so stupid, I'm not upset with her.'

Now Georgie stood beside Wrigley outside the door. 'Eloise, can you hear me? That was incredibly rude of me. Please darling, do come out,' she said rather loudly.

'Mum, I can hear you. Please just give me a minute. I'll be right there.' Ellie felt terrible. 'I can't believe this. I'm in another loo again feeling like an imbecile,' she whispered to the wall.

Wrigley turned to Georgie. 'What should we do?'

'I'll tell you what to do.' Poppy had arrived on the scene and now the three of them stood huddled outside the door. 'Both of you stop clinging to this door and leave the girl alone.'

Poppy pushed the others aside and moved close to the door. In a very patient and calm voice she said, 'Now, Ellie, not to worry, take your time and when you're ready, we'd love for you to join us for dessert.'

'Thanks, Poppy, I'll be there in a moment, I promise. But do take Wrigley and Mum with you.'

'You heard her,' Poppy said, 'back to the table with the lot of you.'

At last Ellie was left alone. She looked in the mirror. There was a hint of sarcasm in her voice as she leaned forward a little closer to the mirror: 'Well, here we are again Ms Hart. Another bloody fiasco, let's see if we can finish up the evening in a civilised manner, shall we?'

There was a very faint tap on the door again. 'Ellie, it's Jean-Louis, everything *très bien?*'

'Yes, Jean-Louis, everything's fine.'

'Ellie, I do not mean to disturb, but instead of one cake for your birthday mother, I make favourites for each one. I make for you my chocolate soufflé and it is warm now, but not so in a few minutes. You understand, *oui?*'

Ellie quickly opened the door. 'The warm bittersweet chocolate soufflé?'

'*Oui,* and just for you, lavender ice cream, your favourite, no?'

'Jean-Louis, I'm ready to return to the scene of my discontent.'

'*Pardon?*'

'Never mind, you're the best.' Ellie gave Jean-Louis a peck on the cheek and left the loo seduced by promises of a very special serving of cake and ice cream.

When she entered the private dining room everyone began to speak at once. Ellie quickly silenced them with apologies for her outburst.

Ellie's mother spoke up first. 'I'm sorry, Ellie, none of us had any idea about Preston.'

'Of course you didn't, Mum. I didn't even make the decision until today.'

'Then he doesn't know yet?' asked her mother.

'Afraid not. Maybe Poppy can offer her expert advice for a soon-to-be ex-girlfriend. I hope I don't wimp out.'

'My dear, you are certainly not a wimp. I have a feeling it will be much easier than you expect,' Poppy said confidently.

Wrigley had been noticeably quiet since Ellie had returned. She looked over at him and saw that he was staring into the fire.

'Wrigs, I hope I didn't throw off the timing for my soufflé,' she said.

'Your soufflé? What about your mum's apple tart and custard?' he teased as he turned to her. 'As a matter of fact, your timing is impeccable.' Wrigley leapt up to help Jean-Louis as he entered with a cart full of desserts. *'Voila!'*

For the rest of the evening each of them swooned over their individual desserts. Jean-Louis accepted accolades for his mastery of each one. Poppy's almond cake was dense and sweet. The stewed autumn fruits were a perfect complement to the richness of the cake. Wrigley had his usual, sticky toffee pudding with vanilla ice cream, and Jean-Louis joined Georgie with her tarte tatin and warm custard sauce.

'Mum, close your eyes for a minute.'

'Oh Ellie, please, I'm too old for that.'

The entire table groaned with dissension. Outnumbered, Georgie sat back in her chair with her hands in her lap and eyes closed like a schoolgirl expecting a treat.

Ellie pulled the empty dessert cart over and placed the rosewood box on top of it. She opened the box so that her mother's first glance would fall upon the beautiful ivory tiles. Poppy giggled while Wrigley helped Ellie roll the cart in front of Georgie.

'All right Mum, open your eyes.'

At first Georgie couldn't respond. But as her eyes adjusted to the box in front of her, she gasped and clasped her face in her hands.

'Oh Eloise, is it what I think it is?'

'Yes, Mum, an old one, an original, 1923.'

'But ... what ... where did you find it?'

'Mr Evans found it for me.'

'Of course, I might have known. That Dai Evans can find anything. Thank you, dear, it's very special.'

Wrigley and Poppy gathered around the gift, excited to see the objects of their favourite game. Meanwhile, Eloise tried to explain to Jean-Louis that mah-jongg bore absolutely no resemblance to dominoes.

Wrigley knelt down beside Ellie's chair and said softly, 'This was a very nice evening for your mother. The set is beautiful. Very thoughtful of you, Ellie.'

'Well Wrigs, I'm pleased I could do something right.'

Wrigley frowned. 'What do you mean by that?'

'I haven't exactly been right about anything else lately, have I?'

Wrigley stood up. 'You know what you need Ellie? You need a good old-fashioned Sunday outing. We haven't had a long chinwag in a while, let's catch up. I'll take you to Sunday lunch. I've been meaning to try a place in Bedfordshire.'

'You know, Wrigs, that sounds really nice. I was going to do a little work tomorrow, but I can catch up on Monday.'

'No worrying about work tomorrow, all right?'

'Hmm. No promises. Mum looks a bit knackered, I'd better see her home. I'll settle with you tomorrow then, if that's all right.'

'There's no settling this. It's my treat.'

'No, Wrigley, tonight was my idea, part of her gift. I've been so neglectful of her lately.'

'Sorry, can't hear a word you're saying. I'm absolutely deaf and dumb to any other discussion.'

'That's really kind of you, Wrigley. But what will I have to do to make it up to you? I won't have time this week to be your slave or anything.'

'Not a bad thought, actually. Go. See your mum home, come back here and by then I'll be ready to drive us home.'

'Wrigley, are we tired of commuting to Chorleywood?'

Wrigley laughed. 'Of course we are, but we love Chorleywood.'

Ellie stood and walked over to her mother. 'Come on, Mum, ready to go?'

'You needn't come with me, Eloise, I'm certainly able to ride in a taxi by myself.'

'Save your breath, it's late, I insist, so say good night. Poppy, we'll drop you off too.'

Everyone said their goodbyes and inundated Wrigley and Jean-Louis with compliments for the evening.

Ellie dropped Poppy off first at her Kensington flat and then took her mother to her little mews house in Marylebone.

Ellie asked the taxi to wait as she escorted her mother into the house.

'Eloise, I know your spirits are low tonight, but I must say that I think you've made a wise decision.'

'I'm not even going to ask you to explain that, Mum. I'm not really up for listening to any Preston-bashing tonight.'

'I wasn't going to "bash" anything, Ellie, I was just trying to say … Never mind.' Georgie sighed. Her daughter was so difficult to talk to sometimes. It was exasperating to intend to say something complimentary about Ellie's decision, only to be met with a dismissal. 'Thank you for a wonderful evening, Ellie.'

'Don't thank me, thank Wriggers. He wouldn't hear of my paying the bill, can you believe that? He adores you.'

Georgie bit her tongue because what she really wanted to say was, 'No, it's you he adores, you thick-headed young lady.' Instead she said somewhat seriously, 'Yes, Eloise, I can easily believe it.' She hoped Ellie would someday see what a good friend he'd been to her.

'Well, I'm off then, Mum. Take care.'

'Thank you very much again for the mah-jongg set. I'll send a little note to Dai, too. Perhaps you might come for dinner one day this week after work.'

'Oh, I don't know, Mum, pretty busy this week, but I'll try.'

'I can meet you in the City if you like, dear.'

'Mum, it's not that, I have to come to the West End anyway to change trains ... oh never mind, we'll see. Good night, Mum.'

She's just so difficult to talk to sometimes, Ellie thought as she hopped in the taxi.

On the way back to Chorleywood both Ellie and Wrigley were quiet. They rode comfortably together without speaking, having long ago dismissed forced chat in their friendship. When Wrigley pulled up to her house she realised how tired she was.

'Thanks for not mentioning Preston. I didn't really want to talk about him tonight.'

'You're not the only one,' Wrigley said.

Ellie frowned at him.

'Sorry, sorry. I'll pick you up at ten in the morning then. Do you want me to call you?' Wrigley asked.

'No, I'll set the alarm.'

'Ellie, last seating is at twelve-thirty, we can't be late.'

'I'll be ready, I promise.'

As Ellie made herself ready for bed she added one step to her nightly ritual. She placed a pen and small blank notebook on her bedside table. She anticipated the arrival of Mr Fairchild tonight and wanted to be sure that she wrote down as much as she could remember in the morning.

◆

Ellie awoke on Sunday morning having slept soundly through the night. There were no dreams at all to write down or think about. Puzzled, she thought that maybe the two dreams were just that. Two dreams that happened to have the same setting and character and nothing more. Still, as she padded around her house, taking her time getting dressed, the elegant man's face stayed in a corner of her mind.

It was a perfectly beautiful late autumn day. The air was very cool and fresh and the sun was shining.

'So, where are we going, Wriggers?'

'It's a surprise.'

'You know I don't like surprises.'

'Course you do. Always have.' Wrigley smiled at her.

Ellie looked over at Wrigley and opened her mouth to speak, but then closed it as if she had changed her mind and looked again at the road in silence.

Wrigley exited the M1 and began a series of turns and roundabouts that eventually led them to the foothills of the Chilterns in the rolling countryside.

'Wriggers, why didn't you bring Chutney? He would have loved running about in the countryside.' Ellie referred to Wrigley's pride, a tan Briard who'd won medals for mischievousness.

'No dogs allowed, I'm afraid.'

'Oh Wrigley, we're not going somewhere posh, are we? You didn't tell me to dress up.'

'Ellie, calm down. You look fine.'

'No, I don't. I must have put on at least a stone. I was getting dressed last night and couldn't zip up my dress.'

'You looked smashing last night.'

'I did? But can you tell that I've put on some weight?'

'Honestly? Yes. But you still looked smashing.'

'I don't know how it happened, suddenly my clothes don't fit.'

'Oh, you're barking. I've been telling you for ages that you eat like a 12-year-old.'

'What does that mean?'

'You know very well what I'm talking about, Ellie. Your Monday-night pizza fests with the girls at work, for one. Then you go all day without eating, only to indulge in some rather nasty junk food when you get home at nine o'clock at night. If you ate at my restaurant every night of the week, where, if you remember, I have offered to cook for you anytime, that would be a hell of a lot better.'

'Are you having a go at me?'

'Well yes, I suppose I am,' he said cheerfully.

'Well I've been under a lot of pressure lately.'

'Even more reason to eat more sensibly.' He paused. 'But you still looked fabulous.'

'Are we there yet?'

Wisely, Wrigley dropped the subject. 'Yes, just about.'

'I know where we're going – John Bunyan territory. We're going to Houghton Conquest to try out that pub you've been going on about.'

'It's more of a restaurant than a pub. But you're right.'

Just as Wrigley turned onto Conquest Road he said, 'It's a seventeenth-century country inn.'

'Stop the car.'

'What?'

'Please, Wrigley, pull over.'

Wrigley found a safe place to pull over at the side of the road. 'Are you all right?'

'Yes, just hang on a minute.'

'Ellie, you've been awfully, well … dramatic lately. Does this have anything to do with Preston?'

'No. Yes. I don't know. Do we have time for a walk before lunch? I think I need some air.'

'Right, I'll just go ahead and park at the inn, we're almost there, and then we can walk from there. We've plenty of time.'

'Thanks, Wrigs.'

They pulled up to the old country inn and Ellie jumped out of the car. Wrigley noticed that she took a good look at her surroundings as if to make sure she was really there.

He took her arm in his and walked closely beside her. 'All right then, Ms Hart, do tell me. What is troubling my old friend?'

Wrigley's unconditional and undivided attention helped Ellie to ease into telling him about her dreams of Mr Fairchild. She relayed how she felt she might be going a bit loony and was afraid to tell anyone what was happening to her. And then, while she was on a roll, she poured out her feelings about her insecurities at work, the reports she had received from her colleagues, and then finally wound down with her decision to break it off with Preston.

When she finished she looked up at Wrigley and asked, 'Well?'

'I think I might be jealous,' Wrigley said.

'Jealous?'

'I only wish that I, a simple man who loves nothing more than to plant things in the earth only to pull them up and set them upon a plate, could have my own personal gardener. A gardener from the seventeenth-century no less, who could teach me about ...'

'Wrigley! You haven't taken me seriously!'

'Oh, but you are so wrong. I am serious. Don't you see, Ellie? You've got to listen to this man. He has shaken you up and you needed a good shake. It doesn't matter who he is or that he only appears in your dreams. For heaven's sake, you could be having nightmares every night like some poor old blokes, instead of gardening lessons.'

'You are so right. He could be chasing me with a pair of his large gardening shears!' They laughed. 'I'm a bit peckish, is it time for lunch?'

Wrigley and Ellie made their way into the inn. They waited for their table in the dark-beamed bar which was panelled in Jacobean oak.

'I read somewhere that this place is supposed to be haunted,' Wrigley said.

'Don't tell me, the ghost of the gardener serves drinks on Sunday.' Ellie felt herself relaxing.

'No, two ghosts, one male and one female. A draught is felt as they walk by and a spectral hand can be seen stirring the drinks.'

'Wrigley, you're very entertaining, did you know that?' Ellie paused. 'Thanks for listening to me today.'

'Listen, Ellie, right now you feel pretty badly about Preston, but I just want you to know that, well, in all seriousness, I didn't think he was up to snuff.'

'No surprise there. You're so predictable, Wriggers, you've never liked any of my boyfriends.'

Wrigley looked at her for a moment and then stood up quickly. 'I'll just check on our table.'

They were led into the conservatory restaurant.

'Oh, it's lovely, isn't it, Wrigley?'

And it was. Persian rugs covered the floor and the large picture windows boasted swagged curtains and a view of the orchard garden. Large hanging plants brushed against them as they made their way to their table. The room was full of Sunday lunchers, but Wrigley had managed to wrangle the nicest table for two in the restaurant.

Ellie began to relax and enjoy herself as she and Wrigley chatted away the afternoon. Wrigley was genuinely interested to hear more about her project at work.

'I hadn't realised the full scope of the project, Ellie. Doesn't Human Resources take care of diversity issues?' he asked.

'Not in my universe. HR has its hands full. Do you realise how diverse a diversity department can be?' They laughed as Ellie continued,

'Take me, for instance, you've no idea what I've had to put up with. Remember when I was promoted? Some of the men in my department were furious. They hate having female team leaders. It's taken me three years just to get my bloody team balanced. I had to fight tooth and nail to get an older man, and I use the word "older" loosely, a Sikh from Bombay on my team. He's fantastic. He always brings an insight to the table that none of the rest of us could possibly contribute. It's absolutely ridiculous that there is so much discrimination. Let's see, you've got your age discrimination, then there's race, gender and let's not forget sexual orientation.'

'Such forward thinking, Ellie.'

'It shouldn't be, though.'

'Do you want a pudding?' Wrigley asked.

'After last night? What about you?'

'Of course.'

'Me too.'

'What you're trying to do for your company is very challenging, I admire you for it. You're venturing into turbulent waters. You remind me of my father.'

'Wrigs, that's the nicest thing you've ever said to me. I loved your dad. How's your mum?' Ellie asked.

'She's all right, she misses him. It's just been two years since he passed. She'd love to see you sometime.'

'We could take our mothers on an outing before it gets too cold.'

'They'd love it. You're the one with the busy schedule though.'

'Hang about, Mr Six-Day-a-Week maniac. You plan it, I'll be there.'

'Done. Ready to go?'

They spent a little time walking around the area before they journeyed back to Chorleywood. As the Forager rolled up to Ellie's house, she leaned over to give Wrigley a friendly kiss and thanked him for the loveliest weekend she could remember having in a very long time. He watched her open her door and wave to him as she stepped inside. He sat outside her house for a moment; frustrated, he laid his head on the steering wheel. What am I going to do about Ellie Hart? he thought.

◆

On Monday morning Ellie arrived at the office early with hopes that she could do a bit of catching up. Even though she'd been absent only two and a half days the previous week, it felt like two weeks to her. She was having great difficulty getting anything done. A constant flow of people filed through her office door and Floris, Ellie's second in command, practically parked herself in Ellie's office all day. Jasper called her in for a quick meeting for which she was completely unprepared. She was aware beforehand that she needed a few documents and at least 15 fact-finding minutes for the meeting, but she had been so busy micro-managing everyone else that she neglected her own needs. Ellie felt like a scolded schoolgirl when Jasper impatiently dismissed her from his office.

Floris was waiting for Ellie when she returned from her meeting with Jasper.

'What *is* it Floris?' Ellie asked impatiently. 'You've been hovering about all day.'

Trying not to show her own frustration, Floris calmly asked Ellie for a minute of her time. Floris was a very focused and highly motivated woman whom Ellie had been grooming as her replacement for well over a year – if everything went well.

'Ellie, I've been thinking about the new off-site training programme. I'd really like the opportunity to head that project. I feel very capable and I've had a lot of experience in this area.'

'I don't think so, Flo. It's just too new and this is the first time we've offered this kind of programme.'

'I understand, Ellie, but quite frankly, you've had your hands full lately and we're getting a bit behind on it. The Women's Conference and the closing dinner are just around the corner as well. I need some numbers.'

'I'm well aware of the schedule, I'll take care of it. I'll work on some figures. Anything else?'

'The team wants a special meeting.'

'What about?'

Floris squirmed a bit in her seat, pushed her dark curly hair away from her eyes and said, 'They want to discuss the cost-cutting exercise.'

'Oh, for heaven's sake! Now? I told everyone we'd discuss it in the future; we have too much to do right now.'

'Ellie, they think you'll just keep putting it off.'

'I don't give a toss what they think. All right then?' Ellie looked at Flo and the door. Flo took the hint and excused herself.

She hadn't meant to snap at Floris, but Ellie was experiencing that familiar feeling of being pulled in too many different directions. It seemed that she couldn't walk a straight line any more for being distracted by myriad twists and turns.

It was the end of the day before she was able to sit in front of her computer to do the tasks she had hoped to accomplish much earlier in the day. Soon, however, five of her colleagues appeared at her office door with their coats on.

'Ready to go?' asked one.

Ellie looked at her blankly.

'Monday night ... pizza ... hello?'

Ellie sat for a moment looking at them and then back at her desk, which was piled high with work. She enjoyed the Monday-night pizza routine with the other women; it was her social touchstone when she became too embroiled with her work. However, tonight it felt like an added pressure. She had often wanted to skip the evening but hated to disappoint her friends and always acquiesced. Perhaps, she thought, this is another one of those distractions that I could do without for a while. Another hour at my desk will certainly be more effective than a few slices of pizza.

'C'mon then, Ellie. We're hungry,' another of the women said popping her head inside the door.

Ellie stood and walked over to the group. 'I'm really sorry,' she said, 'I've got some catching up to do here.'

Groans of protest from the group made it difficult for Ellie to stand her ground.

'You've never missed a night, Ellie. Must be a Preston evening,' one of them teased. 'Is he meeting you here and you just don't want to tell us?'

Ellie smiled a weak and rather unconvincing smile at the mention of Preston and just shook her head no.

'Go on with the lot of you. Have a good time.' She shooed them away.

During the rest of the week Ellie slowly began to catch up on her work. She turned down several invitations for after-work drinks from her colleagues and a shopping excursion during the course of the week, which she certainly never enjoyed anyway. She was surprised to find that her focus improved. She also realised that it wasn't necessarily the amount of time that she formerly spent with Preston that had drained her of her energy, but that the actual worrying and frustration he caused had been the true distraction.

Wrigley, on the other hand, made good on his promise to offer her dinner whenever she felt so inclined. She stopped by his restaurant a couple of nights during the week after work, and, as usual, he was a gracious host. It proved to be a relaxing, easy way to end her day. She even managed to meet her mother for dinner at Wrigley's one night, which pleased her mother no end.

Her dreams during the week were Fairchild-free and Ellie wondered again if maybe she had seen the last of her odd friend. She still slept with a pad and pen by her bedside and a piece of paper with Mr Fairchild's instructions sat at the bottom of her bag. She had acknowledged the need for change and she was doing a pretty good job of weeding out a few serious distractions. But was that it? she wondered.

By Friday Ellie felt her grasp on the work ahead was a bit stronger. She was actually looking forward to the planning meeting with her team. That is, until the bubble she had been manoeuvring around in all week burst.

As soon as she entered the meeting room Ellie could sense the tension. 'What the crap is going on in here?' she said to herself.

Not one to play games she immediately addressed the group. 'All right then, out with it, what's up?'

Floris spoke first. 'I believe I can speak for the team, Ellie. We're trying to avoid a last-minute panic here and we're all feeling a little overwhelmed.'

'If this is about the cost-cutting exercise …'

'No, Ellie it's not. We know that Flo spoke to you about that earlier.' The handsome Paresh spoke up. He was a striking man, tall and well built. The Sikh's turban made him tower over everyone seated around the room. He continued, 'I don't think any of us are ready for this planning meeting today. We're still trying to catch up with last week's meeting. We have several very important events coming up soon, as you well know. The problem is we don't work as quickly as you do. None of us are very productive with the off-the-cuff, last-minute approach that seems to work so well for you.'

'That's right,' Floris said. 'We need to have more information sooner. For example we've had several proposals for our off-site training but we can't respond until you approve the budget.'

'We don't want to constantly chase you, Ellie, we know that you have a lot on your plate right now, but we can't keep delaying certain decisions,' another team member said. 'We need some more face time with you. We're just trying to avoid rash decisions.'

Ellie was silent. She looked around the room. Over in the corner sat her youngest and newest team member.

'Margaret,' Ellie addressed the young girl, 'whatever is the matter?'

Margaret, the perfect English rose, sat twisting a tissue in her hand, and appeared to be holding back tears. Her translucent skin looked a little pinker than it should and her whole demeanour, which was normally bright and even perky, had collapsed in the chair. Margaret looked through the strands of her blonde hair but could not lift her head up, nor could she speak.

'Margaret?' Ellie waited for a response.

Finally, Margaret raised her head and huge tears welled up in her eyes. 'I'm afraid ...' she gulped, 'I'm afraid I'm going to lose my job.'

'For heaven's sake, Margaret. Why on earth would you think that?'

'I have a report due for Mr McMurty next week and I'm nowhere near ready.' Margaret managed to spew the words into the room, looking around her as if the team were going to jump at her. She still had not looked at Ellie.

'Well, what is it going to take for you to get the report ready, Margaret?'

'I've been trying to meet with you. I need to speak to you about it.'

'But that doesn't make sense, Margaret, you know where my office is by now, don't you?'

'You're always so busy. I just ... I don't know ... I can't seem to find the right moment to speak to you. I didn't want to bother you.'

'Please, Margaret. We'll talk about this later. Don't worry. I *will* help you with anything you need to finish your report. You are not going to lose your job, all right?'

'Yes, Ellie, sorry, everybody.'

Paresh, who was sitting closest to Margaret, smiled at her and mouthed, 'It's okay.'

Gratefully Margaret nodded to him.

'All right then. I've certainly heard all of your concerns,' Ellie continued, 'and I assure you that I take them all on board. I'd appreciate it if each of you would state your points and any questions in writing as soon as possible. Let's call it a day, shall we?'

Ellie left the room. Her team sat staring at the door as if they expected her to come straight back.

'Did we make a mistake?' Floris looked at Paresh.

'No,' he said thoughtfully. 'We did the right thing. We were all experiencing the same thing to a degree.' And he then turned to the group. 'Weren't we?'

Yes, indeed, they all agreed.

◆

Ellie was a tad angry, feeling a little guilty and a lot upset. She left the office feeling lousy. Just when she thought her work life was beginning to improve, her team proved to be almost dysfunctional. She was aware that she needed some time to assimilate today's meeting, but instinctively she knew that she bore most, if not all, the responsibility.

Ellie was tired and wanted to get home early. She phoned Wrigley on her way back to Chorleywood to tell him she wouldn't be coming by for dinner tonight. She thought she heard disappointment in his voice, but he was understanding and amiable. Funny, she thought, I feel a little disappointed too now that I think of it. After today's meeting, she had a feeling that this would be mostly a working weekend for her.

Later that evening after a take-away curry and a long bath, Ellie settled down on her sofa in front of the television. She popped in a DVD of her favourite series, but couldn't keep her eyes open long enough to see the first five minutes.

Soon Ellie found herself standing in a pile of soil. A light breeze blew her hair away from her face and with the breeze came the most foul smell she believed she had ever had the misfortune of smelling.

'What is that horrible smell?' Ellie shouted.

Upon first glance it looked as if her garden no longer existed. All she could see was earth – everywhere. Dirt piled high in one corner and in another area she saw a trench where the soil looked fluffy and rich.

Stones and rocks had been moved to one side and then she saw Mr Fairchild with a spade in his hand.

'Ah, there you are. I am so pleased you have arrived. Better to stand downwind today – away from the barrow.' Mr Fairchild waved to her.

Ellie quickly stepped away from the wooden wheelbarrow. 'What's in it?' she asked.

'Very old horse manure,' Mr Fairchild said proudly. He reached into his pocket and pulled out a fine linen handkerchief. On one of the corners of the small piece of cloth was embroidered a tiny, long-stemmed red rose with two green leaves.

Ellie marvelled at his reliable good cheer. 'Fancy that. What about all this dirt then?'

Mr Fairchild presented the handkerchief to Ellie and motioned to her nose.

'Cover your face with it if you wish,' he said.

'Mmm. How lovely, it smells of roses.' She held the handkerchief to her nose.

Mr Fairchild explained: 'Preparing the soil is the most important step in gardening. Digging is a vital step in the preparation. Digging also gives one time to think – which is very important, Ellie – to have time to think.

'The work is quite hard but the rewards are numerous,' he continued authoritatively. 'Otherwise, without preparation you really are wasting your time.'

Mr Fairchild slowly and methodically continued to dig. Each time his spade hit a rock Ellie helped him remove it from the earth and place it to one side. As they worked together she followed his lead in taking breaks. He seemed to know at just which point her back could take no more.

At one point Ellie asked if she might have a go at the digging. Mr Fairchild graciously handed her his spade. But Ellie and her spade were not very compatible. Mr Fairchild made it look so easy, yet she was buckling under the weight of it.

'Preparation can be a bit daunting, I admit.' Mr Fairchild watched Ellie as she struggled. 'It can be a very challenging proposition sometimes; nevertheless, you will be lying in a hammock not long from now resting. You will be pleased with the low maintenance required in the future.'

Sooner than she would have thought, the entire garden had been dug, trenched and was ready for the wheelbarrow full of dung. Mr Fairchild began to fork in the fertiliser, again working slowly and methodically. His movements back and forth, back and forth, calmed Ellie.

'Another very important part of the preparation is to give the plant what it needs to grow. If the soil isn't fed well from the beginning then it will require you to play ... what is the phrase you young people use ... catch-up? That can be quite disastrous really.'

'I never knew it took so much preparation to just plant a seed,' Ellie said.

'Well you certainly know how much work it takes to begin a project, don't you?' he asked.

'Oh, well I never thought of it that way.'

'And would it be true to say that there have been suggestions from several quarters as to your need for a little improvement in the preparation area?' Mr Fairchild asked very gently.

Ellie smacked her palms to her forehead and continued to mildly beat herself on the head. 'Of course,' she said to herself, 'I didn't see it coming.'

Still Ellie could feel her armour coming up. 'I work very hard, Mr Fairchild. I work weekends and late nights.' Her voice became much louder and shriller. 'Some weeks I have no time for myself or anyone else. I haven't complained and I love what I do, but are you trying to tell me that I've more work to do, that I have to work even harder than I am already?' Ellie's face was now a very bright red and there was a drop of perspiration on her upper lip. It could be said that she had just had yet another outburst.

Mr Fairchild was silent. He slowly walked over to a pail of water that was resting under the apple tree. He washed his hands and face and still said nothing. He brought another large bowl of water to Ellie and put it down beside her. Then, he went back to the apple tree and disappeared behind it for a moment. He then reappeared with a wicker basket. On top of the basket was a Linsey-Woolsey plain-woven cloth, which he spread on the only patch of grass left under the tree.

'I would not interfere in any way with your work and am by no means suggesting that you should consider working harder.' Mr Fairchild continued to relieve the basket of its contents. 'In fact, I was endeavouring to illustrate how to create more free time, not less.'

On the cloth Mr Fairchild had placed a selection of farmhouse cheeses, several beautifully ripened pears and apples and a huge chunk of homemade bread.

'Preparedness is the hallmark of a true professional, Ellie,' he said with gravity in his voice. 'For people like your good self who must cultivate it, it is the difference between longevity in the garden or the quick demise of the plants, or, perhaps in your case, attaining your goals within your place of employment ... or not.'

Mr Fairchild placed a lovely plate of food in Ellie's hands.

'Everything in your garden depends on how you prepare it. The very roots of the flowers and plants need room to grow; they need water, food and sunlight. You are meant to be in charge, and if you are not, then nature will most definitely take its course. The same would be true for your place of work.'

Ellie knew he was right, as painful as it was to hear.

'They call me "Miss Wing It" at work. I've even adopted the name for myself. I must admit that it is getting harder and harder to play catch-up, never mind getting ahead,' she admitted.

Ellie looked at the simple but elegant lunch that Mr Fairchild had laid before them. She recognised that preparedness had reigned with Mr Fairchild today.

'I apologise for my outburst, Mr Fairchild.'

'Apologies accepted. Do you favour lilies, my dear?'

'Well, yes I do actually.'

'Excellent. The white lily happens to be my speciality. They love a light soil with a bit of lime rubble in it. I think they should be planted in pots, though. Do you agree that a natural garden is preferable to a formal garden?'

'Yes, Mr Fairchild.' Ellie yawned. She suddenly felt very tired. 'I quite fancy a natural garden.'

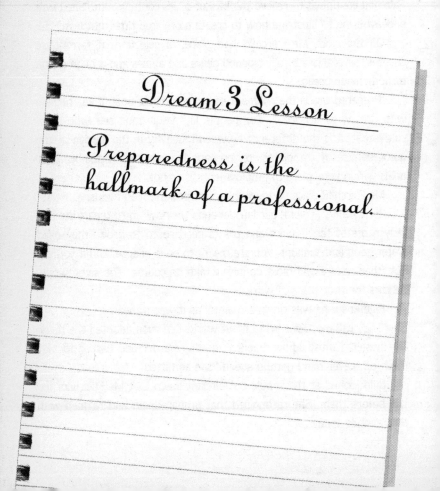

Dream 3 Lesson

Preparedness is the hallmark of a professional.

The Seeds of Change

Ellie awoke on her sofa where she had spent most of the night. She squinted at the clock and saw that it was four o'clock in the morning. Rumpled and still sleepy, she made her way into her bedroom, yawning and trying to remember her dream.

She picked up the pad and pen beside her bed and tried to recall a few of Mr Fairchild's last words to her. She scratched her head, muttered and then wrote *preparedness* and *hallmark*. Ellie promptly fell back to sleep.

On Saturday morning, a little bit later than normal, Ellie began her usual loads of laundry. As she sat staring at the machine, the previous night's dream was very much within her consciousness. She had never really considered herself an 'unprepared' person. On the other hand, it seemed that her colleagues in New York thought so. Of course, she knew she had earned the nickname of Miss Wing It; still, she managed to get things done and considered herself a reliable person. 'But I think Mr Fairchild was speaking of something else, some other level of preparedness,' she said to herself.

The ring of the phone interrupted her thoughts.

'Ellie, how are you, darling?'

Speaking of being unprepared. It was Preston.

'Oh, all right, Preston,' she managed to say.

'Why don't I come over? It's been too long.'

Ellie was furious. 'Preston, the last time I spoke to you, which was over a week ago, you cancelled an engagement that was important to me. And now, a week later, you call me at the last minute expecting to see me? What would you think if you were me, Preston?'

'Well, just think of it as if I had been on a short holiday and now I'm back.'

'No, *you* just think of this: I am now going on holiday, except I won't be back.'

'You're not serious, Ellie.'

Ellie calmed down a bit, 'Yes, Preston, I am. This isn't working for me and I dare say it probably isn't working for you either. I don't really have anything else to say about it right now.'

'Now come on, Ellie. Don't be a silly girl, you don't know what you're saying, darling.'

Angry again, Ellie put the phone down – something she had never done before.

The phone rang again instantly. 'My name is not "darling", she was almost screaming into the phone, 'and as for the silly bit, the silly bit was wasting my time with you.'

'Umm, Ellie? Just wanted to know if you wanted to go for a coffee. That's all.'

'Oh Wrigley, I'm sorry, I thought you were Preston.'

'Undoubtedly.'

'A coffee? Yes, I need to get out of here.'

'Great, I'll pick you up in fifteen, all right?'

Ellie stood outside waiting for Wrigley, the air was very cold and it was a grey morning. She smelled the sweet burning wood from nearby chimneys and vowed to warm herself up with her own fire when she returned home.

As soon as Ellie slid into the car seat she ranted, 'Bloody hell, Wrigley. Damn him. Damn that man. What a cheek!'

'I'm sorry he's upset you.' Then, gently: 'I take it you've enlightened him about your decision.'

'Not very well, I'm afraid. I would have preferred to tell him in person, but he made me so angry.'

'I thought we'd drive over to Rumbles for a spot of breakfast,' Wrigley gently suggested.

Ellie noticed his careful tone and placed her hand on his arm. 'I'm all right, Wrigley. It's really okay. I wasn't expecting him to call this morning. I just wasn't ready. I lost my temper with him.'

'What did he say to you to make you scream into the phone like that?'

Ellie relayed the short conversation to Wrigley. He remained silent and kept his eyes on the road.

'Go ahead,' Ellie said, 'say it.'

'What?' Wrigley asked.

'I told you so.'

'No, but I will say this: Preston Wilcox is a big girl's blouse.'

Ellie laughed as they entered the car park and made their way into the restaurant.

Over breakfast Ellie was hesitant to tell Wrigley about her most recent dream. It wasn't an easy subject for her and she was embarrassed to bring it up again. But eventually, she did. Wrigley, who was immensely relieved that she was able to move on from Preston – his least favourite subject – was genuinely interested.

'Your Mr Fairchild certainly has you pegged,' Wrigley said.

'Got that right.'

'So do you have any ideas yet?' Wrigley asked.

'Ideas for what? Colour-coding my life?'

'Getting yourself organised and being prepared doesn't have to be like that, Ellie.'

'I know … I just … Well, do you think I have to change my entire life?' she asked seriously.

Wrigley laughed. 'Let me see if I can explain what being prepared means to me.'

He paused and took another bite of his eggs and toast.

'All right, see if this makes sense to you. All the advance prep work we do in the kitchen is my security. That way, when the inevitable lunch or dinner crisis occurs in the kitchen, I've no reason to panic. I can never prepare for or avoid the unexpected, but at least I know that I've done everything possible to keep a mistake or problem in the kitchen from becoming a disaster at the customer's table. Are you with me?'

'Umm, yes I think so. But don't you consider the work you do even before you enter the kitchen a part of the preparation? How many times have you tried to drag me to one of those early morning markets on the weekend?'

'Very good. But that's the fun bit for me. I love that stuff. That's not work, that's play.'

'Sorry, Wriggers, being prepared is not on my list of playtime activities.'

'Just think ahead, Ellie. Maybe spend a little time over the weekend thinking about how you can make next week easier for yourself. Start slowly.'

'You're asking me to rewire my brain.'

'For some reason there's something going on with you right now that brings an elderly gardener into your dreams. It's quite extraordinary really. If I were you, I'd pay close attention. You've set some pretty tough goals for yourself. Maybe you do need to do a bit of rewiring to make them happen.'

Ellie became very quiet and played with the spoon in her cup for a moment.

'This is hard for me to say, Wrigley. It's not as if I can just conjure up Mr Fairchild when I need him. I ... well, I ... oh shit, I think I need a little help,' she blurted out.

Wrigley waited before responding – he could tell by looking at her that there was more to come.

'I know it's asking a lot, but, want to spend your day off tomorrow pulling the latent organisational gene out of me?' Ellie asked hesitantly.

'Only if you don't cook. I'll bring sustenance and you bring a good attitude.'

'Really? Are you sure? You don't have plans for tomorrow?'

'I haven't the foggiest idea what we'll be doing but I'm willing to give it a whirl. Now let's get going, I've got some playing to do.'

◆

Late Sunday morning Wrigley arrived at Ellie's house with his arms full of boxes and with Chutney in tow.

'Couldn't bear to leave him behind today,' Wrigley said. 'You'll be very impressed with his manners.'

'Wrigley, what's all this then?'

'Food magazine reading for me. What do you think I'm going to do while you're working? In this box, incredible ingredients for lunch and a late tea or dinner. And, of course, Chutney's toys.' Wrigley seemed absolutely pleased as punch to be there.

At the mention of his name, Chutney's ears perked up and he sniffed around both Ellie and Wrigley waiting for something to happen to him. Wrigley pulled out a very tattered-looking stuffed duck, which Chutney promptly wrestled out of his hands and settled on the floor with it hanging from his mouth.

Ellie had made a fire earlier, trying at least to make this Sunday workday a little cosier.

'All right then, where do we start?' she asked.

'Well, whenever Jean-Louis and I get a little scattered we always sit down and talk things over first. Then we end up prioritising all the things we need to do. So why don't you just start with that?'

'But everything I do is a priority.'

'It can't be, Ellie. Some things just must come first on your calendar. Don't they?'

'Well yes, but nothing is more important to me right now than getting a green light for Diversity. That's my priority now in spite of the fact that I have loads of other important things going on as well.'

As Ellie talked to Wrigley about the special events that were coming up, she realised just how anxious and stressed she felt about work. Once again she was feeling overwhelmed with how many things needed her attention.

'And let's not forget, there's still the feedback from my last trip to New York to contend with,' Ellie continued.

'Miss Hart, when all else fails, make a list.'

'Make a list?'

'Yes, just list everything that you need to do and prioritise it.'

'It just sounds so simple.'

'It *is* simple. Sometimes when we're overwhelmed or incredibly busy we just forget the most obvious solutions. Look here, Ellie, I've known you for almost your entire life. I don't have to sit in your office to be pretty sure that you leave everything to the last minute and then operate out of emergency mode. Frankly, I don't know how you've done so well for this long – except for the fact that you're clever and talented, of course.' He smiled. 'We had a server at the restaurant once, I'm sure you'll remember him, Eddie from Manchester?'

Ellie nodded her head.

'Eddie was a terrific server. He loved the work too. Loved announcing the specials, knew a lot about food and wine, and he was a good, hard worker. But Eddie had one really frustrating, irritating flaw. He was always late for work. Couldn't show up on time if his life depended on it. So, unfortunately, he wasn't entirely professional. Are you still with me?'

Ellie had been completely silent and seemed to be sinking a bit in her chair.

She nodded again. 'Difficult for me to hear.'

'I know. So, the morning you called me to take you to the airport, which I was happy to do, I became a little concerned about how Miss Wing It would be able to maintain her effectiveness. And that's what you want, isn't it, Ellie, to be effective?'

'Yes, of course it is.'

'It seems to me that you're being pushed, if not shoved, to the next level. Your boss, your co-workers and colleagues are all asking you to change. Maybe you're having a little resistance to that. But I don't hear anyone, including Mr Fairchild, asking you to change overnight.'

'You're right. I know you're right. I need to do things differently.' Ellie opened her laptop and stared at a blank document page. She looked up at Wrigley, who motioned to the kitchen and mouthed the word 'lunch' as he crept out of the room.

An hour had passed before she knew it. She had created a long list of work that needed to be completed before the end of the month and another list that included the following month. At times she struggled with wanting to 'do' instead of sticking with her list. She became distracted by how quickly her creative mind wanted more activity instead of the mundane, disciplined task of methodically taking one day at a time.

Wrigley had been almost unnoticeable until she heard him going through the cupboards in her kitchen. He sounded a tad impatient when he stuck his head out of the kitchen door and said, 'Your kitchen is crazy. How do you function in here?'

'You know I don't.'

'Right.'

'I'm starved, is lunch ready?'

'No, your highness, it's not. Another half hour.'

'Smells lovely.'

'Back to work,' Wrigley said.

Ellie scrolled down to a copy of Tilda's appointment and scheduling diary. Tilda did a good job of scheduling, but it had been a long time since Ellie had taken a comprehensive look at her schedule. There were a few changes that she wanted to make. Usually she would try to keep the changes in one of her many mental compartments so that she could quickly move on. But now, she slowed down and made herself write down the changes. She then looked again at her list.

'Prioritise? *Everything* is important,' she insisted.

'Pardon?' Wrigley yelled from the kitchen.

'Talking to myself,' she yelled back.

Ellie stuck with it despite the restlessness she was feeling. Staring at the long list made her a little anxious. But soon something began to click. Every time she looked at anything on her list related to the Women's Conference she felt a slight pang of panic.

'I've got it! Wriggers, I've got it.'

Wrigley ran into the lounge with a tea towel in one hand and a pair of scissors in the other.

'What are you doing with those scissors?' Ellie asked.

'Cutting herbs. What's wrong?'

'It's the Women's Conference. It's an albatross around my neck, Wrigley. I'm not giving it enough attention and I need to make it a priority this week.'

'Excellent. Let's call this a breakthrough and time for lunch.'

'Let's sit by the fire. I'll help you.' Ellie stood up and stretched.

There was really nothing for her to do. Two plates had already been filled with a beautiful salad of roast chicken, field greens with fresh herbs, quail eggs and strips of sharp Parmesan.

'This looks wonderful, Wriggers. Did it take you all this time to make this?'

'Not really, I was doing a little prep – I stress the word prep – work for later.' He offered her the basket of bread.

'No thanks, I bought scones for tea. I'm trying to cut down a bit on the bread.'

'I'm impressed.'

'What I want to know is how you keep so fit, Wriggers. You're such a foodie; it doesn't seem fair that you haven't put on any weight at all.'

'Fair? Surely you jest. What I do is hard physical labour. Really, Ellie, your lack of knowledge about restaurant work is amazing. And maybe you've forgotten that I swim almost every other day.'

'Oh yes, your very posh London club, I had forgotten.'

'Why don't you come as my guest? We could go early one morning.'

'No thanks, change topic please.'

'I'll never give up.'

'I think it's time for me to get back to work.'

Ellie took their plates into the kitchen while Wrigley put another bundle of wood on the fire. Chutney woke up from his nap and Wrigley took him out for a short walk as Ellie settled down in front of the fire to continue her work.

'One week, if I can just get through one week without having to play catch-up that would be an improvement.'

She began with her schedule for Monday. Soon she was printing out reports, budgets, lists and made several pages of notes for various members of her team. She took the luxury of uninterrupted time to make decisions that she had been putting off for weeks. Wrigley plied her with steaming cups of tea as if he were in domestic bliss.

Four hours later she was weary but deeply satisfied. She looked up at Wrigley who now sat quietly on the floor by the fire surrounded by mounds of his treasured magazines.

'Famished?' He looked up at her through his glasses.

'Absolutely.'

'Want to go for a walk with Chutney before tea?'

'Sounds lovely,' Ellie said.

'I've been thinking about something you said earlier,' Wrigley said as they grabbed their coats. 'It sounds like your private office has an open-door policy. I imagine you sitting at your desk with people coming through a revolving door all day.'

'Fancy that,' Ellie said ironically, 'a manager with an open door. What's wrong with that?'

'Nothing, I suppose.' He paused, 'Unless you need a minute or two to yourself during the day. There are such things as boundaries, Ellie.'

The sun had set and the temperature had dropped to send a frosty little shiver through Ellie. They turned back and headed towards Ellie's house with Chutney prancing around them.

'I usually only close my door for emergencies, for instance when I throw a wobbly, or when there's a need for privacy. Wait a minute. Remind me, why are we talking about this?' Ellie asked.

'It just sounded as if you are constantly interrupted. Would it hurt to have a little private work time?'

'Well, I don't know,' Ellie teased, 'I have a feeling it's not something I placed on my high-priority list. Close Door Monday at eleven.'

'I'm just saying that a few minutes of peace might be helpful. It also sends a strong message. When I'm not available at the restaurant sometimes my staff solve their own problems. Look at your resistance, Ellie.'

'They already complain that they don't get enough time with me. You're right though. Ridiculous, isn't it? I'll have a think about it.'

They spent the early evening in front of the fire where Wrigley served a late tea. He had prepared a smorgasbord of delicacies for them to leisurely munch upon and they polished off Ellie's scones with French jam and Devonshire clotted cream.

'Wriggers, you are definitely some lucky woman's dream. When was the last time you had a date?'

Wrigley didn't take his eyes from the fire. 'I don't know, some time ago, I imagine.'

'I remember. I think it was Miss Impossible, wasn't it?'

'How could I forget? There was no pleasing that wench.'

'Yes, but she was beautiful,' Ellie reminded him.

'Oh really? It became impossible to see her face through that sour expression.'

'Hence her alias. So, no one since then?'

'No, not really.'

'Oh come on. All of those women who swoon over you at the restaurant?'

'They do not swoon – besides they just want a good table.' Wrigley began to clear the plates away.

Ellie stood up to help and noticed that Wrigley seemed a little sensitive about this subject.

'Sorry, Wrigs, it's just that it's been a long time since your break-up with Ann and you haven't really been serious about anyone since.'

Wrigley stopped walking towards the kitchen and turned back with his hands full of dishes to face Ellie.

'I know,' he said quietly, 'I know.'

'Is that it then? Are you still thinking about her?'

Wrigley began to chuckle and shook his head from side to side.

'What?' Ellie asked, surprised by his reaction.

'No, Ellie.' Wrigley barely made it to the kitchen without dropping the dishes. 'I have no forlorn thoughts of Ann.' He hesitated a moment. 'Speaking of exes, you've not even mentioned the old geezer today.'

'That would hardly be hospitable of me now, would it? You've spent your only day off with me, holding my hand through a work crisis and feeding my face. Wouldn't it be a bit rude of me to be mooning over Preston all day? But don't think I haven't noticed that you've changed the subject.'

'I told you, I'm just not seeing anyone right now.'

'All right, all right. Don't get your knickers in a twist. Just asking.'

They finished the washing up and Wrigley began to take his boxes to the car.

'Thanks for all your help today, Wrigley,' Ellie said as she followed him outside.

'Pleasure, treasure, let me know how your week goes. Come by for dinner if you want.'

'Thanks, I probably will. Listen, I apologise if I was being a nosey parker.'

'You weren't, Ellie.' Wrigley looked at her and was about to speak again but Chutney was barking in the front seat. He took that as a sign and decided it was time to go home.

'I think he's saying bye for now.' Ellie reached in the door and gave Chutney a nice rub.

'Night, Ellie.'

'Night, Wrigs. Careful home.'

On Monday morning Ellie opened her wardrobe to discover that she had forgotten to take her suits to the cleaners. 'Shit.' Her hands quickly moved through the hangers looking for anything resembling an acceptable work outfit. She admitted to herself that the contents of her wardrobe did look a little tired. 'Not today, please not today.'

Until two minutes ago she had actually been eager to get to her office. But now she sat on the bed with her head in her hands. This was not the first time Ellie couldn't find anything to wear to work. She thought something must be wrong with her for she didn't care about clothes the way every-single-other-woman-she-had-ever-met-in-her-life felt about them.

'I believe in uniforms. I really do. Why can't we all wear the same thing? Ten suits, ten blouses and the same shoes. We can all walk around like Stepford workers. I'd really fancy that!'

Her fantasy was not helping her get dressed. She stood again in front of her wardrobe and stared. She eyed the red suede skirt. Her hands reached into the wardrobe and just stroked it for a minute. 'Well, why not? No important meetings today. I don't really have a choice this morning, now do I?'

She slipped the black turtleneck over her head and vowed to deal with this dilemma once and for all. She knew she needed new clothes but she wanted to lose a little weight first. She zipped up her skirt and thought that maybe she was imagining it, but she could just possibly have lost a little already. 'Hmm. I wonder if suede stretches.'

◆

By the time the office began to hum with people Ellie had completely forgotten that she wasn't wearing one of her rather tired old suits, or one of her newer suits that didn't fit her properly. She was unaware that when she walked through the halls and offices, she splashed a bit of colour around her. As she made the rounds of her team members' desks they shot glances at her as she departed. When Tilda came into her office, she stared at Ellie without speaking.

'What?' Ellie asked.

'Um nothing, nothing.'

'Don't have time for this, Tilda,' Ellie said in a singsong voice.

'Everyone's commenting on your outfit,' Tilda said very quickly.

'Surely there are more important things to talk about.'

'You look nice today, Ellie.'

'Thanks, anything else?' she replied without looking up.

'And I noticed the changes in the schedule. Did you do that?'

'Yes, Tilda.'

'Anything wrong with my scheduling?'

'No, Tilda.' Ellie was becoming impatient.

'Just checking.'

Throughout the day her team members took turns spinning through Ellie's revolving door. Ellie had made so many decisions over the weekend that they couldn't resist asking time-consuming questions about her motives. They wanted detailed explanations of the changes she had made for the upcoming Women's Conference. Many of the requests that had cropped up in last Friday's meeting, Ellie had already addressed either in a note or a report to her staff. Yet, she still felt encumbered by their insatiable appetite for more attention.

Even Paresh, who was normally independent and self-motivated, needed nanny time. He was skittish about being responsible for interviewing potential presenters for their first off-site training programme. Ellie made a note – a real one, not a mental one – to set up interviews for him. It was easier than taking the time to coach him through the process.

Oddly enough, the only team member she hadn't laid eyes on was Margaret. Soon, however, Ellie caught sight of her walking past her door and called out to her. Margaret entered her office looking like a deer caught in the headlights.

'Something wrong, Ellie?' she asked, sniffling from a rather nasty cold.

Ellie thought how much Margaret reminded her of a younger, less jaded Daphne Marchant. She smiled when she remembered how Daphne had always frozen when she was called into a superior's office.

But that didn't last long. Daphne soon started to learn the ropes, and what followed was a strikingly new 'Daphne Unleashed'. Ambition and success soon became second nature to her. That was when she and Daphne were good friends, before her move to New York.

'No, Margaret, nothing is wrong. Now is a good time to discuss your report for Jasper. How can I help?'

'Oh.' Margaret was unprepared for this. 'I'll just go get my notes.'

'No, no need to, just tell me what you need.'

'The report is about how to make the company's ethos more easily understood to investors.'

Ellie began to laugh. 'Wait, stop right there.'

'Pardon? What's so funny?'

'He's testing you.'

'What? I don't understand.'

'McMurty is testing you, Margaret,' Ellie said.

'For what purpose?' Margaret was truly perplexed.

'Not sure exactly, probably to test your endurance levels. He knows this is a busy period for us. Who knows? Maybe he's testing your skills for another department. Don't worry about it. Just do the best you can. I'll get you a few similar reports. They should help.'

'Are you sure about this, Ellie?'

'Oh yes, positive.' Ellie smiled. 'He did the same thing to me a few years ago – similar topic, just about the same period in my career here.'

'Go on. Did he really?' Margaret blew her nose.

'Yes, trust me on this.'

Margaret passed Floris on her way out of Ellie's office. Floris had just arrived, having been out all day on appointments.

'You must have worked the entire weekend, Ellie.'

'No, just part of it.'

'I've had a look at everything on my desk. It's fantastic. I can go ahead with all of the arrangements for the Conference. Do you want to include spouses and dates for the closing dinner like last year?'

'Yes, it's in the budget and it worked well last year, don't you think?

Actually I've already made the invitation list and written the first draft for the invites.'

'But I could have done that, Ellie.' Floris was surprised.

'Look, you were complaining about the tight schedule, it was easier for me to just go ahead and do it.'

'Yes, I know, but I was just waiting for a nod from you.'

'Floris, I'm busy.'

'Of course, Ellie.' Floris always knew when to exit. She'd been through this dozens of times. Trying to catch up with Ellie when she was on a roll was daunting.

'By the way, Floris,' Ellie said as Floris was leaving, 'try to find a new caterer for the same figure. Last year the food was very disappointing.'

'All right, Ellie.'

Ellie made a note: *Ask Wrigley – caterer – WC.*

Alone for the first time that day, Ellie was surprised to see the lateness of the hour. The result of her weekend preparation was heartening for her team and it was clear that everyone had benefited from her efforts. That is, everyone but Ellie.

'I think Wrigley was right after all. The revolving-door syndrome was a bit much today.' The tasks on her list that were related to her own work had not received attention that day. She was so busy catering to her staff that now she would need to stay late to catch up with her work.

The Monday-night girls stopped by her office on their way to dinner.

'Oh come on, Ellie. You're not working again tonight, are you?'

'I'm afraid so, Virginia.'

'Oh don't be such a boring old fart. We never see you any more.'

Virginia, who worked in another department, had been a friend of Ellie's since they both joined the company six years ago. They had drifted in and out of closeness depending on the trajectory of each of their careers. When Virginia was promoted to department head she had little time for anything other than adjusting to her new position. Now it was Ellie's turn and she knew that Virginia would understand the inevitable late nights at work.

'A girl's gotta do ...' Ellie began.

'What a girl's gotta do,' Virginia chimed in and then waved goodbye.

Ellie sighed and ensconced herself in her chair ready to do battle with Diversity research. Focused on her work, she did not see Jasper McMurty standing just outside her door. Jasper stood watching her for a moment before making his presence known.

'Working late again, Ellie?'

Ellie jumped. 'Fright of my life, Jasper!'

'Sorry, just wanted to tell you that Friday is a good day for the Diversity update ... my office at eleven. Good night, Ellie.'

'Kaboom!' Ellie said when Jasper was gone. 'Friday?' She was not ready for another meeting with Jasper. She could have asked for more time, but something had told her that was not a good idea. 'Better to work late all week,' she thought. 'But, oh, that bloody commute!'

She hesitated at first, then Ellie phoned her mother.

'Hi, Mum.'

'Hello, darling how are you?'

'Fine, thanks. Listen, Mum would you like a roommate for a few days?'

'Of course, I'd love to have you. Should I get theatre tickets?'

Ellie rolled her eyes but tried to speak patiently. 'No, Mum, I'll be working late all week. I just want to cut down on the commute for a few days.'

'Oh, all right then.' Georgie hid her disappointment.

'Thanks, Mum, I'll be over tomorrow night. Don't worry if I'm late.'

'Eloise, I forgot. I've got the mah-jongg group tomorrow night at my house. I hope we won't disturb you.'

'No, not to worry. Bye now.'

◆

On the train to Chorleywood Ellie made a list of all the things she needed to pack to make sure her week in London ran smoothly. 'This list-making is getting a bit over the top. Is it really only Monday?'

Later that evening Ellie stood in the middle of a nightmare. Except she was actually wide awake, standing in the middle of her bedroom next to a pile of clothes, suitcases and bags.

'What was I thinking?' Packing to spend the rest of the week at her mother's highlighted two things. One, that she was crazy and two, that she was crazy. She never decided what to wear until she stumbled out of bed each morning. It was torturous to have to plan her wardrobe for the whole week at work. Locked into very few clothing choices due to the fact that most of her clothes were either at the cleaners or soon on their way there, she was left with no choice but to be creative.

'Okay. Pretend that you're travelling for business,' she said to herself. But that didn't work either. She was well aware that she got away with wearing the same thing over and over when she travelled.

'Sod it. I'll have to squeeze in time for a bit of shopping this week.' That was not all she would have to squeeze into. Finally she chose a grey suit that was very uncomfortable due to the weight she had gained, then lost, then gained, then ... The suit must have been bought during a thinner incarnation for she could just about manage the skirt's zipper and the sleeves of the jacket pulled a bit. She chose a few more items to get her through the next couple of days, vowing not to forget to pick up her clean clothes. 'What a bloody bother!' She tried to remember which days there would be important meetings to attend.

'Stop this. Stop this right now,' she told herself. As tired as she was, Ellie took out a printed copy of her schedule for the week and checked it to see which days she would need to make more of an effort with her appearance. 'Definitely Friday, definitely for the meeting with Jasper.'

By the time she was ready to hop into bed, Ellie's things were sitting by the door ready to be packed into her car the next morning. She had certainly not broken a habit of a lifetime, but she had at least begun to crack the outer layer. And as she fell asleep that night, she was satisfied. It seemed to be the small things that counted.

The remainder of the week felt like Groundhog Day for Ellie. She performed in warrior-like fashion as she made every effort to adhere to her schedule. She slipped and slid in the muddy grounds of corporate deadlines and demands. She went down fighting and stood up again begging for more. Or so it seemed to those around her.

Jasper was particularly demanding of her during the week. Just as a team member required more clarification or permission to act, Jasper came along and demanded her undivided attention. It was of no concern to him that she was stretched like a very weak rubber band.

Even with the preparation she had accomplished over the weekend, it was still difficult for Ellie to keep her head above water. She had assumed that the week would go more smoothly and, granted, many important things were being accomplished; however, why did it seem that she was the only one who was working at this speed?

Each night she stayed late catching up on her research and doing her best to prepare for Friday's meeting with Jasper. By the time she arrived at her mother's house she was truly knackered. Her mother always waited up for her and usually prepared a light supper. On one of Ellie's late nights Wrigley came by with plates for all three of them and they sat in front of the telly catching up on the news while munching on Jean-Louis's smoked salmon sandwiches.

There was something about being away from Chorleywood for a few days that gave Ellie a more objective viewpoint. Wrigley and her mother were laughing at a very silly television advert when, for a moment, Ellie was able to step outside the picture. She was struck with the realisation of how incredibly fortunate she was. Her mother and her best friend had been stupendously supportive of her during these past hectic weeks. Ellie made a mental note – 'Do something for Wrigs and Mum and don't forget.'

On Thursday at lunchtime Ellie left the office and stepped out into an unusually bright early winter day. She left her colleagues standing in her office speechless that she would actually go out for anything other than a business lunch. Tilda double-checked her schedule thinking that maybe she had overlooked a lunch meeting. But, no, Ellie Hart was actually leaving the office for a while.

Walking quickly around the City, it never ceased to amaze her how much the area had changed. Now one could indulge in hip top-notch restaurants, high-end shopping and services that were unheard of years ago. Time for three errands was ticking away on her mental clock.

First stop, a very upmarket kitchen store was sure to have a lovely gift for Wrigley. She already knew what she wanted to buy for him. Ellie made a beeline for the copper cookware from France. She hadn't a clue what was so special about them, but had seen Wrigley and Jean-Louis make such a fuss over them that she knew this would be the perfect gift. She came to an abrupt halt when she saw the selection – it was huge. Quickly she looked for sales help, but alas, some things never change - no luck there. Then she eyed a sweet-looking little pot with a very long brass handle, in fact, a very, very long handle. 'Hmm,' she said as she read the sign, 'a Flambé Ladle. Sounds very Wrigley.' She finally found someone to help her who was surprisingly gracious when asked to wrap and deliver it to the restaurant.

'Excellent. Next.' Ellie stopped by a speciality florist she had read about in *Time Out* and ordered flowers for her mother. The owner promised her he would create something special using a combination of calla lilies and peonies, her mother's favorites, and artfully arrange them in some ingenious fashion is some ingenious container.

Lastly, there was no time left to shop for anything more than a blouse for her meeting tomorrow. She would have to wear her black suit, but at least she could try to find something different to wear with it.

After having purchased gifts in two wonderful speciality shops, Ellie didn't notice that she walked into the first generic clothing store she could find. The disparity between the two was not at all obvious to her. She also began to worry about the time and picked up her pace, scurrying around the shop moving from one rack to the next. She couldn't make up her mind between a dusty blue, cotton-stretch, casual-looking blouse and a cream silk blouse that was a little more formal. She certainly had no time to try them on, so she held them up to her in front of the mirror without even taking off her coat. Undecided between the two, she frowned and quickly thrust the blue one on the counter.

On her way to the office Ellie realised that she had forgotten to eat.

'A sandwich will have to do.' By now her cell phone was ringing constantly, and with her sandwich in one hand, and her cell phone in the other, she tumbled into the company's reception area.

For the remainder of the afternoon Ellie tried to concentrate on organising her work for the next day's meetings. Not to her surprise, there were crucial phone calls, and the ever-present unexpected tasks to face, which kept her in the office later than she would have liked tonight.

Tilda stopped by Ellie's office on her way home and asked for a word with her.

'I don't know if this is a good time to bring this up, but have you had the opportunity to discuss my salary increase with Jasper?'

'No, Tilda, I haven't, but I told you, I will do.'

Tilda sat silently for a moment as Ellie continued her work.

'What is it?' Ellie looked up to see Tilda still there.

'You said that last month, Ellie. Do you think you'll be speaking to him soon?'

'Yes. Please, Tilda, I want to leave here before midnight. All right?'

Tilda looked at Ellie for a moment and then stood up. 'Good night, Ellie.'

Before Ellie turned out the lights in her office she checked her desk one more time. Everything she needed for her meeting with Jasper was in order. She could hardly believe it. As she left the office she placed copies of her notes on the desk of Jasper's assistant who promised to put them on his desk in the morning. 'He won't believe it either,' she thought as she switched off the lights and summoned the lift, 'bloody marvellous.'

Friday morning arrived so quickly Ellie felt sure it was still Thursday night and she had just put her head down on her mother's pillow. She took a few moments to sip the tea her mother had made, allowing Georgie the pleasure of spoiling her daughter these last few days. Ellie brushed off her black trouser suit and looked around for where she had hung her new blouse, but she couldn't find it. She had a pretty awful feeling she knew where it was. Her new blouse was neatly folded, still sitting in the bag on the floor in her office.

'Dammit to hell!' she said under her breath. 'And I don't have any more clean clothes here.' She quickly pulled out a rumpled white blouse from her bag and gave it a shake. It was a terrible feeling to put on a grubby white blouse.

When she reached the office she kept her coat on while she ran to the loo to change her blouse. Ellie awkwardly took off her coat, then her jacket, and then her white blouse. She opened the carrier bag and took out the new blouse, which by now had become wrinkled from sitting in the bag overnight. She shook it and furiously patted it, hoping to somehow force the wrinkles to smooth out. She bumped her elbow on the wall of the tiny stall as she put her arm through the sleeve.

'Oh no, it doesn't fit. I can't believe it. It doesn't fit. This is supposed to stretch!'

She managed to get the blouse buttoned, but even though the fabric gave quite a bit, it was still very snug around Ellie's chest and through the arms.

The loo was beginning to fill up with early morning tea- and coffee-drinkers. She put her jacket on and stepped out to have a look in the mirror. 'Well, if I don't breathe and maintain perfect posture I should be all right.'

A little before eleven o'clock, Ellie stood outside Jasper's door and waited for the meeting to begin. She was a little nervous but her apprehension was certainly nothing like the anxiety she had felt after her meeting in New York.

The door to Jasper's office opened and he ushered her in immediately.

'I like what I read this morning, Ellie. The programmes you've created for this new department look very good. I particularly like the mandatory training programmes. The direction you're taking is a strong one. How close are you to completing the budget?'

'I'm almost there. I can be finished early next week.'

'Tuesday on my desk?'

'Yes, of course.'

'All right then, please sit down.' Jasper motioned towards the chair in front of his desk.

Ellie tugged a bit on her shirt and sat down.

'How close do you think you are to making another presentation in New York?' Jasper asked.

'Well ... what do you think?'

'No, I'm asking you what you think. When will you be ready?'

'Couple of weeks? No, that interferes with the conference. Three weeks?' she asked.

McMurty phoned his assistant to check his schedule. Ellie had not realised that in today's meeting they would be planning her next presentation already.

Jasper hung up the phone and looked at Ellie as he folded his hands and placed them on the desk in front of him.

'Three weeks, Ellie. Will you be ready?'

'Yes, I'll be ready.'

'There will be another presentation the following week.'

'Excuse me? Another one?' Ellie was more than mildly surprised.

'Yes, you're going to present to the UK top brass the week after you return from New York.'

'So this is it then.'

'Yes, I'll ask you again. Will you be ready?'

Ellie was silent for a moment. She took her time to respond, knowing that a commitment today was a final step.

She looked up at Jasper and nodded her head. 'Yes. I'm certain.'

'All right then. I want to give you something to think about as you continue to prepare. People don't like change, Ellie. As innovative and creative as members of this company may think they are, when it gets down to the bottom line, they will resist. Don't diminish the weight of the kinds of changes you are introducing.'

Ellie furiously scribbled Jasper's words.

'Have you begun the transition process with your team?' Jasper asked.

'I've thought about it. I haven't implemented anything yet.'

'I suggest you start that ball rolling soon. You need the transition to be a painless process. Start slowly, it shouldn't be too abrupt.'

Ellie's heart skipped a beat and she thought, 'He's actually talking about this as if it were going to happen!'

'Right, I'll do that.'

'One more thing, Ellie. You're making your team look good instead of letting them be good. You've got to remedy that very quickly if you want to move on.'

Ellie heard what Jasper had said but just sat staring blankly at him. She hated it when he did that. He was famous for throwing one-liners out to the wind and he then expected you to catch them and do something with them.

'All right then, Ellie? Budget Tuesday morning.'

'Thank you, Jasper. I'm very excited.'

'Good, good.' Jasper had one hand on his phone and the other gave her a friendly wave goodbye.

When she stood up to leave her papers fell to the floor. Flustered by the mess, she quickly bent down to pick them up. Just as she stretched out her arm to retrieve the papers, a button popped off her blouse. Of course it had to be the button that was positioned right at bra level. A very strong blush rose from her neck to her face. She looked up at Jasper, who fortunately was already on the phone with his back turned, looking out of the window. She grasped at her jacket and closed it around her exposed bra and was able to button her jacket before Jasper turned around to see her still there.

Ellie stood up very tall, and with her head held as high as possible, exited Jasper's office with her papers held tightly against her chest.

Once she had returned to her own office and had changed her blouse yet again, Ellie took a moment to contemplate her meeting with Jasper. She said to herself, 'That was a good meeting. In fact that was a great meeting! Yes. Yes. Yes! About bloody time too, Hart.'

Even though she had spent many hours preparing she still had not expected Jasper to move her project forward so quickly. And although it was a short meeting, it was a very powerful one for her. The wheels were finally turning and everything was moving in the right direction – except for that last comment.

'What's the matter with my team?' she thought. 'How can they look good and not be good?'

Floris interrupted her thoughts when she strode into the office and sat down across from Ellie.

'I've got the caterers down to a choice of two,' Floris said.

'Oh, that reminds me.' Ellie looked at her watch and picked up the phone and called Wrigley.

'Wriggers, it's me.'

'Ellie, I was just going to call you. I'm mad for the flambé pan! You didn't have to do that, you know.'

'You didn't have one, did you?'

'Yes actually, three, but it doesn't matter.'

'Are you serious? I'll take it back ...'

'No, no,' he laughed. 'Ellie, I'm just kidding. I adore it.'

'Another favour.'

'Shoot.'

'Women's Conference, two weeks, closing dinner, very bad food last year.'

'Mm-hmm, what's the question?' Wrigley was no fool and knew exactly what was coming.

'What about catering the event?'

'Are you crazy? I'm not terribly fond of that kind of entertaining; in fact, we're no good at it. That's why I have a restaurant.'

'Sounds a bit snobbish to me. How about a few recommendations then.'

'Bit short notice. But I can certainly have a gander for you.'

'Slave for two weeks, thanks, Wrigs, call me later.'

Floris sat through the entire conversation pinching the skin between her eyebrows, trying to stave off an approaching headache.

'There then. We'll have a few more to choose from,' Ellie said.

'Fine, Ellie.' Floris stood to leave.

'What's wrong, Floris?'

'Nothing, Ellie, I'm very happy that you have a friend in the business. Perhaps you could have saved me the time and effort by telling me you wanted to do this yourself.'

'Hang about. I'm just trying to help. What's the problem?'

'No problem, Ellie.' Floris did not sound convincing. 'Shall I put you and Preston down for your regular places?'

'No.' Ellie paused. 'I don't know yet. In any event, it won't be Preston.'

'Oh.' Floris was caught in an awkward moment; this was news to her. She softened a bit. 'Well, let me know, please.' She then left the office.

I don't know what that was about, but whatever it was, it was highly unnecessary, Ellie thought.

------◆------

The Friday afternoon team meeting felt dirgeful. Gloomy faces abounded and the energy in the room seemed lackadaisical. Ellie chose to ignore the atmosphere for the time being and to get on with the meeting.

Usually the procedure was that each team member gave a short report of the week and a prospectus for the following week. Ellie then gave notes and comments to each team member. Today, however, she instinctually felt the need for something different. She wanted the meeting to be freer-flowing and less structured, hoping that the lethargic atmosphere would shift.

Ellie expected to learn from this meeting that the team was beginning to catch up a bit on their work. She had hoped that the work she had done over the weekend would pay off in this meeting. She also expected the planning and details for the Women's Conference to be almost complete by now, but there were still loose ends to take care of.

Something is wrong here, she thought. She continued with the meeting and then opened the room to discussion. Everyone went through the motions and did what they had to do. They managed to wade through the issues of the week, but there wasn't one person in the room who could offer any decisive feedback.

'Is there anything else then?' Ellie glanced at Paresh and Floris, the most senior members of her staff, who were very subdued.

'It's been a very long week, Ellie,' Paresh said.

'Yes, I know, why don't you all go then – have a good weekend.' Ellie watched them file out of the conference room.

'Paresh, Flo, could you stay a minute please?' Ellie asked. 'If there is something on your minds and you have something to say, then I want to hear it.'

Paresh and Floris looked at each other. Paresh spoke first in a very calm and friendly voice.

'We've been talking amongst ourselves. We think it might be helpful if you could just let go of the reins a little bit, Ellie.'

'Wait a minute. I haven't left this team yet, you two.'

'No, that's not quite what we mean,' Floris said. 'The caterer thing, Ellie, that was a perfect example. I am perfectly capable of finding a caterer, yet you undermined me and called your friend.'

'Floris, I didn't undermine you. I told you, I was just trying to help.'

'I think what Floris is trying to say is that when you give her a job to do, just let her do it,' Paresh offered.

'What about you, Paresh? Anything to say?'

'I think we all feel a little like we can't do anything as fast as you, or as well as you. I'm very excited about the off-site training programme. I really want it to be my own project – with guidance of course – but something I achieve on my own.'

'Yes, and I know other members of the team feel the same way,' Floris added.

Ellie sat leaning on the conference table with her arms folded, listening, trying to understand.

'Thank you both,' she said. 'I promise you I will give your comments serious consideration and we'll continue this discussion next week.'

Both Floris and Paresh looked immensely relieved and were grateful for how well Ellie had responded.

'Ellie, I know your friend Wrigley is a great chef, I'd be happy to have his recommendations.' Floris smiled at Ellie.

'Thanks, Flo. I'll probably call you over the weekend, time is getting tight.'

The three colleagues left the building together. It was the first night all week that Ellie arrived at her mother's before ten o'clock.

------◆------

Ellie decided to drive back to Chorleywood after dinner with her mother. The flowers she had sent were on the hall table and she was pleased with the result. Georgie fussed over them and fussed over her; a sure sign to Ellie that it was indeed time to go home.

The traffic had still not died down completely and Ellie found herself becoming drowsy on the road. Thankfully, her phone rang and she could hear the buzz from the Friday-night crowd of Wrigley's restaurant.

'Hi Ellie, is this a good time to speak?'

'I should ask you that, it sounds mad there.'

'It is, just wanted to tell you that I emailed a few caterers to your laptop.'

'You're good. Now I have to find someone to go with me to the dinner. Any ideas?'

'What about me?'

'Well, that would be fun, but it's on a Friday night, Wriggers, you can't leave the restaurant can you?'

'I might be able to manage it. Jean-Louis can handle it. I'll have to speak to him of course, can I let you know tomorrow?'

'Yes, but, Wrigley, are you sure you want to go to one of these things? It's not exactly a laugh and a half.'

'We'll make it fun, Ellie, we always do.'

'All right then, but don't say I didn't warn you.'

For the remainder of the drive Ellie focused her thoughts on the events of the day. She spoke out loud through several yawns to keep herself alert on the road.

'Very, very good meeting with Jasper. Good meeting because I was MORE PREPARED, MR FAIRCHILD,' she shouted in a moment of spontaneity. Then, almost in a flash, her flamboyant speech became subdued. Jasper's advice repeatedly swirled through her mind. 'I'm making my team look good instead of letting them be good. Hmm. But I'm not an idiot, am I? Don't answer that. Isn't it my job to keep everyone on their toes? Aren't I ultimately responsible for keeping our department running like a highly efficient machine? What's to remedy?'

Ellie pulled into her driveway and allowed her thoughts to wander to the prospect of a good night's sleep in her own bed, in her own house.

She stepped over the week's mail and dropped all of her things on the entrance-hall floor. She was halfway undressed by the time she reached her bedroom; exhausted, she fell into her bed. She had only been asleep for a few minutes when she thought she heard a noise. There, she heard it again. It was a heavy thud, a sound that she thought came from outside the house. She bolted up in the bed and slipped on her bathrobe and a pair of shoes. She crept down the stairs, frightened at the thought of an intruder. Slowly, she made her way into the kitchen where out of a lack of any other impulse she hoped to find a very large knife. But she couldn't find a knife in the dark because Wrigley had completely rearranged her entire kitchen.

She moved over to the kitchen door that led to her garden. Just as she reached it she heard another thump. She looked out of the window, her eyes struggling to adjust to the very dark, moonless night.

'Oh, oh, oh,' was all she could say. She could just make out a figure bending over something in her garden. When the man picked up a lantern and turned towards her she could finally see who it was.

'Mr Fairchild!'

Ellie opened the door and ran out into the garden. There he was, completely at ease and not at all surprised to see her.

'Mr Fairchild, what are you … ?' Ellie stopped moving, stopped talking and, as her eyes adjusted, became very, very still.

Ellie's garden had changed quite a bit since the last time she saw it. Gone were the mounds of dirt and the empty trenches. Gone was the sour smell of the manure. Mr Fairchild had placed lanterns all around and their glow revealed young buds, sprouting green stalks and beautiful pots of lush green plants. It was a young garden, but it was very much … a garden.

Mr Fairchild stood next to an old, beautifully carved stone bench.

'Good evening, Ellie. Lovely evening, isn't it?'

'Okay, okay,' Ellie said to herself. 'Whew, umm … okay, just go with it, Ellie. This is a dream, it is just a dream.'

As Ellie moved closer to Mr Fairchild she was amused to see that they were both in their dressing gowns. However, Mr Fairchild's dressing gown put hers to shame. His long velvet robe fell to the ground and landed in an elegant puddle at his slippered feet. The colour of the luxurious fabric was an appropriate midnight blue. His head was covered with a soft woven nightcap that matched the white frilly undershirt he wore beneath the dressing gown.

He motioned for her to sit and as he did so the long and heavy sleeves of his dressing gown moved through the night air with a graceful welcoming gesture. Ellie, in her rather tatty, thick terry cotton bathrobe and an old pair of plimsoles, was not unaware of the contrast.

They sat for a few moments in silence while they drank in the charms of the setting. Mr Fairchild had placed the stone bench (probably the source of the thuds and thumps) under the apple tree, which afforded a view of the entire garden. It dawned on Ellie that she was privileged to witness such a scene. She thought that this must be creativity in its most simple but powerful form.

'Yes,' said Mr Fairchild, 'it is very mysterious isn't it? A great deal of care and work and then, as if by a miracle, our tiny little charges thrust through the earth.'

'There you go again, Mr Fairchild, are none of my thoughts private?'

Mr Fairchild, amused, said nothing.

'Mr Fairchild, why are we out here in the middle of the night?'

'In addition to the fact that it is a rather bewitching time of night to be outside, we do have a bit of work to do.'

'Thought so,' Ellie muttered.

Mr Fairchild reached down beside him and picked up a paper sack with a thin gauzy cloth over it. There was also what looked to be a thin white sheet or cloth of some kind that he placed underneath his arm. They walked towards the plantings and pots and lanterns.

Ellie looked more closely at all of the work that had been done and all of the planting that had taken place. 'Did I miss something? Did I miss planting time or something?'

Mr Fairchild's laugh rippled out of him. 'That's very amusing, Ellie.' And he walked toward the rose bushes, leaving her to sort it out for herself.

'What we do next is very important, Eloise. Come closer please and help.'

He began to unfold the large white cloth. 'It is time for my little assistants to begin their work now. Please hold the bag for me and be very careful, do not tip it over and handle it with care.'

'What's in it?' Ellie asked, highly intrigued.

'Carefully lift the cloth just a bit and you will see.'

Ellie knelt down by one of the lanterns and lifted one end of the cloth.

'Bugs? Bugs? You've got bugs in here, Mr Fairchild?' Ellie held the bag from her distastefully.

Mr Fairchild was busy draping the large white cloth over the rose bushes and a few other rows of plants.

'Lady beetles to be exact. Also called ladybirds and ladybugs. They are nature's pesticide. It was once believed they came from heaven to save the farmers' crops.'

'What are they for?'

'As I said before, they are our assistants. They feed on plant-harming insects, especially aphids. They work for us. They possess a beautiful colouring that also brings cheer to the garden.'

Now completely out of sight underneath the huge cloth, his long shadow moved along the garden like a ghost taking a slow walk.

Ellie walked towards the white cloth with the bag of ladybirds in her hands.

'Careful, my dear, the ground is damp. One must always water the area before releasing the lady beetles.'

He continued, 'The other reason we are here tonight is because these wonderful insects only like being released after sundown or before sunrise. They navigate by the sun and so tend to stay put in the evenings and early mornings.'

Ellie listened to Mr Fairchild and tried very hard to hear the lesson – she knew there was one somewhere – but she was having trouble with her own navigation. The ground was indeed damp and she wasn't as graceful under the cloth as Mr Fairchild.

'This little garden, your garden, has been hard at work producing. I think it's time for a little help, don't you? It's time to release them, if you'll please do the honours. Now, Eloise, now. Let them go. Let your assistants go to work.'

She gently lifted the cloth and sat the bag on the ground. After a few moments the little red spotted bugs flew out of the bag into their new home.

Mr Fairchild and Ellie emerged from the cloth and sat down together again on the stone bench.

'Now then,' Mr Fairchild said as he rubbed his hands together, 'I have planted dill and fennel and there are pots of scented geraniums. These will provide an enticing environment for our helpers. It is perfectly acceptable to bring them in, but now we must coax them to stay with us. We want to do everything we can to attract the lady beetle population!'

Ellie was very quiet again, although she was sure that Mr Fairchild could hear her thinking furiously.

Mr Fairchild placed his hand on her shoulder. In the kindest and most sincere voice she had heard from him yet, he helped her to clear the jumble of confusion that existed in her heart and her mind.

'It is impossible for you to do everyone's job, Eloise. You must let the people who work for you do just that – let them work. Your fears and insecurities about how they perform are preventing all of you from learning. A sense of achievement does not mean that everything must be done today. Making plants prosper in the most unpromising conditions is a challenge, but you have shown that you are capable of meeting the challenge. However, to go to the next level, you must let go. Become the one who delegates. Learn to delegate by letting go.'

Ellie felt as if she might cry in front of Mr Fairchild. Must be the tension from the week, she thought, or maybe I'm just tired.

'No, my dear, you have just planted a few seeds of change.'

The light began to change and it slowly became darker. The lanterns began to lose their light; they flickered and spat until Ellie and Mr Fairchild sat in complete darkness.

Ellie opened her eyes on Saturday morning but did not move a muscle; she kept her gaze straight in front of her. 'Stay calm, just remain calm.' Slowly she crept out of bed. Her bathrobe was lying on the chair. She gave it a pat. 'Good, good. Okay, just go downstairs now.'

She was hardly breathing by the time she reached her kitchen. Leaning on the table in front of her kitchen window she looked out onto her garden. It was the same garden that had been there for a long time. There was no sheet, there were no lanterns and no stone bench. She sighed a huge long sigh and made herself a strong pot of tea.

Up the stairs she went with her steaming cup of tea and as she entered her bedroom she walked by something that she had not seen on her way down, nor did she notice it now. Her old plimsoles were still sitting where she had left them before she left for her mother's house, except that now they were caked with mud.

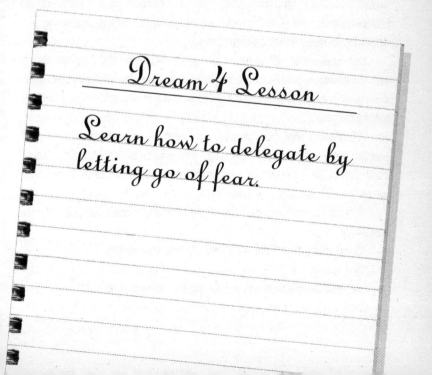

Dream 4 Lesson

Learn how to delegate by letting go of fear.

Miss Understood 5

Ellie enjoyed a few moments of peace and quiet before she began her busy Saturday. She curled up in her favourite chair by the fireplace and drank her second cup of tea. Last night's dream was very much on her mind. She was able to remember most of it and began to record it in her notebook.

For some reason her thoughts began to drift towards her father. Rupert Hart had died six years ago, almost the same time she began to work for the company. Although her parents had nurtured her independence, she now looked back at his death as the beginning of a sobering journey towards self-reliance.

She knew that her independent spirit was partially responsible for her promotions within the company, but now she realised that there was probably a control issue that she had not recognised – a double-edged sword.

'They're all spot-on – Jasper, Mr Fairchild, even my staff,' she said, staring into the fire-less fireplace. 'I'm afraid to let other people do their jobs. Do I take over and interfere because I think I can do it better? Am I afraid to let them fail? Or am *I* afraid to fail?'

Such deep thoughts on a Saturday morning were interrupted by the telephone.

'Good morning, Ellie, it's Floris. Is this too early?'

'No, not at all.'

'I've got all four caterers lined up for meetings today.'

'Don't tell me, I know already, they're upset about the late notice.'

'Well, just a bit! But times are hard and they all want the job, so we're lucky.'

'All right, are they all prepared to have samples for you to test?'

'I don't know, hadn't thought of that.'

Ellie felt a surge of adrenaline. She bit her lip; she desperately wanted to join Floris today.

'Ellie, you still there?'

'Yes, Flo, hang about a minute, I'm just thinking.'

Ellie paced in front of the fireplace.

'Okay, Flo, if it were me, I'd call them all back and ask for food samples. If they can't do that today, they have until Monday to get it together. Otherwise, take them out of the race.'

'Yes, of course, I don't know what I was thinking. We have to taste the food, right?'

'No, *you* have to taste the food, Floris.'

'Do you want me to call you back later with the results?'

'YES!' she wanted to scream but didn't. 'No, Flo, I'm sure you'll make the right decision.'

'Oh.' Floris was caught by surprise. 'Are you sure?'

'Positive.'

'All right then, Ellie, have a good weekend.'

After Ellie hung up she actually felt a little shaky. She hoped she wouldn't worry about this all weekend. Exactly one day ago, she would have been dressed and in her car by now on her way to meet Floris.

'Oh God, I hope she makes the right choice.'

All day long as Ellie went about taking care of things in her house that she had neglected all week, she thought about how she was going to learn how to delegate. It was now obvious to her exactly what Jasper had meant by his remark. Well, obvious thanks to Mr Fairchild. She made her team look good by not giving them more responsibility. No, not quite, she thought, not only do I not give them more responsibility,

I don't even let them get on with their regular duties without butting in all the time.

All right, I need a little help here. I need to find a way to break through this habit of not letting go of anything. Who, she wondered, is really effective at delegating?

Daphne Marchant was the answer to that question. Her old friend Daphne was a demon when it came to getting the best out of people. She knew that other department heads and managers thought she must be terribly difficult to work for, but Daphne's team was fiercely loyal. Ellie remembered her own surprise when she overheard one of Daphne's staff members talk about how she loved working for her. Before Daphne left for New York, her team had had the most promotions for three years running.

Daphne had literally soared to the new position that led to her New York transfer. And in so doing had alienated many of her friends in London. Ellie wondered if she should, or even could, break the ice. Would it be right to do so now that she needed Daphne's help? Ellie sat with the phone in her hand. She looked up Daphne's number and noted the time: 'Too early to call now anyway.'

A brisk walk to her local newsagent helped to clear her mind a bit. Mr and Mrs Bovery always looked after the shop together on busy Saturdays and Mrs Bovery never failed to bring in her baked goods on the weekends to sell to the crowd. They tempted Ellie with a home-made Cornish pasty and Ellie could not resist. 'They'll make a lovely lunch, Mrs Bovery. Your pasties are the best.'

'Well, if I do say so, they aren't half bad. That young man, the chef, friend of yours, popped in this morning and bought a tray full.'

'Wrigley? Wrigley was here this morning?'

'Oh yes, I forgot his name,' she said with her plump pink cheeks smiling and wisps of her snow-white hair falling into her eyes. 'Bright and early he was. Off to a local farmer's garden.'

'Yes, that's Wrigley.' Ellie laughed.

'Now don't forget your milk, Ellie, you always leave it on the counter and then have to trot back in here later.' Mr Bovery feigned a frown.

'Thank you, Mr Bovery.' Ellie smiled because she had indeed forgotten her milk.

The sky began to darken as Ellie walked back to her house. She picked up her pace and sheltered her bags from the first drops of rain. By the time she reached home she had made the decision to call Daphne.

The phone rang until Daphne's voicemail picked up. Uncomfortable leaving a message, Ellie just hung up. She would try several more times during the day but never managed to catch Daphne at home. Ellie thought that Daphne must be out doing something terribly New York-ish.

Over the weekend she worked on the budget for her next presentation and looked over her schedule for the week. She pored over it, trying to figure out how to delegate more responsibility to each member of her team. It was difficult to imagine becoming more hands-off, but she made a valiant effort.

She also made two important decisions about the future of her staff. She wanted to promote Floris. She felt sure now that Floris was the right person to be her replacement – if Ellie was able to pull off the launch of a Diversity Department. And she chose Paresh to go with her as her number two. She was still unsure about the future of her other team members, their placements remained to be seen.

Still unable to reach Daphne, Ellie resigned herself to the fact that the timing was not right yet. By Sunday evening, she was worn out but pleased with herself. 'What I wouldn't give for a holiday,' she said out loud. But she knew that there was no holiday in her future for quite a long while. All in all, it was a very Chorleywood-ish weekend.

---◆---

Monday morning Ellie returned to her office from a manager's meeting to find a memo on her desk.

TO ALL MANAGERS

RE: 360-DEGREE REVIEW

We are implementing a new reporting system in order to assess how you are impacting people. Your peers, your staff and other managers will be asked to answer questions regarding how they are experiencing you as a person and co-worker. The reports are always anonymous and are purely for developmental purposes.

Your 360-degree review could be the most useful piece of information you will receive this year.

'Bloody hell,' Ellie said, looking at the memo. 'Not one of these. Not now!'

Tilda ran into Ellie's office with her hands full of papers and a pen sticking out of her red curls. 'Morning, Ellie. People-clash on the seventh floor!'

Ellie quickly headed out of the room. 'Small or large, Tilda?'

'Medium, I think.'

'Man or woman?'

'Both.'

Ellie's week had begun. She participated in the resolution of a screaming match that had begun on the seventh floor between a woman who accused a man of inappropriate remarks and the man who denied them. It was rare that a disturbance like this one became so public. Usually these dreaded matters were talked over in the privacy of an office.

'Don't tell me we don't need a Diversity Department. The goal is to prevent this nonsense, not be a referee.' Ellie stood next to a department head in the lift when it was all over.

The man turned to her and nodded his head. 'Quite right. I couldn't agree more.'

At the end of the day Ellie held an impromptu meeting in her office for several members of her staff. They were all surprised when she handed to each of them lists of specific new tasks and responsibilities.

'I'm going to try to stay out of your hair. I know that is probably hard for you to imagine, but just do the best you can on the points I've listed for each of you. If you need help or have any questions, you can always ask me anything.'

A few subtle looks between the team crisscrossed the room, but no one reacted.

'We'll discuss this further on Friday. In the meantime, anyone who is working on the conference should wrap it up by Wednesday. That's it.'

Tilda stayed seated as the others left the office. She had not received a list and Ellie had barely acknowledged her presence in the meeting.

'What is it, Tilda?'

'Can I speak to you for a moment, Ellie?'

'Yes, of course.'

'Do you mind if we close your door?'

'Not at all, go ahead.'

Tilda closed the door and sat down next to Ellie.

'Did you manage to mention my salary increase to Jasper last Friday?'

Ellie sighed and put her forehead in her hand, 'I'm really sorry, Tilda, I ...'

Tilda calmly interrupted, 'It's all right, Ellie. I've decided to give you my notice.'

'What? But Tilda ...'

'No, I've thought about this for quite a while and it just isn't working out for me here.'

Ellie remained silent.

Tilda continued, 'It's not really the money, although that would be helpful. It's just, well, I don't think we're a good fit any more, Ellie.'

'Tilda, you know I don't want you to go. Can we talk about this first?'

'We are talking, Ellie.'

'Yes, but I mean what would you need to stay on?'

'I'm not really sure. I haven't thought about that, I just think of leaving all the time, not staying.'

'Please do think about it, Tilda. Is it me? Is it the company?'

Tilda couldn't raise her eyes to meet Ellie's.

'I see. Listen, Tilda, I'm truly sorry that you are so unhappy. I do hope we can work this out. Will you give me a month? If at the end of the month you're still unhappy, then I won't try to stop you.'

'I don't know, Ellie. I don't really want to go, but I don't feel like I have a choice.'

'But you do Tilda, there is a choice. If you give me this month to get things sorted and it still isn't working for you, I'll actually help you find another job.'

Tilda sat quietly for a moment. Ellie was wringing her hands out of sight under her desk. 'This is not good,' she thought, 'this is really not good.'

'All right Ellie. I owe it to both of us to give it another go.'

'Great! And Tilda, we'll continue this discussion after you've had a think. I'll think about it too. If you can be more specific with me that will help us both.'

'I'll do that, Ellie.' Tilda rose to leave. 'Staying late again?'

'I'm afraid so. Good night, Tilda. And please, don't worry, I really want this to work out.'

Ellie took a deep breath and mentally put the Tilda shock on hold. She worked steadily for a couple more hours. Famished, she was on her way to the kitchen in search of her favourite chocolate biscuits when her mobile rang.

'Hi, Ellie, where are you?'

'Hi, Wrigley, on my way to the chocolate biscuits in the office kitchen.'

'Don't do that. Why don't you come by for a proper meal? The theatre crowd is gone, it's not too busy.'

'Is there a ride home in this offer?'

'Of course.'

'Deal, see you soon.'

'Resist the biscuits.'

'What biscuits?'

By the time Ellie arrived at the restaurant the coffee-sipping stragglers were the only customers left. Soon they left and Jean-Louis and Wrigley joined Ellie for a light supper. Ellie tried to relax as she listened to the friendly banter between Wrigley and Jean-Louis, but now the blow of Tilda's attempt to resign hit her fully.

When Jean-Louis retreated to the kitchen Ellie said to Wrigley, 'You and Jean-Louis get along really well don't you?'

'Smashingly well.'

'Why is that?'

'Well, we always communicate with each other. It's not easy sometimes, but the lines are always open. Sometimes, when Jean-Louis gets excited I can't understand a word he's saying – but I always know what he means. Does that make sense?'

'Yes. What about the rest of your staff?'

'It's a matter of being clear with them about what I want. I just can't afford any misinterpretation. What's this all about, Ellie?'

'Tilda wants to leave.'

'Oh, I see. Why?'

'I don't really know yet, except that she has probably had her fill of me.'

'Why? Have you been hard on her lately?'

'No more so than anyone else. It's been insanely busy, you know that.'

'Well you're on the right track if you're thinking about having a good old natter with her. Maybe you can change her mind – that is, if you want to.'

'Do you think I could be hard to work for, Wrigley?'

'Jeez, that is not a fair question, Ellie. I doubt if any of your staff have ever seen you playing with the garden hose in a red spotted bathing suit. But I do remember your being rather bossy with the Gordon twins and very demanding at age ten in the town library.'

'Take me home, you barmy man.'

'My point exactly.'

◆

Tuesday morning found Ellie in Jasper's office, at which time she presented him with her completed budget for the Diversity Department. He, in turn, handed over a rather ominous-looking envelope.

Ellie looked at Jasper as she took it from his hands, 'This is very official-looking.'

'It's your 360-degree review.'

'Oh.' Ellie raised her eyebrows.

'Just remember that it is meant to help.'

'Thank you, Jasper.'

Tilda eyed the envelope as Ellie strode by her desk. She and Ellie were far too busy to be uncomfortable with any remnants of the previous evening's discussion. Ellie walked back to her office and promptly put the envelope on her desk with every intention of returning to it later in the day. As the result of her new hands-off experiment the flow of traffic through her office was slightly lighter, but Ellie couldn't resist checking up on the progress her staff was making. She wandered in and out of offices; she fought the urge to take over and tried to limit herself to answering questions. There was the usual crisis or two – however, she held back from the actual caretaking and followed her instincts to direct.

She had not ignored the envelope sitting on her desk – each time she passed it she felt a flutter, but she did put off opening it until the end of the day. The offices were quiet and there were only a few people scattered around working late. Ellie turned on her desk lamp for more light and fingered the metal clasp for a moment, more nervous than she thought she would be.

The reports were in the form of a standard questionnaire. There was room left after each question for written comments, but the responses had been typed in order to avoid the handwriting being recognisable. She quickly scanned the papers. Ellie's mouth flew open as she read a few of the words at random:

'Abrupt ...'

'Demanding ...'

'Intolerant ...'

'Scattered – but better of late ...'

'Impulsive ...'

'Ungrateful ...'

'Nothing is ever good enough ...'

'She doesn't keep her promises ...'

Shocked, she hastily put the papers down and then picked them up again. She managed to sit down and then, slowly and methodically, she read every single report. It was very, very difficult to read what her peers and staff thought of her. It was very personal but she felt that without exception each person had tried to be honest. There were positive remarks as well. She was pleased that at least most people thought she was hard-working, well-meaning and loyal. However, the negative feedback was very disturbing to her, especially since she had been trying so hard over the last few months to improve.

'It would be helpful if Ellie could allow her team to take more responsibility.' Another read, 'It's as if she doesn't completely trust our judgement.'

'It's obvious this was written before this week. Give me a chance here,' Ellie said.

She tried to detach herself emotionally as she read the anonymous words until she came across the report of the person who said that, *'Ellie doesn't keep her promises.'* This person also wrote that she thought Ellie was dismissive and impatient and that, *'Sometimes she acts as if she isn't concerned about the welfare of her staff.'*

Those have to be Tilda's words, she thought.

Ellie began to feel nauseous. The knot in her throat meant that tears were on the way, so she walked quickly towards the ladies' loo with her head down, praying not to run into anyone else.

She ran into the loo and made so much noise banging first the door to the loo, then the door to the stall, and was crying so loudly, that at first she didn't hear the sounds coming from the very next stall. As she gasped for breath in between sobs, in what should have been silence, there could be heard another sob. The synchronised sobbing in the loo softened a level or two as both women now became painfully aware of their situation.

Ellie's stall was out of loo paper and she was desperate to blow her nose.

'Oh sod it!' she said under her breath as she struck out at the loo-roll holder.

Ellie looked down and the woman next door was holding a huge wad of loo paper in her hand, which hung in the air dangerously close to the floor.

'Cheers,' Ellie said, still crying and sniffling and blowing her nose.

After a short time they both calmed down and there were a few moments of very uncomfortable silence. The silence was especially loud after the reverberating weeping that had bounced off the walls.

Then Ellie heard a faint giggle from her neighbour. And then a very small chuckle erupted from Ellie. The snickers and giggles soon bellowed out into full-force laughter. When Ellie had the thought that she had no idea who was next to her sharing in this mad experience, she laughed even harder.

Finally the laughter subsided and Ellie spoke first.

'Okay. Out on three. One, two, three.'

The doors flew open and both women stepped out at the same time and faced each other.

'I don't believe it!' Daphne Marchant said.

'What are you doing here?' Without thinking Ellie opened her arms and wrapped them around Daphne, who responded by wrapping hers around Ellie. Then in a moment of awkward disbelief and confusion they parted as quickly as they had come together.

'Oh!' Daphne said.

'Oh!' Ellie echoed.

'Well if this isn't just awkward as hell. Just look at us,' Daphne said, looking in the mirror. 'What a fright we'd give someone.'

They did look frightful. Both of their noses were bright red, their faces were blotchy and Ellie's mascara was smeared underneath and all around her eyes. Daphne wore waterproof mascara – of course.

'What are you doing here?' Ellie asked.

'A bit of business and the conference. Actually, I tried to call you.'

'I tried to call you too,' Ellie admitted.

'Didn't leave a message?' Daphne asked.

'No.'

'Neither did I.'

They splashed cold water on their faces and tried to tidy themselves up.

'I'm glad that it was you who found me here blubbering like an idiot,' Daphne said.

'What about me? I must have sounded like the wailing chorus of some Greek tragedy.'

They laughed again.

'What are the odds of us being in here together like this?' Ellie asked.

Suddenly, Daphne burst into tears again. Ellie had never seen her like this.

'I'm sorry, Ellie. I'm sorry we lost touch with each other.'

Ellie was sorry too but she couldn't imagine that this was the reason Daphne was inconsolable.

'I don't know why I'm telling you this, but ...' Daphne was struggling to purge herself of some repulsive thought. 'I DON'T LIKE WHO I'VE BECOME!' More tears.

Astounded that the loo had become an early-evening confessional, Ellie didn't know what to say. She had momentarily forgotten her own tears, which had brought her to this moment.

'Are you unhappy in New York, Daphne?'

'No, it's not that. I love New York, and I love my job. I've just ... oh, I've done some bloody stupid things and made some very bad mistakes.' She was off again.

Ellie waited for her to calm down.

Daphne took a deep breath in and tried to explain. 'I'm in a compromising situation.'

'Look, Daphne, are you sure you want to tell me this? I mean, after all, it's been quite a while since, well, you know.'

'I think you're the only person I can tell.'

The loo suddenly felt very lonely to Ellie. She put her arm around Daphne, 'Listen, Daphne. We're going to get out of this loo. I'll go out to see if the coast is clear, then we'll go into my office, all right?'

Daphne nodded and held her hand out for more loo roll. Ellie quickly complied and then stuck her head out of the door. The floor looked empty now so she stepped out to make sure they could make it to her office.

The two scurried to Ellie's office and she dimmed the lights and closed the door.

'Here.' Ellie moved the chairs around to face the wall instead of the glass partitioning that faced the public areas. 'If anyone does pass by they'll only see our backs.'

'A new position has opened up in Singapore.' Daphne was eager to speak. 'They need someone to head the entire Asia Pacific office. Ellie,

I want that job more than anything I've ever wanted in my entire career.'

'Singapore – really?'

Daphne nodded. 'But guess who else is in the running.'

'Gosh, Daphne, I don't know.'

'Tyler.'

'No! Our Ty the Guy?'

'He knows how badly I want it. I was really stupid one night after work. I let my guard down, and you know how manipulative he can be, and I told him. Of course that was before I knew he wanted it too.'

'So he's making your life a misery.'

'Yes, but there's more.'

A little bit of colour had returned to Daphne's high, hollow cheeks and her large brown eyes were a little less tortured. Her long arms lankily draped the chair and her even longer legs stretched towards the floor like a cat in a good long stretch. Daphne had the kind of hair that, no matter what she did to it, or what state she was in, always appeared as if it was supposed to look exactly as it did. Tonight, she sat twisting strands of it with one hand while still clinging to her tissue with the other.

'When Ty and I both found out we were up for the same position we began eyeing each other in the halls and in meetings – you know, normal stuff. But one night I was working late and I walked by his office and heard a strange noise. At first I was terrified that someone was in there stealing something, but then I heard a woman's voice. To this day I don't know what made me do it, maybe I thought someone was using Ty's office or something, I don't know, but I opened the door.'

'Oh no,' Ellie said.

'Thank God they were still fully clothed, but there was my little Alice, one of my staff, locked in a huge snog with Ty the Guy.'

'What did you do?'

'Nothing, closed the bloody door and got the hell out of there.'

'Isn't he engaged?'

'Yes,' Daphne said dryly.

'I take it you've still not reached the climax – so to speak.'

'You can say that again. About a week later Alice came into my office and of course I know what it's about, or at least I think I do. Turns out, their little intimate moment was really only that, but now Alice can't untangle herself. Tyler Elliott won't leave her alone. Seriously won't leave her alone. She's accusing him of harassment.'

'Oh shit. Do you believe her?'

'Of course. But then Tyler approached me. He told me that he's not harassing her, that he and Alice were just, I think he used the term "horsing around", and when she lost interest he left her alone. So they both want to use me as a witness. Tyler knows that if this gets out of hand he might lose his job and then, without a doubt, Singapore is mine. Even if they put someone else in Ty's place, I'll still get it. I just know it. Tyler is my only real competition.'

'Not complicated enough, is it?'

'Not half, and what's more, I don't want the job of my dreams to come to me this way.' Daphne teared up again. 'I'm stuck in the middle because I opened that damn door. One single action put me in the middle of this mess.'

'What will you do?'

'I don't know yet. But look at the time. I've been terribly selfish. I'm sorry. I completely forgot that you came into the loo with your waterworks on full as well. What's that all about then?'

'Sounds like you have enough on your mind, Daphne, I'll be all right.'

'Oh sod that, come on then.'

'All right, but I'm a bit peckish, you?'

'I could kill for a curry.'

'That sounds good, the posh one in Soho all right with you?' Ellie asked.

'Divine, but can we get a table at this late notice?'

Ellie smiled. 'I have connections.'

Ellie rarely asked Wrigley for this kind of favour but it was worth it. Soon they were seated at a quiet table for two at Daphne's favourite Indian restaurant. When they had ordered, Daphne again pressed Ellie to confide in her.

Ellie chose not to tell Daphne about her dreams; it had been a long time since the two had been close friends and she was a little shy. She did, however, tell her that she was striving to make changes at work and within herself. That was why, she said, the 360-degree review was so difficult to swallow.

Daphne turned out to be a very good listener. It was a relief to Ellie to be able to speak to someone who was actually in the company and knew many of the players. Ellie finally reached the topic of her presentation in New York. She decided not to skirt the issue of how tough the feedback reports had been, including Daphne's. But Daphne was unfazed and continued to listen.

They were well into their curries and masala dosas and a little bit of everything else when Ellie laid down her fork.

'That's it. I'm finished.'

'But you have a plate full of food.'

'No, I mean that's the extent of my lament.'

'Oh, okay, well do you want my thoughts?'

'Yes. I think.'

'Stop that, it's not bad at all.'

Pulling off a piece of naan, Daphne continued, 'There are a couple of things going on here. Firstly, you've outgrown your position. You work very quickly and you feel that you have to stop and nanny, which distracts you and irritates you. But you won't admit that.'

Ellie interrupted, 'But ...'

'No, let me finish. Most of your team members need a hand-holder, someone who works a little more slowly and deliberately. That's okay, that's fine, it's time for you to move on and hopefully their next manager will do that. But, and this is a big but, it doesn't give you an excuse to be abrupt and impatient with them while you're still there. They're dead right about that – you always were impatient. It's about finding a way to get what you want without sounding too demanding. Now, it's good that you're learning how to delegate, that's crucial and you'll need that skill when you move on. All right so far?'

'Yes, carry on.' Ellie was amazed at her sharp assessment.

'You're incredibly and surprisingly good with people. But, well, I'm dying to be vulgar here.'

'Don't,' Ellie said.

'No, I won't.'

'Go ahead.'

'You've got yer head up yer arse, old girl.'

'Bloody hell.'

'Here you are, you want to teach the world to sing, yet you can't keep your own assistant happy.'

'Ouch.'

'Do you ever give them pats on the back?'

'Oh, for God's sake Daphne, you know there's no time to be nice. That must sound awful. But you know what I mean.'

'I beg to differ there. It doesn't matter if the entire corporate business culture is rude and curt; in the long run it's more productive and makes for a better, more creative atmosphere to employ a little empathy. They're frightened of getting it wrong and making mistakes. It may take a little more effort to slow down and acknowledge their successes, but you won't get the best out of them any other way. Damn, this curry is marvellous.'

'You make me sound like a monster.'

'The person described in these reports is not the Ellie Hart I know. Just try bringing more of yourself to work. Believe me, it's good advice.'

Daphne was on quite a roll and didn't give Ellie time to respond.

'Now, about that Diversity idea of yours. It is absolutely bloody well ridiculous that our company does not have a Diversity Programme. Really, in this day and age, how archaic. There are companies in the States and all over Europe that have had Diversity Programmes for over fifteen years and longer.'

'Well thanks a lot for speaking out at my presentation, Daphne.'

'Ellie, that wasn't for me to do, at least not in your first round. I do think that you're the right person for the job. You just need to get your act together. I know, I know, you're working on it, but you've got to be sharp when you come back to New York. Did you rehearse last time, or did you do your Miss Wing It thing?'

'Kind of sort of.'

'You've got to know that material inside out, Ellie. If Tyler is still there – that sounds weird, doesn't it? – if he's still there, he'll come after you.'

'Why? Why is he being such a git about this?'

'Well firstly, he simply doesn't want the kind of changes in the company that this programme would bring. And then there's the fact that you're a woman; if it were a man presenting this he wouldn't react in the same way. He'll try to do something, I'm not sure exactly what it will be, but if I were you I'd do some serious troubleshooting.'

'You mean look for holes, that kind of thing?'

'Exactly. Do you want a pudding?'

'I'm trying to cut back … but I have an idea. Why don't we stop by my friend's restaurant for dessert?'

'Do you mean Wrigley's? You used to speak about him but I never met him. That sounds good.'

They continued their discussion as they paid the bill and stepped out into the clear cold night. The streets were jammed with London's night traffic and they walked to the corner and talked while keeping an eye out for a black cab.

'Do you know what I think is really interesting? It seems to me that these hurdles are all about communication really,' Daphne continued. 'I mean, everything is about communication these days. Every *action* is about communicating something. Tyler's reputation communicates to me that he is the guilty party, not Alice. I failed to communicate support for you at the presentation. In that case, my inaction was a strong message. And you, Ellie Hart, have a huge desire to communicate very specific issues to the entire working world. I don't think you've really tapped into that yet.'

'Daphne –' Ellie stopped in her tracks, 'what are you talking about?'

'Haven't a clue, but it sounded good, didn't it? Seriously, think about it. You're obviously communicating to your team that you are offhanded, hard-nosed and short-tempered. That's not who you really are. At the meeting in New York, you seemed intimidated and unsure of yourself. There was not one person there who can do what you can do. You need to trust Jasper; he knows what he's doing. You've got to show up in that next meeting. Speaking of which, what about your clothes?'

'My clothes?'

'It may sound boring, or superficial to you, but it really does matter. You'll be representing the company in a different way if this gets approved. You can't hide out in your office all day if you're going to be head of a department.'

'All right, all right, you do go on.'

'Well, it's been a while, making up for lost time.'

'I despise shopping.'

'You are very unusual, Ellie. I'm going to be around until after the conference. If you want any help, I'd love to hit some of the London shops.'

'Thanks for the offer, I suppose I do need some new things.'

They arrived at the restaurant but Wrigley had already left for the evening. Jean-Louis was happy to see them and made a royal fuss over Ellie's guest. He brought them a beautiful presentation of dessert samplings and Ellie felt no guilt as she indulged.

'So, are you still seeing that filthy-rich cad?' Daphne asked.

'Recently terminated.'

'Oh, I'm sorry.'

'I felt like such a fool. It seemed that everyone else knew that our relationship was a farce except for me.'

'Love is not only blind, it is deaf and dumb.'

'What about you?'

'No, thank you very much. I'm off men for a while.'

'Aren't we a pair then?'

Jean-Louis joined them for coffee. 'Wrigley will be so sorry to miss you.'

'Yes,' Ellie said, 'where is that boy?'

'Very tired he was, the home bed called to him. I want to tell you, Ellie, did you know Wrigley wants to explode?'

'Pardon, Jean-Louis?' Ellie glanced at Daphne who was trying very hard to suppress a laugh.

'*Oui*, he wants to explode.' And then Jean-Louis spoke a string of French that Ellie couldn't understand. He ended with his arms held out and said, 'Bigger place.'

'Oh, I see, you mean *expand*, Jean-Louis.' Ellie laughed first, and then Daphne and Jean-Louis joined in.

'*Oui, oui*, expand, expand, so sorry.'

'Really, well that's interesting. I didn't know that.'

'He won't ask, but maybe you help to think with him?'

'Of course, I'd love to help. Thank you, Jean-Louis, for telling me – you're a good friend to him.'

'*Merci*, Ellie. And you are a very good lady.'

'All right, you two, stop your dribbling over each other,' Daphne said.

'What means this dribbling?' Jean-Louis asked.

'It was short for thank you so much for the dessert and your very delightful company. Good night, Jean-Louis.'

'I go now and call taxi for you. Wrigley will box these ears if I don't.'

'I must meet this friend of yours, he sounds refreshingly decent. And what a change that makes. Recently I've felt as if I'm surrounded by nothing but wankers. Do I sound as bitter as I think I do?' Daphne asked.

'Yes, but you're forgiven. You'll meet him at the conference dinner. I'm dragging him along to get through it. Daphne, I want to ask you about something you said earlier. I don't mean to pry but you said that you didn't like who you've become. What did you mean by that?'

'Oh please, Ellie.' Daphne rolled her eyes. 'We may have had a lovely reunion here tonight, but I am well aware that I've treated you very badly. I'm ashamed of my behaviour.' They slid into the black cab.

'I'm not faultless in this, Daphne. I don't believe that's the whole story though, is it?' Ellie asked.

'Too clever. No, that's not the whole story.' Daphne leaned forward and closed the partition. 'A couple of years ago I was under an extreme amount of pressure at work. My boss was absent a great deal for health reasons and I literally ran the department. It was a tough year in our offices, there were more projects than there should have been, a staff shortage, it was difficult. I was completely shattered. I worked constantly at such a pace that I lost my perspective. I felt very vulnerable and I made a mistake. I had a fling with someone in the office. I should have known better than to ever, ever let that happen. I've paid for it ever since.'

'Tyler.'

Daphne was silent for a moment and then nodded. 'Stupid, very, very stupid. He's bad news, Ellie. It was a humiliating experience. I feel safe in saying that I don't think he likes women very much. Anyway, it's possible that I may have to disclose that very sad episode if he and Alice don't straighten themselves out. So there you have it, probably more than you wanted to know.'

'I don't know if this helps, but you're certainly not alone. All of the offices in Europe have had a tough time with this sort of thing. We have far too many problems with it. People on the outside who think sexism in the corporate world doesn't exist any more should spend a week in our office. We're not all playing by the same rules, are we?'

'Abso-bloody-lutely – and of course I know that. That's why I can't believe I put myself in that situation.'

'What do you think will happen?'

'I don't know, maybe they'll work something out. He's not stupid, but he has a huge ego. I don't give a toss what happens to that nasty sod, but I do care about how this will affect Alice.'

The cab approached the station and Ellie and Daphne found themselves rushing through their goodbyes.

'Thank you for listening, Ellie.'

'I'm really glad you were in that loo, Daphne. Do you still have the same flat?'

'I can't give up my flat! It comes in handy and my mum stays there when she comes in to town.'

'Let's try to continue this – would you like to have dinner or something before you go back?'

'That would be really lovely – maybe on the weekend? And don't forget, the shopping offer stands when you're ready.'

Ellie hurried to catch the train and waved once more to Daphne as the black cab left the station. She was glad to board the train and settle into her seat. The lull of the moving train helped to decompress her mind, for it was spinning from the day's events.

'Oh my God! I don't believe it. Please take this image away. Tyler and Daphne, I don't believe it.'

The shock of seeing Daphne dulled the degree of disappointment she felt from reading her reviews. Now, with the peace of the train ride, her thoughts would not stray from the searing words of her peers and staff. ' "Purely for developmental purposes", the memo had said – great, thanks very much.'

It was eleven o'clock before Ellie finally pulled back the duvet and slid into bed. She took the reports to bed with her, thinking that if she re-read them before tomorrow, she might be able to better understand what to do when she walked into the office in the morning. Should she call a meeting? Should she try to speak to Jasper? 'Daphne was very helpful tonight, but it's still not clear.'

The lamp on her bedside table burned a soft light, the papers were spread out on her bed and a few of them were still in her hand when Ellie fell asleep.

She pulled the duvet up over her for she suddenly felt a shiver. Then she thought she felt something cold in the bed.

'What in the …?' But it couldn't be the bed that felt so cold, because she now noticed she was on a hard surface, very unlike her soft bed. She opened her eyes and found herself sitting on the cool stone bench in her garden.

'How daft, I never get it right away.'

She looked around for Mr Fairchild but he was nowhere to be seen. She waited a few moments while she kicked her crossed leg impatiently.

'Hmm. Where is he?' When she stood up something fell off her lap. She bent down and saw the envelope of reports on the ground.

'Well that's odd. Why did I bring these?'

She walked around the garden looking for Mr Fairchild and did not notice how beautifully it was growing.

Now she became a little frustrated that she was alone. She didn't want to be in the garden alone. She wanted to see the gardener and she wanted to hear him speak to her again and she couldn't understand why he wasn't there.

'I'm not leaving.' She sat down defiantly on the bench, folded her arms and waited. There was still no sign of the man. She then took the papers out of the envelope and began to read them again.

'Your papers must be very important. I do not recall your ever bringing anything with you to the garden before,' Mr Fairchild said.

Ellie jumped up and looked to see where he had come from.

Mr Fairchild was standing by the apple tree as if he had appeared from behind its large trunk.

'I am terribly sorry,' he said, 'I did not mean to startle you.'

Ellie said nothing.

'Eloise, have I upset you?'

'You're usually here, I was confused, that's all.'

'I believe if you examined your feelings more closely you would also add angry and frustrated and disappointed. Might I be correct to assume that?'

'Well, yes.'

'Then would you agree that my absence and delayed arrival communicated a powerful message to you?'

'Yes, Mr Fairchild, although I'm sure I don't know what that message is.'

'All right, Eloise.' Mr Fairchild laughed at her indignation. 'Enough then of my demonstration's mysteries. Come, please walk to the other side of the garden with me.'

A table had been set up in the corner of the garden. But she had not seen it earlier. 'Okay, okay,' she said to herself, 'I get it, he has his magic bits and bobs.'

'In my day we knew very little about the plant world. I was very fortunate to play some small part in the discovery of such wonderful workings of nature. My generation was quite pioneering. We came to learn that each plant needed particular treatment to survive. We were constantly experimenting, trying new things. It was necessary to learn how to communicate with the plants. And when the communication went well, I could grow things that others could not grow. I learned how to make barren trees bear fruit. I had the luxury of watching things grow, studying them daily.'

As he spoke, Ellie watched as Mr Fairchild lovingly potted bulbs. One would think that the bulbs were priceless the way he handled them. His fingers seemed to speak to the precious soil in the pot.

Mr Fairchild nodded towards Ellie's papers and continued, 'The papers you brought with you – their meaning and purpose is very important for you. They are teaching you about the power of communication.

'The plants need someone who is reliable, they need clarity from me, their humble caretaker. They also need me to communicate to them effectively. And long ago, when I did not know the true meaning of communication, I constantly sought to experiment until I became effective. I took pains to discover what they needed to grow and thrive. I chose to make them my life. I could not afford room for misinterpretations. Could you please retrieve the watering can?'

Ellie looked around and found a very large watering can sitting next to the table.

'Thank you, my dear. In the world that you have chosen there are many different ways to communicate. Unfortunately, there are also many different traps for not doing so effectively. Perhaps you might think of a few to tell me about.'

'My reviews say that ...'

'Pardon me for interrupting, I would be interested to hear your own views on this matter.'

Ellie took a moment to gather her thoughts.

'I usually work very quickly and I always feel the need to communicate as quickly as I work. Whether that communication is verbally in person, or in an email – oh, do you know what that is?'

Mr Fairchild nodded that he did indeed.

'I'm sure that I don't always take enough time to think about a response. Sometimes I don't have time to give long explanations to people.'

'Yes,' Mr Fairchild said. 'What else?'

'I've recently learned that I don't think I show my staff enough appreciation and I suppose I can be quite demanding. I feel terrible. No wonder my reviews were scathing.'

'You see, the desire to communicate must start with a seed of authenticity. The authentic desire to communicate is what brings power to the communicator. You might also encourage and coax this from others. My intense curiosity about the plant world led to my dialogue with it. If you are genuinely interested in your subject, it will tell you what to do, what it likes and what it needs. It is your duty to comply with the needs of your chosen interests.'

'With what I have on my plate, there's no time to mess around then – I'd better get on with this immediately.'

'Best to work in a timely fashion. Speed is not the goal. Plants grow in their own good time; there is nothing I can do to speed the process. I can, however, hinder their growth if the lines of communication are not kept open and healthy.'

'And also, Mr Fairchild,' Ellie said, 'if I don't go about this in the right way, then those whom I wish to affect will sense something false or manipulative.'

'Very good. Well put, Eloise, but I do not think you have the problem of being inauthentic. It is the *way* that you communicate that needs fine-tuning. Just remember. Every word, every action, every inaction is a communication. You are being asked to take an in-depth look at yourself. It is not an easy task; however, I hope you will welcome it. One more thing – your language is quite atrocious, my dear.'

'You sound like my mother. I never curse out loud at work – I wouldn't dare do that.'

'Yes, but mark my words, one day you will slip. One day your habit will have its way with you and it will be at a most highly inappropriate occasion.'

Mr Fairchild wiped his hands on his apron. 'Now, we must not keep these pots outside for they will freeze and then they will not blow for 20 years!'

'They will not what? Blow?'

'Yes, blow, bloom. They would never speak to me again if I left them out in the cold.'

Dream 5 Lesson

Never underestimate the power of communication.

Posh  Frocks

Ellie woke the next morning with a little bit of an emotional hangover. She had slept the entire night with the review reports scattered about her. She took her time getting out of bed, stared up at the ceiling, and gave herself a moment to think. Her dream made her realise how deeply the opinions of others had affected her. It was like a great secret that had finally been revealed to her.

As she lay thinking about the days and months ahead, a sense of gratefulness came over her. After all, shouldn't she be grateful for the opportunity she had been given to change? Wasn't it better to learn these lessons now, rather than later? Wasn't it better to accept the criticism and get on with making the changes, rather than fall flat on her face from not making the effort?

Once again she opened her wardrobe to face the five-minute staring game she always played with her clothes. Daphne's offer was beginning to look more appealing to her, she realised. 'This routine is becoming very old.' She said out loud. 'Even *I'm* sick of these clothes.'

When she got to the office, the first thing she did was cajole her way into an unplanned meeting with Jasper. His assistant, who was fiercely protective of his schedule, squeezed Ellie in for a nine-thirty.

Jasper knew why Ellie paced in front of his office. He knew why she was now sitting in front of him. But what he was surprised to see was an Ellie Hart, minus the nerves and very much a focused human being.

'I'm very grateful for the reviews, Jasper. I'm here to discuss them and I'd like to know if you have anything to add. I want to do whatever it is I have to do so that I can go forward.'

'Good attitude, Ellie. There's a bigger picture here. Whether or not you see it now is not important. What is important is that you take this opportunity to grow. This is your no-pain-no-gain moment.'

'I understand.'

'Anything else?'

'I've had some thoughts about the future of my staff. Would you like to hear them?'

'Not unless you're having a problem.'

'No I'm not. That's it then. Thank you, Jasper.'

'You're very welcome, Ellie.'

When she got back to her office she asked Tilda to come in and close the door.

'Close the door?' Tilda asked. 'It's ten.' Tilda referred to the busiest time for Ellie's revolving door.

'I know, Tilda, it's all right, they can wait.'

Ellie noticed Tilda's blue suit. It was a striking colour of mauvy blue that made her sea-blue eyes and red hair stand out even more.

'Please, sit down, Tilda. I want you to know that what I am about to say has very little to do with our conversation and your desire to leave. Nevertheless, those things have prompted me to discuss my ideas with you now, instead of a month from now. You were right; I simply forgot to speak to Jasper about your salary increase. I have no excuse for that. This is what is on my mind. If Diversity gets off the ground, and believe me, I'm going to do everything I can to make sure that it does, I would like you to come with me, but not as my assistant. I have always seen your potential as that of being a team member.

'Again, that does not excuse the fact that I ignored your request for a salary increase. If after the month, you've decided that you don't want to come with me, I'll put in a great recommendation for you, which will support a salary increase, which I've no doubt you'll get. However, I would much rather give you the promotion that you deserve and start out on a more solid footing in the new department. I honestly believe that Diversity will be a better department with you on board. Think about these things and we'll see how it goes.'

'I'm very surprised, Ellie.' Tilda drew in a long breath. 'I was thinking last night that maybe I just haven't been able to hold up under the pressure. Quite honestly I stopped thinking about a promotion months ago. I really would like to work this out, but ...' Tilda was having a little trouble finishing.

'I know,' Ellie said. 'You want some time to think about it and you especially want to see if things remain as stressful as they've been, and ... you want to see if I'm going to make a few changes.' Ellie smiled. 'And I don't blame you, Tilda. I think that's a very clever thing to do.'

'Thanks, Ellie, I appreciate your understanding.'

'Now, will you ask Floris to come in here please, she's lurking about out there.'

'Everything's in place for the conference if you want an update now,' Floris said when she entered.

'Absolutely. Let's have a dekko.'

Ellie quickly scanned the charts, schedules and reports that Floris handed to her. 'This looks very good, Floris. Well done. What's the empty space on the speaker's list?'

'Oh that.' Floris cleared her throat. 'Several of the heads suggested that you fill that spot. They want you to speak at the dinner.'

'I don't think so. On what topic?'

'Your choice.'

Ellie looked down at the papers. 'Who was your catering choice? I don't see it here.'

Floris leaned over and found the page for her. 'Your friend's recommendation. Really nice man, great food and a discount.'

'Bravo.'

'You've changed the subject.'

'I can't do it, Floris, not this time. I'm leaving for New York the following week; I probably won't even make it to many of these events. Why don't you do it?'

'Me? Really?'

'Why not? Unless you'd rather not.'

'I'd rather, I'd rather! What should I speak about?'

'Hmm, what about calling it "The Gatecrashers"? Twenty minutes on the history of women crashing the party. Let's see, men – the invited guests, women – the gatecrashers. That should bring down the house.'

'That's brilliant, Ellie.'

'Thanks, Flo, but not really, I recently read an article written by a female investment banker who was constantly harassed. Why don't you take the positive angle though, you know – how far we've come, that kind of thing?'

'Will do, Ellie.'

One by one her staff filed into her office. Ellie welcomed them and concentrated on listening and making suggestions. She took her time and consciously gave each of them more attention than usual. They noticed the effort.

Paresh, whom she had not seen all day, came in towards the end of the afternoon.

'I'm here to pick up some of what everyone else is getting.'

Ellie laughed. 'I'm trying, Paresh, I'm trying.'

'Seriously, every person who has left your office today has a different kind of look on their face.'

'I think it's called shock. I'm just trying to give everyone a little extra time today. Thought it might help boost the morale around here.'

'Here's how you can boost mine. Lunch on Friday – two people from every department working on the conference have been invited to the Saddle and Reins Club. I think we should make an appearance.'

'Please don't ask me to do that.'

'I know it's impossibly late notice, but it's one of those terribly hurried and eccentric decisions from the top.'

'What is it they want us to do?'

'Not a thing, as far as I know; the person who called me just said to show up when I asked her.'

'They must just want an update. What's wrong with a simple memo? All right, all right. Consider yourself boosted.'

'Thanks, Ellie. I've always wanted to go to this club – apparently it's quite something to see.'

Ellie made the most of an unusual lull in the activity. She asked Tilda to guard her closed door for an hour. She was in the middle of a phone call when Tilda stuck her head in the door.

'Sorry,' she mouthed. 'Daphne Marchant on the line.' Tilda waited for instructions.

Ellie nodded, ended her other call and picked up the other line. 'Are we still friends?'

'Hi, Ellie, are you busy?'

'Manic.'

'I won't keep you. Did I have a dream last night, or did I really tell you all of my darkest secrets?'

'I'm the first to admit that the line is blurry, but no, you were not dreaming.'

'I feel like the "morning-after girl". I realised this morning that last night was very unusual and I might have burdened you with more than you bargained for.'

'No regrets here and you know you don't have to worry about confidentiality with me,' Ellie said.

'No, you are the most brilliant secret-keeper. But thanks for saying it. I actually called to thank you for last night, you were a great help.'

Ellie sat staring at her computer. 'I really didn't do anything. Where are you?'

'Two floors up, one office over on your right.'

'That's scary that you know that. Listen, I remembered a bit of research I've done recently for Diversity. Did you know that most sexual harassment cases are settled quietly and that sexual discrimination cases are not? Companies don't like their dirty laundry aired in public.'

'Oh?' Daphne asked. 'And discrimination is clean laundry?'

'Something like that, but I thought that might interest you. I wouldn't worry too much.'

'I'll try.'

'You were a help to me as well. You pushed a few dusty buttons last night, but I needed it.'

'You've been having a tough time, haven't you?' Daphne asked.

'Uh, yup, you could say that.'

'Just remember what I said about your next meeting in New York.'

'I will. Do you want to speak over the weekend then and plan something?'

'Sounds good. I better go now and whip a few young lads.'

Daphne hung up to the sound of Ellie's laughter.

The rest of the day and the day following were so busy that Ellie could barely remember returning home late each evening.

On Friday, as planned, Paresh arrived at Ellie's office to escort her to lunch. Ellie gave him a double-take. 'Gosh, look at you.'

Paresh, who always appeared well turned out, looked particularly handsome today. Ellie was surprised to see him in a suit. Although he often wore a jacket and always wore a tie, Friday's were not normally suit days. It seemed to Ellie that he was standing much more erect; even she could tell that his new suit fitted like butter on toast. Its colour was the darkest of charcoal greys. The shirt he wore was deep lavender and had a subtle sheen. His tie, which was dark aubergine, sported cream-coloured spots.

'Thank you. Must be the new suit. I have a friend in the business who let me in on a spectacular sale. I thought the Saddle and Reins Club deserved it. Are you ready to go?'

'Yes, just give me five minutes, I'll be right back.'

Ellie grabbed her bag and ran to the loo. Paresh's new suit intimidated her. Should she have dressed differently today? 'It's just a stuffy old club, for heaven's sake, she said to herself.' She found her lipstick and a tube of mascara but they didn't help much. Ellie still looked a bit rumpled and thrown together. It wasn't that she had forgotten about the lunch meeting, she just hadn't been aware that she should have made an extra effort with her appearance. 'I'm not going to worry about this. It's Friday, after all.'

But Ellie was dead wrong. It *was* Friday; however, this was the Saddle and Reins Club and when they arrived she could immediately see that both the women and the men had dressed for the occasion. Not surprisingly, Ellie felt out of place.

She put on a brave face as they entered the old carriage house. The Saddle and Reins was more of an old dining club in which the reception and lounge ran heavily to a horsey theme. Various horse accoutrements were perched rather importantly on the brick walls. There was a clubby atmosphere with deep-seated leather chairs and a gigantic roaring fireplace. Famous foxhunting prints competed for attention on the walls.

Drinks and finger-food starters were served in the lounge as Ellie tried to remain engaged in the various conversations. She was having trouble focusing, becoming more uncomfortable minute by minute. At least she could see that Paresh was going to make an excellent number two; she watched him work the room with the confidence of a seasoned politician.

Just when she thought she would crawl out of her skin from the sideways glances she was receiving from the other women, they were ushered into the dining room.

'I think they've led us to the wrong room,' Ellie said very discreetly to Paresh. 'It seems they have mistaken a Victorian bordello for a dining room.'

They strode across a plush carmine carpet, which clashed slightly with the crimson velvet chairs. The stark white linens screamed, 'Here are your tables.' To Ellie's displeasure there were two mirrored walls, which threw back her reflection any which way she looked, and this was not a good day for reflections. The other two walls were covered in a dusty rose damask paper. The mirrors reflected the hand-painted ceiling where garlands of roses, ferns and oddly coloured pastoral scenes had been painstakingly applied. From the busy ceiling hung Moorish chandeliers with pierced brass insets of jewelled glass, which, in Ellie's mind, contributed to the bizarreness of the room.

'A bit garish, don't you think?' she whispered to Paresh.

'Too right!' he whispered back. 'How disappointing.'

When they were seated the meeting began immediately. The luncheon, Ellie and Paresh found out, was actually a pre-launch meeting for the Women's Conference. Paresh and Ellie looked at each other, both perplexed that somewhere down the information chain they had been ill informed. Luckily, and thanks to the hard work of Ellie and her team, the previous Wednesday's deadline for completion had left her fully prepared for this meeting. Still, she was furious. How could this have happened?

The item of the day that she was not prepared for was the fact that she had just heard her name called. She looked up at the speaker, who stood staring at her, waiting for her to rise and give an update on her team's contribution to the conference. She turned to look at Paresh, who leaned over to her and said, 'I had no idea. No one told me!'

She would not normally have had a problem with this kind of public speaking; it was simply a report on their progress and to convey that they had done their jobs well. The problem she had was with the way she looked today. Ellie was very embarrassed to walk to the front of the room; she knew her colleagues would stare at her and judge her appearance. Daphne was right. She could no longer hide in her office.

Ellie winged it; she presented a short, efficient account of her team's share of the planning for the conference. She applauded Floris and Paresh, to whom she gave most of the credit for the smooth completion of their assignments. She even made a joke about the time crunch with the caterer. When she finished, she tried very hard to keep from running back to her seat.

When Ellie returned to their table Paresh handed her a note: *Very sorry! I'll find out what happened. You did marvellously well.*

Ellie nodded her head to acknowledge the message. She wondered if she might be foaming at the mouth from the day's continuing disasters. She didn't want Paresh to think that she was blaming him, so she struggled to keep her temper under control.

The elderly staff glided in and out of the room, quite like ghosts whose purgatory was to serve hungry company employees who relished free lunches. Ellie found herself without an appetite and moved her fork around on her plate, still stinging from the walk to the podium. When the pudding was finally served and she was not even tempted, she took it as a sign. She felt compelled to look at her reflection in the bevelled mirrors to determine if she stuck out as much as she feared. Her best hope was that she might see someone interesting-looking staring back at her. Ironically, her vision became blurry and she gave up.

At the end of the programme when they were on their way out, Ellie heard several complimentary comments about the décor of the dining room. 'Lovely,' said one woman, 'I'd love to hire this room for my wedding reception.' Another said, 'It's so gorgeous here, couldn't you just sit in this room all day?'

Paresh followed Ellie as she swiftly marched into the street out of sight of the others. She could contain herself no longer.

'Shit!' Ellie paced the kerb. 'Shit, double shit!'

She turned on her heels and said to Paresh, 'Please make it your Friday-afternoon quest to find out which bloody wanker is responsible for that major cock-up. Find out which of those imbeciles didn't inform us that I was expected to give a presentation. That was a bloody launch, for Christ's sake. I should have known! I should have known – the Saddle and sodding Reins Club – you just don't "show up" and do nothing! What a load of bollocks that information was.'

She stopped ranting and walked away from Paresh. 'I just lost it.' She put her hand to her forehead. 'I can't believe I just lost it.' If she were honest with herself, Ellie knew that a part of her frustration was from having a very bad hair day. Of all days to get caught out and not feel good about herself, it would have to be on a day when she stood before a roomful of people.

Quickly she turned back to Paresh. 'I'm sorry, I am so sorry. I've had a disastrous day all around.'

Paresh was visibly relieved that it wasn't him with whom she was angry. In fact, he didn't care who it was as long as it wasn't him. 'Quite all right, Ellie, you have a right to be angry. Not to worry, I'll find out what happened. Leave it to me.'

He hailed a cab and when the two had settled in for the ride back to the City, Ellie became a good deal calmer.

She had enough presence of mind to be aware of the fact that she needed to change the atmosphere before they returned. She had set a terrible example. Mr Fairchild was right, she thought – I did slip – and I will slip again if I don't watch myself.

She purposely instigated a good laugh with Paresh by describing the décor of the dining room at the Saddle and Reins.

'There must be something wrong with my taste level because I thought it was just awful. Is it me? Did you hear those women going on about how beautiful it was?'

'You have a more discerning eye, Ellie. You know what's right.'

Ellie looked at him. 'You certainly wouldn't know it to look at me today.'

'It can be very hard for one to see oneself accurately,' he said tactfully.

'You did all right. You are very well turned out today without being ponced up, which I don't have time for at all.'

'But I told you, I had help.'

'You're very kind to say that, Paresh.'

Paresh was silent for a moment. He kept glancing over at Ellie as if he were about to speak, but changed his mind and looked away. Finally, after several tries, he managed to say something to her that he had wanted to say for a while.

'I'm very grateful to you, Ellie.'

'Good heavens, for what?'

'You've given me opportunities that, quite frankly, I never thought I would have. I never told the hiring gods in this company what happened to me at my previous job.

'It was a real boys' club,' he continued. 'There were literally a handful of women working in our department. When the lads tired of handing out insults to the women, they'd have a go at me. One day one of the men called me "Bombay" and unfortunately the rest thought it a great laugh and it stuck. As I was one of the newest members of the team it was always, "Bombay fetch this", or "Bombay will do it". I took my complaints through the proper channels but as you might guess, they were completely ineffectual.

'My position on your team is bliss compared to what I left behind. I have a great deal of respect for you and a personal stake in what you are trying to achieve. The reason I bring this up now is because I know you've made a gigantic effort with very little support. Also, although we've already discussed that I would like to join your new team, if it turns out that I am not right for it, I want you to know that I am deeply grateful that I have had the opportunity to work with you.'

The taxi had stopped in front of their building. Ellie, on the verge of tears, asked the driver to wait for a few moments.

'Um, well!' She fought to compose herself. 'I'm touched by what you've said. I'm not too surprised that you've found some of your experiences at work to be so rotten. Sometimes we have to rebuild our self-esteem, don't we?' She shook her head slowly. 'I suppose we all have our issues.'

Ellie paused a moment before she continued, 'I was going to speak to you about this soon, but as we're here running up the meter on the taxi, now seems to be perfect timing. I *would* like you to be a part of my team. Actually, I'd like you to be my number two. So I suppose you'll have to suffer with a promotion, Paresh.'

The cab driver opened the partition. 'I've turned off my meter, luv, but would you be so kind as to hop out soon?'

'Sorry, sorry,' Ellie said to him. 'Be right out.'

'What? Really? But I thought you'd take Floris with you.' Paresh did not attempt to disguise his delight.

'I can't discuss Floris's position with you because I haven't spoken to her yet. As I said, this was an unplanned conversation.'

'Of course, of course, I didn't mean to question you, I'm a little ... well ...'

'Does that mean you accept?'

'Of course! I accept, yes, yes, I accept.'

'Good.' Ellie smiled. 'We'd better go in now.'

Ellie and Paresh stepped out of the taxi. The driver had turned the meter off from the moment they pulled up to the kerb.

'Thank you very much, I hope we didn't keep you too long.' Ellie gave him a generous tip.

'I always do one good turn a day. Cheers, luv. All the very ...'

As they stepped out of the lift Paresh said to Ellie, 'If you need any help with your next presentation I can devote some time to research, or whatever you need. I'd be happy to.'

'Thanks, Paresh. As a matter of fact, I could use your expertise on something I'm working on for my next meeting in New York. If you have a minute after our meeting today, I'd appreciate it if you would come by my office.'

'I will do.'

Ellie wanted to conduct the Friday meeting in a quick, efficient manner so they could all go home early if they chose to do so. As she looked at her schedule for the next week she saw that she was left with no choice but to delegate duties if she was going to meet her own deadlines. She glanced at the time and then sprang from her chair to have a peek at the room to see if it was ready.

The conference-room table had been prepared to her specifications. Tea and coffee, cold drinks, assorted biscuits and fresh fruit had been laid out for their meeting. Ellie arrived a little early and sat working as they entered.

'What's this then?' Floris asked.

'I'm starved.' Margaret grabbed a biscuit.

Even Tilda, who had no idea Ellie had organised the food, smiled and poured herself a cup of tea. The last of her staff trickled in and each of them selected something to eat and drink. I should have done this a long time ago, Ellie thought, such a small gesture, yet they all appreciated it enormously.

The meeting went smoothly, hastened by Ellie's eagerness to dole out the responsibilities for the following week.

'I'm going to be out of the office for a few hours next week.' Ellie looked at Tilda. 'Tilda, I'll let you know my schedule as soon as I can, I just don't know it yet. If any of you need anything I'm sure Floris and Paresh will be able to help you.'

Ellie asked Paresh to fill the team in on the day's lunch meeting, which he did beautifully, without going into any of the gory details, and then Ellie called her meeting to an end. To her surprise, her staff lingered for a while and chatted about the upcoming conference; they included Ellie in the conversation and asked her to tell them what the Saddle and Reins was like, which she did quite humorously. Ellie was relieved to see them in better spirits and thanked each of them for producing such good work.

As promised, Paresh stopped by Ellie's office after the meeting.

'Please come in and sit down, Paresh. I don't think I'll need to remind you about getting back to me with the name of the person who told you about the Saddle and Reins lunch.'

'Absolutely not.'

'Good. Now, I have something special planned for my next presentation in New York. I thought that ...' Ellie said as she closed the door to her office.

The train was wall-to-wall with commuters returning home on a Friday night. It had been so long since Ellie had taken one of the rush-hour trains that she had lost her commuter legs. She couldn't make it to the seats fast enough, so she stood for much of the journey. She couldn't wait to get home, drop her bags down and take off her work clothes.

By seven-thirty Ellie was in her house, sitting in her favourite fireside chair eating a bowl of cereal. A documentary on the telly about sleep disorders was actually doing the trick for her. Soon her eyelids became very heavy and she drifted off in the middle of hearing various cures for the ailment.

At first she thought she was flying; instead, it appeared she was floating above an old London street. The street itself was dimly lit from gas lamps and there were neither cars nor buses anywhere to be seen. Ellie heard the sound of heavy hooves all around her. Carriages drawn by the large owners of the clopping hooves began to draw up to a property that sat among a row of terraced houses. This house, the one with a single lantern above the large front door, was in the process of accepting the company of several well-dressed gentlemen.

One modest carriage, a hired carriage, stopped in front of the house and a man who looked familiar to Ellie carefully stepped down into the street. He paid the coachman and then walked towards the house. In his hands he very carefully carried a parcel. In fact, he behaved quite protectively towards his parcel and did not even remove his hat immediately upon entering the house.

Ellie followed him, because it was obvious to her that she was neither seen nor heard. She noticed a plaque upon the wall in the entry hall of the fine old building. Upon it was a coat of arms and underneath the plaque, a brass sign read: *The Royal Society, established 1662.*

The meeting was called to order, which was a true necessity due to the fact that every single gentleman appeared to be speaking at once. The minutes were read from the previous meeting, after which point the gentlemen were asked to present their papers. Ellie looked for the man she thought she recognised and found him still holding his precious parcel. He and another man stood up and walked to the front of the room. The men turned to face the audience and Ellie gasped. The man holding the package was Mr Fairchild. Granted, a younger, more robust and plumped-out Mr Fairchild, but certainly none other than he.

Although Mr Fairchild did not appear to be as wealthily dressed as many of the other men, he was, at this age, just as precise and neatly attired as ever. Tonight he appeared to be wearing his very best suit of clothes, consisting of a very fine black brocade coat with a matching long waistcoat. A crisp lace edged the collar of his white shirt and the large stiff cuffs, which were turned back over the sleeves of his coat. His breeches, the plainest garment of all, were of a plain black finely woven wool.

His companion appeared to be speaking to the group; however, Ellie could not hear what he was saying. She shook her head to clear it for now she could not hear anything at all. Mr Fairchild began to unwrap the parcel and very carefully he produced to the group a dried, pressed flower.

'A dried flower?' Ellie said disbelievingly. 'A dried flower?'

The scene before her quickly disappeared and abruptly she found herself in the garden. Mr Fairchild stood before her in the same black suit of clothing and in his hand he held the flattened flower. Tonight, he was glowing; a light shone around him where he stood, very still and quietly powerful.

'Maybe it's just my eyes.' Ellie rubbed them and yet he was still there, smiling at her patiently.

'My dear, lovely Eloise. Do come near and hear my story. Do you remember the last time we were together I explained to you my curiosity about plants?'

'Yes, Mr Fairchild,' Ellie replied as she moved towards him.

'When I was a young man, my intense curiosity and deeply strong desire to learn about the world flowers inhabit led to, shall we say, a rather daunting experiment. I was particularly interested in the sex life of flowers.'

'Why Mr Fairchild, how naughty.'

'Yes, Eloise, but certainly not in the way you are suggesting. However, in my time it was "naughty", as you say, for a different reason. When it was discovered that plants reproduced similarly to animals, much like you, I too was seduced by diversity. In those times, men would venture far to seek new, exotic plants. High rewards were paid to those adventurous men who crossed the seas to bring back varieties of plants not yet seen in our land. Little did I know that one of the most exotic flowers would be found in my own nursery.

'This evening,' he continued, 'you witnessed a night that was very important to me. I had been invited to a meeting held by a scientific institution, a very important institution. I was not a Fellow, nor a member, for I am no scientist. I was invited to the meeting for the sole purpose of introducing my mule.' He handed Ellie the pressed flower.

'This flower is the result of the experiment that created the first hybrid. At the time, it was a blasphemous thing to do. I had tampered with nature and had, in some eyes, interfered with the Creator. It bore down upon my conscience for the rest of my mortal life, yet I could not resist it. Therefore, Eloise, I do know a little about taking risks and pioneering.'

Ellie made not even a feeble attempt to speak.

'On the evening I was to be presented to the Society I took great pains to ensure that I was appropriately attired. I had no room in my being for worry, or self-consciousness about how I physically appeared to the audience that evening. My desire was to appear as well turned out as possible so that I could then forget that aspect of my presentation. My goal was to focus the attention of the group towards the mule and my companion's words. I could ill afford to arrive over-dressed or uncared for – I wanted nothing to distract from the task at hand. I was certainly not the most fashionable man in the crowd, nor was I the least. I employed every possible tool to appear credible. Ah, I hear your thoughts coming towards me already. No, Eloise, you are entirely wrong. It is not such a lot of fussing.'

'But why, Mr Fairchild?' she asked earnestly. 'Why is it so important? I understand that one must be well groomed and certainly not tatty, but I have to admit I still don't understand why this clothing thing is so important. I need some new clothes, so what? So does everyone eventually. Isn't it my work that counts? Doesn't the fact that I'm loyal and work hard say much more about me than my clothes? Why all this fuss about it? If people don't like me for who I am and what I produce, then too bad.'

'Yes, it is too bad, Eloise. But too bad for whom? It might not seem fair to you, but you must take responsibility for how you are going to be perceived.'

Mr Fairchild paused to allow his words to take effect.

'The messages you send via your image can determine how you are perceived professionally,' Mr Fairchild said. 'You must make the effort. People appreciate effort. I am certain that you can readily recall the feeling of walking into the luncheon today. You did not feel confident, far from it, you felt out of place. You've come so far already, Ellie. Think of the beautiful flowers in your garden, they are ready to bloom, so are you. It is such a waste of your precious energy to neglect this aspect of yourself.'

'I'm thoroughly admonished and chastised, Mr Fairchild. I am behaving quite childishly, aren't I?'

'No, Ellie, you were just in need of clarification, that is all.'

'Are you really the father of the hybrid then?'

Mr Fairchild laughed, 'The word did not even exist at that time in relation to plants, that is why it is called my mule. Some say that my intense curiosity led to an "accident" in my nursery and then I deliberately recreated the accident. Others say that I intentionally impregnated a carnation with the pollen of a Sweet William.'

'Fascinating. Which was true?'

Mr Fairchild smiled, leaned towards her as if to tell her the answer, but instead, gently plucked the pressed flower from her hand. His image began to fade.

'Oh come on. Please don't go. Mr Fairchild, what a tease you are.'

Ellie saw something floating through the air. She tried to catch it but it evaded her as it fluttered around her. It looked like Mr Fairchild's mule. When it fell to the ground she bent over to pick it up and saw that it was a paper flower with words transcribed on the long stem: *The messages you send via your image can determine how you are perceived professionally.*

Dream 6 Lesson

The messages you send via your image can determine how you are perceived professionally.

Ellie vs. the Volcanoes

7

'All right, all right! I get it,' Ellie said in her sleep. She jumped when she heard the telephone ring. 'What's that, where am I?' She looked around to find that she was still in her chair. 'Hello?' She looked at the time as she picked up the phone – it was only nine-thirty. She couldn't believe it, surely it must be morning, she thought.

'Ellie, Daphne here. Are you busy?'

'No, not exactly, I just had the most bizarre dream.' Ellie turned down the sound on her television, which was now blaring out a sitcom.

'Sorry, did I wake you?' Daphne asked.

'No, no, it's all right, I just nodded off in front of the telly. Actually, your timing is perfect. I was going to ring you tonight anyway. I've really got to do that shopping thing.'

'Good for you. We can start tomorrow if that works for you.'

'What do you mean "start"? You mean start and finish don't you?'

'No I do not, miss. You do know that this is going to take more than one day, don't you?'

'Okay, all right,' Ellie said reluctantly. 'What do I have to do?'

'To do this right, we should have a little breeze through your wardrobe and see what you need. Then we'll make a list. So, I should come by your house in the morning, bright and early. Next, we go into the West End and have our first look-see. Now, depending on …'

'Hang on, hang on. This must be what it's like being one of your staff. Please go slowly, this is not something that comes easily to me.'

'Sorry. Tell you what. Why don't you pick me up at the station at around eight in the morning, or whatever time the train gets in closest to eight, and we'll take it from there. We'll go to London by train – I don't think we need to deal with traffic and parking.'

'Eight? That early?'

'We'll lose the day if we don't. Come on now, this will be fun.'

'Mmm, sure, lovely. Thanks so much, Daphne.'

'Pleasure. See you tomorrow.'

Ellie padded to the kitchen and placed her empty cereal bowl in the dishwasher. She looked out of her window into her dark garden and raised her hands in surrender.

'Okay? All right?' she asked the night air.

The next morning she rose early, dressed and took the short walk to the Boverys' shop. Mr and Mrs Bovery had not quite opened up yet, but Ellie knocked anyway. Mrs Bovery peeked through the door and opened it wide when she saw Ellie.

'I'm so sorry to trouble you, but I have a friend coming over early this morning and of course, I'm out of everything,' Ellie apologised.

'No trouble 't all. Your friend usually comes around 'bout this time anyway. We always let him in.' Mrs Bovery was as welcoming as usual.

Mr Bovery explained, 'He usually picks up the missus's baked goods to take to his restaurant with him. He tells us that he shares them with his staff, but we think not a morsel sees the outside of his car! Don't we, Mrs Bovery? Yup, there he is now, reliable as a Swiss clock, he is.'

'Wriggers! Good morning.'

'Ellie? What are you doing here at this hour?'

'I have an early-morning guest.'

'Oh?' Wrigley swallowed. He stiffened and said, 'Well I hope your guest appreciates Mrs Bovery's delicacies.'

Ellie smiled. 'I'm sure she will.'

Wrigley immediately relaxed again, and turned to the Boverys.

'Good morning, Mr and Mrs B. What have we got today then?' he asked.

Mr Bovery brought the long flat boxes to the counter and Mrs Bovery opened them to reveal warm oatcakes, sausage rolls and hazelnut shortbread fingers.

Wrigley and Ellie, having nearly depleted the Boverys' stock, walked to the Forager where Wrigley offered Ellie a lift home. The short drive allowed for only a hurried account of Ellie's rekindled friendship with Daphne.

'I was surprised to hear from Jean-Louis that you and Daphne had come by the restaurant. He had a little trouble with her name. Actually, he butchered it,' Wrigley laughed.

'By the way, Jean-Louis told me that you were thinking of expanding, or exploding, as he put it. I would really like to talk to you about that.'

'Ellie, you're too busy right now to …'

'Wrigley, you've been so supportive of me, I really would like to help you with this. Why don't we give it a try?'

'Offer accepted, I'd like that. When some of the pressure is off and you have more time I'd love to talk to you about it. If you two are coming into town today, why don't you stop by for lunch?'

'Wouldn't dream of it. You're far too busy on Saturday, you'll need the table.'

'Nonsense.'

'No, Wrigley, I feel guilty when I'm there on Saturdays.'

'All right, no pressure. Have fun today.'

'Are you mad? This is torture.'

'Ellie, I really think you're going to have a great time.'

---◆---

Daphne's train arrived just after eight. Ellie hopped out to greet her and wondered how Daphne could look so smart at such an early hour on a Saturday morning. She wore a beautiful dark brown suede jacket, that had two leather flap pockets; it almost looked like an old man's hunting jacket. Underneath the jacket she wore an anthracite grey jumper. A fine stripe bordered the neck and the bottom of the jumper in the colour of a deep red wine. And beneath the jumper, the large pointed collar of her blouse stood out boldly. The blouse, which was white, had a tiny aubergine diamond-shaped pattern on it. Her caramel coloured wool trousers fit her brilliantly. Ellie thought the whole ensemble might look a little odd on anyone else, but Daphne carried it off with aplomb.

'Top of the mornin'.' Daphne said brightly.

'Oh please, cheeriness doesn't suit you, Daphne.'

'Look, this will be fun if you let it. I've never met anyone so sour about shopping.'

'I'm sorry. You're right, I think I must be a little nervous.'

They pulled up to Ellie's house, 'No need to be nervous. We'll get this done and then you won't have to think about it for at least another four or five months.'

'What?'

'Oh yes, spring and summer wardrobe.'

'Can't wait.'

Ellie opened the door to her house. They walked in and Daphne exclaimed, 'Wow, Ellie. This place looks marvellous!'

'Oh thanks, I did a bit of a re-furb last year.'

'My gosh, I love your taste. Where did you get that mantelpiece? It doesn't even look like the same fireplace.'

'Jean-Louis helped me find it, it came from an old castle in Brittany. Well, actually the servants' quarters. Make yourself at home, I thought I'd make a pot of tea before we start.'

'Lovely. Was this wood floor always here?'

'Yes,' Ellie said from the kitchen, 'always. It was underneath that horrid carpet.'

'I do envy you all this space. Do you know how much my little one-bedroom on Riverside is worth now?'

'Not a clue.'

'It's worth more than it's worth.'

Ellie appeared with a tray filled with tea and the warm baked goods.

'I guess that's a lot of money then. Let's take this upstairs.'

Ellie laid the tray on a table in her bedroom, poured the tea and made up a plate for them both.

'Over to you now,' Ellie said, sipping her tea.

'No, over to you, my dear. Go to your wardrobe and pick out your most favourite, can't-live-without item of clothing.'

Ellie stood before her cupboard and found herself experiencing the familiar numb feeling. Finally, she chose the black dress that she hadn't been able to fit into a few weeks ago.

'This black dress,' she said.

'Ellie Hart, that is not a black dress. That is a piece of black cloth with four holes in it, one for your head, two for your arms, and a big hole in the bottom from which your legs protrude. I can't believe you still have this thing. Give me that and find something else.'

'You are ruthless!'

'Find something else, please.'

'You sound like a bloody schoolma'am, or hospital Sister.'

Daphne ignored her and pointed to her watch.

'All right, here.' Ellie pulled out the red suede skirt.

'That's better,' Daphne said with her mouth full of food. 'Damned good oatcakes. I know you didn't make them.'

'Of course not.'

'Let's have a gander at that skirt. Quality's not great, but not too bad, good colour for you. Try it on, please.'

'Oh Daphne, do ...'

'You're going to have to get used to this, I won't watch. Go stand over there and change and I'll have a look through your wardrobe in the meantime.'

Daphne's hands flew through the clothes in Ellie's closet as if she were editing the entire costume department of a major film studio.

'Do you know what we need to do here, Ellie? We need to get the taste level that you've brilliantly demonstrated downstairs into your closet. I'm afraid it's nowhere to be found except perhaps in that red skirt.'

Ellie turned to face Daphne and yelped when she saw so many of her clothes piled up on the bed. 'What are you doing with my clothes?'

'I'm thinking Oxfam.'

'But that leaves me with hardly anything!'

'Wrong, that leaves you with the incentive to deal with this.'

'What's wrong with this?' Ellie held up the navy blue suit that she wore every week to work.

'Ellie look at this, do you see that sheen on the fabric? That means it's over, finished, well worn out.'

'It is a bit old, isn't it?' Ellie conceded.

'Ancient. But that skirt looks quite nice on you. Keep it on, I think you should wear it today.'

'I was going to wear my jeans and a jumper.'

Daphne patiently explained: 'We're going into the kind of shops that you're not used to shopping in. I'm not asking you to dress for them, but for yourself. After you try on better-quality clothes the last thing you want to do in the dressing room is to put an old pair of jeans back on. Believe me, it will make you feel better.'

'All right, I won't argue.'

The two continued to work through Ellie's wardrobe for another hour. Daphne was, not surprisingly, very thorough and listed everything she thought Ellie needed.

'This is how I think we should do this,' Daphne said while dialling her mobile. 'Let's see if I can get you into my tailor's for a consultation today – he only sees people by appointment on Saturday. Then we'll do a few bits around the West End. We'll have to plan some time next week for fittings and to finish off.'

'Whoa, whoa, whoa. Fittings?'

Daphne held up her hand, 'Wait a sec. Hello, Mr Timmons? Daphne

Marchant here. How are you? Good, and how is your family? Wonderful, do give them my best. Yes, I'm in London. Yes, thank you, I'd love to come by. I know this is awfully late notice but I'm with a friend right now, and believe me she would really appreciate your time today. Is there any way you could fit her in? I think we can make that. We'll be on our way then. We're about an hour away depending on the trains. Lovely. Thanks ever so much, Mr Timmons.'

Ellie knew when she was beaten. She finished changing into the skirt and jumper, boots and – drat it all – tights on a Saturday afternoon.

'Lovely breakfast, Ellie. Let's go. I'll explain on the train.'

When they were seated on the next train to London, Daphne took out her pad and pen and began reviewing her list while she spoke.

'A few years ago I was in the City walking around at lunchtime and a woman passed by me in the most gorgeous suit. It fitted her so beautifully and it wasn't one of those really predictable women's suits that always look like a man's suit gone wrong. I ran after her and asked her where she bought it. She hesitated for a moment but she finally let the cat out of the bag. His name was Mr Timmons. At the time, he had a little shop in Gracechurch Street; he's since moved to Holborn, which is where we're going now. Although he makes great women's suits, it's not something he wants to advertise – he's a bit of a secret. Anyway, I think you should start with three new suits and two of them should be made-to-measure.'

'All right, I appreciate the introduction, but why? Why do they have to be made-to-measure?' Ellie asked.

'You deserve to know what it's like to wear something that fits exceptionally well, and makes you feel and look good. You'll have a unique, special experience that you won't find on Bond Street, or at any of the rock-and-roll tailors who've taken over Savile Row. When you launch Diversity you'll look like you're expressing who you are in your own quiet and subtle way. And it won't be as pricey as you think; you'll get real value for your money with Mr Timmons.'

Mr Timmons was the quintessential traditional tailor. He was always immaculate, and wore his trademark braces with hand-made shirts and rather over-sized, hand-tied bow ties. His large, round brown eyes peered from behind his bifocals, which he hated wearing and took off at every opportunity. His reddish-brown hair, which, surprisingly for a man of his age, boasted no hint of grey, was untamed, a mess of organised chaos.

He and Daphne put their heads together, poring over fabrics and colours and trying also to teach Ellie as they ploughed through the quagmire of a made-to-measure suit. An hour later, Ellie had been thoroughly and painstakingly measured. Daphne leaned on Mr Timmons to have the first suit ready in time for Ellie's trip to New York without any extra charge, and the second would be ready by the time she returned. When Ellie heard again that she was required to come in for fittings, she tried not to show her panic about being away from the office.

After they left the shop, Daphne checked her watch. 'I think we should grab a quick bite before we go to the West End, it will be a madhouse there today.'

They sat with a view of the Thames and ate a light lunch while Daphne continued to go over the items on the list. Ellie was quick to pick up that this shopping experience was going to be similar to one of Daphne's ultra-organised projects. But she was grateful for it – for she certainly wouldn't have made the best of it on her own.

'Not to worry,' said Daphne. 'You'll pick this up in no time. We haven't really talked budget yet, but I know you can afford to get the essential items. So I don't want to hear any complaints about the dosh.'

Ellie laughed at Daphne's bossiness. 'No complaints.'

'I'll come with you and help you while I'm still here, after that you can just call me if you need to. I think we should hit Knightsbridge and Kensington for late-night Wednesday shopping, we can also go back to the West End on Thursday night for their late night, and a full day on Saturday. Let's check our schedules and see if we can get away from the office early on those days.'

'Are you sure you have time to do this, Daphne? I don't want to intrude upon your time while you're here.'

'I told you, this is something I really want to do for you and I actually enjoy it. It's the least I can do for behaving so badly.'

'You don't owe me anything, Daphne.'

'I know, it's not about "owing", it's about behaving like a good friend. A good friend wouldn't have cut you off the way I did. Especially for no other reason than that my only focus was *moi*.'

'Is that an apology, you old goat?'

She laughed. 'Yes, I guess it is.'

Daphne whisked them to the West End, where they spent the rest of the afternoon. She certainly still knew her way around and introduced Ellie to a whole new culture of shopping. Ellie's fears of being dragged into trendy designer stores where only the fashionistas shopped were soon allayed. Daphne's experience and focus on getting the job done taught Ellie the value of giving her appearance the much-needed attention it deserved. There was no dilly-dallying; although there were fun moments, everything they bought was to fulfil a purpose.

By the end of the day, something had clicked for Ellie. She began to respond to the look and feel of better-fitting, good-quality and sophisticated clothes. She looked at her reflection in the changing-room mirror. The suit she was planning to buy completely changed her posture, she stood more upright and actually looked a bit taller.

Ellie turned to Daphne. 'You know, one of my staff said to me that it's hard for us to see ourselves sometimes. Too right! And, I think it's even more difficult to see ourselves the way others see us.'

'Well the way I see it, you should buy that suit,' Daphne said.

They took a much-needed break while they waited for a rush job on her alterations to be completed. Seated at a table in the café of a small museum, the two women lingered over their tea, relishing the thought of biting into the warm scones that passed them by on their way to some other table.

'When you're ready, we have to talk about your hair and makeup,' Daphne said. 'And I was hoping you'd be ready just about now.'

'I knew this was coming. I'm not going to wear inches of makeup and I'm not spending an hour blow-drying my hair.' Ellie looked at Daphne, who looked very determined; Ellie relented immediately. 'All right, what do you have in mind?'

'Well … we just happen to be a few blocks from my stylist – why don't we pop by? I still see him when I'm in town, but let me give him a call first. He's particularly good at making corporate hair look real. I think you should take next Friday afternoon off, get your hair done, and then on to the makeup artist for a lesson and an application. That would be a real treat for you before the dinner. That reminds me, we've got to find you something to wear to that dinner.'

By the time they left the last shop at closing time, and Ellie had met Brendan, Daphne's hairstylist, they were both completely exhausted. They toyed with the idea of an early dinner but they were both just too tired. Before Ellie stepped out of the taxi laden with carrier bags, she said to Daphne, 'You've made this fun, I actually had a wonderful time. I can't believe I'm saying this, but when are we going out again?'

◆

On Monday morning Ellie walked into the office wearing a very soft tweed skirt. The brown, red and cream coloured flecks of the fabric were subtle, yet still made the skirt look special. It fell just below her knee and there were two large pleats in the front and two in the back. The pleats fell perfectly enough to give the skirt a little swing when Ellie walked. She also wore a deep red cashmere jumper with a uniquely designed square neck. Under the jumper she wore an ivory silk blouse with a soft long collar, which lay easily upon the jumper. The blouse's cuffs were long and they floated out from under the jumper's sleeves. At just about hip level she wore a thin brown suede belt. The colour of the belt matched her new chocolate brown suede boots.

She certainly felt the stares and the double-takes, but this time, she didn't really care. She could handle the attention because she felt good. Her clothes were comfortable, they fitted really well and she finally understood that they were being used to enhance her personality, not overwhelm it. She accepted the compliments as graciously as she knew how.

The first person through her door that morning was Paresh, who looked uncharacteristically agitated.

'Good morning, Ellie. Have you got a minute?'

'Of course. Morning, Paresh.'

'I'm having a little trouble with the woman who left us out on a limb at the lunch last Friday. Her name is Jeanette, and when I called to find out what happened, she virtually denied that she forgot to tell us to have a verbal report ready for the luncheon. She insinuated that I didn't remember the conversation correctly. You know I don't lose my temper easily but I wanted to wring her neck. I'm not sure what to do. Do you want to speak to her?'

'As you might imagine, I would love nothing more that to have a go at her. But I've been thinking about this. You're the one who had the initial conversation with her. I think it's important for you to learn how to handle these kinds of incidents. It's over to you first, Paresh. And of course, I'll help you and I'll step in if it comes to that. First, think about what it is you want Jeanette to do.'

'I want her to take responsibility and I think she owes us an apology.'

'Good. You might not get the apology, but someone has to take responsibility for the muck-up.'

'What would you do?' he asked.

'I would go to her in person and I would be extremely calm and polite, but very clear. Tell her that you are not in the least bit mistaken about the content of your conversation. Tell her that you know how busy she must have been making arrangements to organise the meeting. Ask her to please rethink her conversation with you, to take her time in doing so and to get back to you in person. Tell her that, at the moment, you don't intend to take this matter any further and that you hope you can sort this out between the two of you. Make sure you save that remark for the end and then promptly and politely excuse yourself.'

'That sounds very good, what should I do if she's not alone?'

'Ask to speak to her privately. She'll be more than accommodating.'

'Thanks, Ellie. It seems so simple when you say it, but these kind of confrontations are not easy for me. Sometimes I feel that I need to be more careful than other people.'

'I understand. No, they're not easy. I don't think anyone likes to do it except bullies, and then those are not really confrontations, are they? I'll stand by you on this – it involved me as well. We're still on for four o'clock today, yes?'

'Yes, and by the way, excuse me for saying so, but you look very nice today.'

Ellie smiled at him. 'Thank you. Like you, I had a little help.'

Floris arrived right on time for a meeting with Ellie. Her mouth flew open when she saw her boss standing in her office on the phone. Ellie waved her in and hung up.

'Really nice, Ellie, really nice.' Floris reached out to touch Ellie's jumper. 'Ooh lovely.'

'Yes, it's all right, isn't it, Floris?'

'I have to say that I don't know what this meeting is about. Have I forgotten something?' Floris asked.

'No, no, nothing like that. First I want to say that you've done an excellent job this year. I realise I haven't been very vocal about how pleased I've been with your work. You've helped enormously with keeping the team motivated. You've managed to endure both the changes I've made and the challenging experiences we've had this year, particularly the last several months. I want to speak with you about what happens in the event we go forward with Diversity. I'm sure that you're the right person to head the team after I leave – well, if I leave. And I'm going to strongly recommend you.'

'Oh? Gosh, that's ... well it's not what I expected. I thought you'd want me to go with you. But, that's great!' Floris flew into a tightly controlled dance in Ellie's office. 'That's fantastic. I mean ... I didn't mean that ...'

Ellie smiled. 'I know what you mean, Floris. I don't like the thought of not having you with me, but I really think you can manage this team and the responsibility. I also think it's right for you to stay in this department.'

'Are you taking anyone with you?'

'Yes, I have every intention of taking Paresh, that's what I hope to do.'

'Hate to see him go. But I do understand why you'd take him. He'll be great.'

'He'll be pleased to hear he will be missed.'

'Is there anything I can do to help in the meantime?' Floris asked.

'Yes, as a matter of fact. At last Friday's meeting I told you that I needed to be out of the office quite a bit these next two weeks. Some of that time I will need Paresh with me. That leaves you with the reins. If you need to call me, then by all means do so, but use this time as a testing ground for yourself. Try to gauge whether or not you really want this job.'

'That sounds good, Ellie. I will do that and don't worry about anything here.'

'Good. Thanks, Floris.'

'You've done some kind of remarkable turnaround in, well ... every area, it seems. The team is much happier, they're thinking more creatively and it's because you've made some noticeable changes. I've learned a lot just by observing you.'

'Thank you very much, Flo. I've had enormous support from a variety of people.'

'Still, you did it.'

'Well, I'm just trying to keep at it. I have a way to go yet.'

'You'll do it, I know you will. And by the way, you look great.'

Ellie, still not used to all the compliments on her appearance, blushed just a little. 'Thanks, Flo.'

By the end of the day, Paresh and Ellie had begun what would be the first of many closed-door sessions. Throughout the rest of the week they attended several off-site meetings as well. Ellie's instincts were right on target; Paresh was a good partner to have chosen to assist her with her presentation.

During the week Ellie liaised with Daphne to attend her first-ever fitting for her new suits. To an uneducated eye it looked like a load of fabric lightly held together by big awkward-looking stitching. Mr Timmons asked her to move about, use her arms, walk, and sit to make sure it looked and felt just right. It was hard for Ellie to imagine that the hodge-podge of fabric she was wearing would soon be a suit.

When Ellie returned from her fitting she found Margaret sitting in a chair outside her office. Ellie exchanged looks with Tilda, who was standing next to her.

'Margaret would like to see you right away, if possible, Ellie,' Tilda said.

'Of course, go on in, Margaret, I'll be right there.'

Ellie waited for Margaret to enter her office, while she remained outside with Tilda.

'What's this about?' she asked Tilda.

'I don't know. She won't tell me. She's been sitting out here for half an hour. I couldn't get her to budge. I told her I'd call her when you returned but she wouldn't hear of it. Sorry, I tried to block this pass, but she was determined.'

'That's odd behaviour for her, isn't it? Okay, thanks, Tilda.'

'Margaret? Tilda tells me you've been waiting for me for some time,' Ellie said as she closed her door.

Margaret looked particularly young today. The short plaid skirt she wore made her appear more like a schoolgirl than someone who was just wearing a fashionable skirt.

'Yes.' Margaret cleared her throat. 'I don't know if I'm doing the right thing by coming to you with this. It's always been clear that you dislike gossip, but ... I thought this was different and that maybe you should know about it.'

'Then I'm sure you're right. Go on.'

'I was on the eighth floor yesterday. I needed a bit of information from one of the analysts and I stopped in the ladies' on my way back down. I was just going to open the door to come out of the loo when I heard your name. A group of women had been standing outside the door when I went in.' Margaret then looked up at Ellie with a rather tortured look. 'I stayed at the door and earwigged into their conversation.'

'Ah, I see. Well I can assure you, Margaret, that I am a very boring target for gossip. Whatever you heard and whomever I was supposed to be doing it with is untrue and it doesn't concern me a bit.'

'That's just it, Ellie. It wasn't as much about you as it was about *it.*'

'It being ...?'

'Corrine Baxter.' Margaret looked very uncomfortable. 'Corrine Baxter was making really negative remarks about the diversity project. She said something about how it was going to disrupt everyone's working lives and change the environment in a bad way. She said that things are tough enough without you making it worse and who were you in the first place to try to take this on.'

'I see,' Ellie said.

'I thought you might want to know about it. I don't know what you intend to do about this, but, I'd really appreciate it if you wouldn't mention my name.'

'No, of course I won't, please don't worry about that. I'm glad you told me. You were right to do so, because this is not about you or me, it's about the company. '

Margaret became a little more courageous. 'Well that's what I thought. I didn't think it was right for staff to stand around and undermine an important new project, especially one that is going to help all of us.'

Ellie was mildly surprised. 'Thank you. I didn't know you felt that way, Margaret. By the way, any feedback from Jasper on that report?'

'Not a word.'

'Told you. I appreciate your effort here today.'

Ellie sat at her desk and continued to mull over the information Margaret had given her. She knew Corrine by sight but had never really had any real contact with her.

'So why is she attacking this project?' Ellie said aloud. She would mull over this information for a few days before she decided what to do about it.

◆

On Wednesday morning, the opening day of the conference, Ellie stood in front of her wardrobe and knew exactly what she would wear that day. She chose her new store-bought suit, which she had yet to wear, having saved it for this occasion. It was a black wool gabardine trouser suit. What was so different about this particular suit for her was that it was up-to-the-minute in style, and it made her appear polished – and polish was not something one would have previously associated with Ellie. It was a good-quality suit that fitted her well, especially for an off-the-peg suit that wasn't a size eight! With the suit she wore a very chic, amber-coloured, silk mock turtleneck, which enhanced the green of her eyes and made them sparkle. When she was dressed, she took an extra long look at herself in the mirror. It looked good, *she* looked good and more importantly, she felt good. She could also see that Daphne was right to push her to complete the job with a hair and makeup update. Now she was looking forward to it rather than dreading it.

The conference was being held in various rooms throughout their building, and tonight's first meeting, which opened the conference, was to be the only event Ellie would attend before the closing dinner on Friday night. Most of the events and seminars would take place at lunchtime and during the evenings, so she would be able to pop in and out, but the remainder of every spare moment would now be focused on her presentation next week in New York.

She thought she would probably be the first person in the office this morning, but Jasper was already at his desk. He motioned for her to come in as she walked by.

'Good morning, Ellie. I've just been looking at your report and your request for an additional ticket to New York. I'm not sure I understand why you need Paresh there.'

'Good morning, Jasper. I'm sorry, I was supposed to accompany that report and explain, but you were busy.'

Ellie proceeded to explain what she and Paresh had created for the presentation.

'It's a very good idea, Ellie. You've got courage, I'll give you that. Just make sure it goes as smoothly as possible.'

'Thanks, Jasper. I will. I feel pretty confident about this.'

As she left his office Jasper said, 'Good to see you've done a bit of shopping, Ellie. Well done.'

'Thank you.'

On her way back to her office she relished those few moments she had spent with Jasper. And anyone who might be looking could see Ellie smiling to herself as she walked the halls.

At the end of the day Daphne and Ellie planned to rendezvous before the conference began. Ellie waited for Daphne in the hall of the eighth floor where the largest meeting room had been transformed to accommodate tonight's event. Groups of both men and women were scattered about the halls and public areas. When Ellie spotted Daphne and walked towards her, she passed by a few women who became noticeably silent as she approached them. Out of the corner of her eye, Ellie saw Corrine Baxter at the centre of the group. She also recognised a couple of the other women. Undaunted, she stopped where they were standing and greeted them as a group. Their response was casually chilly – Corrine was, in fact, unbelievably rude and simply turned away to continue her conversation.

'How bloody childish,' Ellie thought.

Daphne was standing beside her now and had witnessed the snub.

Ellie's voice remained even-toned as she said, 'I hope you all enjoy tonight's programme.'

'The bloody cheek!' Daphne said as they walked into the conference room, 'Who was that woman?'

'Her name is Corrine Baxter, she's a PA to one of the managing directors.' Ellie filled Daphne in on what Margaret had overheard yesterday.

'Bloody troublemaker if you ask me. What will you do about it?' Daphne asked.

'I'm not sure yet, but I can't let her carry on with those negative huddling sessions.'

'Too right!'

The evening ran smoothly and the audience responded warmly to the opening speaker. This year's conference theme was 'Gender Champions' and there seemed to be enough head-nodding and alert faces to make Ellie feel confident that the planning committee had made a good choice.

After the opening speaker, there was a short break for drinks and light food before a return to the evening's programme. This was Ellie's chance to do a little networking. She left Daphne and went to search out as many of the top executives as she could spot in the room. One by one she approached them, reintroduced herself to those who might have forgotten her name, or, in a few cases, introduced herself for the first time to those she had never met in person. She waited for them to recognise her as the person who would be giving the Diversity presentation in just two short weeks. She knew they wanted to get a good look at her, but she also was very interested to have a look at them. These were the people who would be deciding her future and the future of the company. To her surprise, she found them very stimulating to speak to. Challenging, yes, but challenging in a way that made her think quickly on her feet.

At the end of the evening, Daphne gave Ellie an exhilarating ride to the station. She owned a 1965 navy blue Aston Martin convertible, which she kept housed in her parents' garage. It was a clear night and she cranked up the heat as they drove through the London streets with the top down.

'I guess I'm still such a Brit at heart. Can't give up the flat and can't sell my Aston.'

'Why should you? You'll be back someday,' Ellie laughed.

'You've changed, Ellie. I saw you tonight chatting up the old top brass. You looked completely at ease. You must feel quite chuffed.'

'I'm never exactly chuffed these days, Daphne. But thank you, I dare say I do feel more confident about what I'm doing now. I know it's right. I just need all the pieces to fall into place.'

'I can't guess what will happen, but you certainly looked the part tonight.'

'This suit's not bad, is it?'

'Not bad at all. Wait until you slip into one of Mr Timmons' suits.'

'I managed to get my hands on the seating charts for Friday night. You and your date are at our table. I hope that's all right with you.'

'Of course, and my date will love it. Guess who it is?' Daphne said.

'Wouldn't dream of guessing.'

'Oliver.'

'Oliver? You're bringing your brother? That's kind of sweet.'

'Isn't it? I told you I'm off men for a while.'

Daphne pulled over at the station amid the stares of late-night rail travellers who rarely saw a convertible in the chill of late-autumn.

Sitting at her desk on Thursday morning, Ellie picked up the phone and dialled Corrine Baxter's extension.

'Hello, Corrine, this is Ellie Hart.'

Corrine answered with a clipped, 'Yes?'

'Corrine, I thought it might be a good idea for the two of us to go out for a coffee sometime today. What time is good for you?'

'What for?'

'I need to speak to you, Corrine.'

'I really don't think I can find the time this week. Maybe sometime next week.'

'Corrine, we *are* going to have this discussion. I thought it would be more pleasant for us to get out of the office and have a chat over coffee. If that doesn't work for you I'll come by your office sometime today. Of course, if you'd like me to check in with your boss first, I'll happily do that.'

There was a moment of silence before Corrine responded.

'No, no, that's okay, I'll meet you in Julia's in an hour.'

'Good. Thank you.'

An hour later Corrine and Ellie sat in the coffee shop around the corner from their offices. Ellie ordered and paid for the coffees as Corrine sat uncomfortably, noticeably agitated.

Corrine was a tightly wound woman. Ellie always referred to her type as 'overly pressed'. Everything looked like one big pinch. Her shoes were pinched, her mouth was pinched and the creases in her trousers appeared immovable. Her hair, also pinched, was dyed a bright yellow blonde, and was a bit stiff from over-bleaching.

When Ellie was seated across from Corrine she leaned into her and in a very concerned voice asked, 'Are you happy here, Corrine?'

Stunned, Corrine could not reply.

'Is everything going well for you here?' Ellie asked again.

'What do you mean? What's that got to do with you?' she asked.

'I think it has everything to do with why we're here. I think it has everything to do with your negative huddling. Your behaviour tells me that you're more engaged in negative campaigning than in your work, Corrine.'

'I'm allowed to have my opinion,' Corrine said.

'There's a big difference in having an opinion and undermining a project. Is there something troubling you?'

'What do you mean?'

'When we're troubled or unhappy in business we often do things that we wouldn't normally do. Some people have affairs they usually regret, some people drink too much. Sometimes, when people don't look forward to coming to work, they find ways to divert their attention from the real problem. Do you know what I mean?'

'I suppose,' Corrine reluctantly answered.

'I'm sure there are days when, like me, you'd rather be at home doing almost anything else. Is that right?'

'Of course there are days when I just don't want to come to work. But that's normal, there's nothing wrong with that.'

'Very normal. I feel that way when I've worked too hard and haven't seen my friends or family for ages. What it is that makes you feel like that?' Ellie delicately and diplomatically tried to soften the pinch.

'It's not just me, you know. A few of us in my department find work almost unbearable when it gets too rough.'

'Too rough?' Ellie asked. 'What exactly do you mean by "too rough"?'

'Why? Why should I tell you? So that I can lose my job?'

'I assure you, Corrine, this conversation is confidential. I'm not here to cause you any problems. I'm just trying to find out if you really have a problem with me, or is it something – or someone – else?'

Corrine was hesitant to respond. She was still trying to gauge whether or not she could trust Ellie. Ellie sat back in her chair as a gesture towards giving Corrine a little time and space.

After a few minutes, Corrine looked down at the paper napkin, that she had pinched into shreds and spoke without meeting Ellie's eyes.

'Sometimes our department head can be really difficult.'

'Do you mean demanding?' Ellie asked.

'No, they're all demanding, aren't they? I mean very difficult.'

'Okay, I see where you're going. I just want to repeat, I promise you it won't go further than this table, if you don't want it to.'

Corrine let the tiniest bit of emotion surface in her face.

'He's a bully. He's disrespectful and completely insensitive. He's like this with everyone, but he's worse with women. What really annoys me is that he's getting away with it.' Corrine's controlled anger was surfacing.

'It's hard to believe, isn't it, Corrine? Some people would find it difficult to believe that in this day and age that kind of behaviour still goes unchecked. But I think I can help. One of the programmes I intend to start within Diversity is a mentoring programme. I think it would be something that would be very helpful to you and the many other women within our company. If you would let me, I could find the right mentor for you, someone who could help you with this problem right now. We can't change the difficult people around us, but we can certainly learn how to deal with them more effectively.'

'Would I be able to learn what to do the next time he shouts at me? Because I end up feeling so powerless. I'm left standing there like an utter fool.' Corrine wiped her eyes.

'Yes, you would, but also you would have a support system that is proactive. I also want to create mandatory training programmes as a way of preventing these problems before they get out of hand. So that women don't have to feel that they'll lose their job if they're being mistreated. I mean really, how twisted is that?'

'I think I must owe you an apology. Here you are trying to do something to help all of us and I've ... well, I'm very embarrassed. Really, this is *very* embarrassing,' Corrine said.

'Let's put this behind us. I'd much rather see you in the halls with your friends talking about something that moves us all forward. If we had to have this little meeting to get there, then I don't mind a bit.'

'Thanks a lot, Ellie. I've got to run back now.'

'You're very welcome, Corrine. I'll be in touch. In the meantime, you take care of yourself.'

Ellie watched Corrine walk down the street. Was it her imagination or did Corrine Baxter look a tad less pinched?

◆

On Friday afternoon Ellie sat in front of Brendan's mirror with a head of wet hair while he and Daphne caught up on their respective lives. When he brought his complete attention to Ellie she was already relaxed from listening to the two of them having a good old gossip.

'I'm terrible with a blow-dryer. If you must know, the last time I tried to blow-dry my hair I was almost fatally wounded,' Ellie confessed.

Brendan laughed. 'I'm sure it wasn't that bad. But I'll tell you a little truth. No one can blow-dry their hair the way a professional can. It's physically impossible. So, I'll teach you what to do in between visits. Just know, my darling, there's nothing wrong with you. Your hair should look good regardless. If it doesn't – then it's a bad cut.'

Well, that's music to my ears, Ellie thought.

He cut into her hair to give it a little texture and cut a couple of inches off the bottom to make it a bit shorter than shoulder-length. He also gave her just a few fringy wisps around her eyes. If Ellie were to shake her head, her hair would fall into place in a subtle but sassy way. Needless to say, Brendan was the answer to her dreams.

Next stop was the makeup studio. Ellie said to Daphne before they entered, 'I don't want to come out looking like a clown. Promise me I'm not wasting my time here.'

'Stop worrying. I told you, if you don't like it I will personally wash it off.'

And so Ellie sat in front of yet another mirror while a very nice young woman named Zelda began by plucking Ellie's eyebrows. Ellie kept one eye on the mirror as much as possible. It seemed to be going well, but Ellie's mistrust of the end result kept her alert. When it was all over, she looked up into the mirror and was truly astounded. Not because she saw the 'Miss After' photograph staring back at her, but because the talented and skilled young woman had truly used the makeup as a tool to enhance. Ellie thought she looked brighter, more alive and sophisticated. Not that it would have been too difficult after the last several months. Her eyes and lips in particular, were much better-defined.

'I told you so.' Daphne beamed.

Finally they indulged in one more salon experience. This one was Ellie's idea. She treated them both to manicures and a cup of pre-dinner tea. Daphne nearly required resuscitation when Ellie told her that this was her very first manicure.

In the late afternoon the two women parted ways to get ready for the evening. Ellie's mother had pleaded with her to dress for the dinner at her house, and it was convenient, but when Ellie arrived, Georgie wasn't home yet. A few moments alone were not unwelcome to her after the long day.

She went to the bedroom and took her new dress out of the wardrobe. The dress was faintly reminiscent of a 1950s cocktail dress. It was made of a crisp, non-shiny silk taffeta in an inky black. It had an unusual slash neck, similar to the better-known boat neck. The slash neck was designed to fit snugly across the collarbone, less revealing then a boat neck, but extremely flattering and very sophisticated. The long sleeves ended in dramatic flared cuffs with a split at the wrist. The body of the dress was plain except at the bodice, where two perfectly placed darts flattered Ellie's bust line. The dress just grazed the bottom of her knees, and was form-fitting. At the centre of the back of the dress was a kick pleat.

Ellie slipped on the new black shoes that Daphne was so shocked she had bought. Ellie had a secret penchant for tall-heeled sexy shoes; her new dress gave her a reason to indulge.

She heard her mother coming in downstairs so she went down to greet her.

'Ellie?'

'Yes, Mum, it's me.'

When Ellie descended the stairs she laughed when she saw her mother's face. It wasn't exactly shock, but somewhere very near disbelief.

'It's all Daphne's fault. We've been doing a little shopping.'

Georgie was swollen with pride. 'Eloise, darling, you look beautiful.'

'Thank you, Mum, but please don't make a fuss, all right?'

'No, of course not, but really, dear, you do look so heavenly.'

'Mum.'

'All right, all right. Do you have a coat?'

'Oh, I almost forgot.'

Ellie went back upstairs to get her wrap. She and Daphne had found a hand-dyed black velvet shawl. It had an iridescent sheen to it and the fabric appeared to move in the light.

When Ellie came back downstairs Wrigley had already arrived and was standing talking to her mother. Ellie stopped on the stairs when she saw him. And he, in turn, stopped speaking when he saw her.

'Hi, Wriggers!' Ellie finally said.

'Wow,' Wrigley managed to say.

'Why Wrigley, I think you are a confirmed clothes horse. I've never seen that suit on you. Is it new?'

But Wrigley could still only say, 'Wow.'

Ellie's smile disappeared. 'Oh no, Wriggers. Do I look that different? I'm not supposed to look like a makeover victim. Daphne promised me I wouldn't. Is the makeup too much? Is that it? It's the dress. It's the dress, isn't it? It's too sophisticated for me. I knew it. Or is it my hair ...?'

'Stop, Ellie! Stop. It's perfect. It's all perfect. You're perfect. Isn't she perfect, Georgie?'

'I'm not really allowed to say,' Georgie said, 'because my daughter is a bit sensitive about compliments, but yes, I'd say she is just about perfect.'

'Okay, time to go. Before I become so perfect that I can't be seen in public.' Ellie gave her mother a kiss and a hug.

'Well you two make a very handsome couple. Have fun now.'

'Night, Mum.' Ellie waved as they left.

Wrigley followed Ellie out of the door, turned back to Georgie and gave her a solid wink.

There were very few occasions in which the employees of Ellie's company saw each other out of their nine-to-five attire. The Women's Conference closing dinner had become one of them. Ellie was a little nervous as Wrigley drove. At least I'm not speaking tonight, she thought.

She leaned over and touched Wrigley's arm. He jumped with the unexpected sensation, which made her laugh. 'I'm sorry, Wriggers, I just wanted to feel the fabric of your suit. What is it?'

'It's moleskin,' he replied.

'It's very soft, it almost looks like velvet.'

The moleskin was a slate-blue colour. The suit jacket was single-breasted and beautifully tailored. His shirt was ivory-coloured cotton with flat-looking pleated tufts running down the front. As a special finishing touch, he wore hand-made Cordovan leather Chelsea boots.

'There's something different about you tonight, Wriggers. I don't know what it is, maybe it's just that you look so handsome in that suit.'

And he certainly did. Although Wrigley always took great pains when he chose his clothes, tonight he had made a special effort. He wanted Ellie to be proud of him when she introduced him to her colleagues, none of whom he had ever met.

'Hark!' Wrigley said to himself. 'She hath thrown me a bone. She thinks I look handsome.'

Aloud he said, 'Thank you, Miss Hart. You just haven't seen me in anything but a very white starched apron for a while, that's all.'

They had been instructed to park a short distance from the actual building. The venue for the dinner was a National Trust property, which had no parking facilities, the only drawback of the entire evening's planning.

As they entered the room Ellie was relieved to see that the caterer had done a very fine job of creating a special atmosphere. The tables were lit with coloured oil lanterns, a nice change from candles, and instead of centrepieces, miniature individual flowerpots were arranged at each place setting. Ellie was quite amused for they reminded her of Mr Fairchild toiling away at his potted lilies.

Tilda was the first person to greet them. Tilda was the 'go-to' girl for the evening, a liaison who would move between all the people who had contributed to the organisation of the evening. Tilda looked bright and sparkly in a royal blue dress, her red hair pulled neatly back from her face.

She shook Wrigley's hand and was truly delighted to finally meet the voice on the telephone.

'I'm having a smashing time, Ellie. Thank you for giving me this responsibility.'

'Not at all, Tilda, I'm pleased to see you so happy.'

Tilda leaned over to her and whispered, 'I don't think I'm going to explore any other job opportunities, Ellie. I'd really like to stay. Let's talk about it next week, all right?'

'Of course, you know I'd love for you to stay. Carry on then, we're going to move along to our table now.'

Ellie and Wrigley were not the first to arrive at their table. Daphne and Oliver were already seated, as were Floris and her husband Spencer. Everyone stood when they saw Ellie, and Daphne gave her a huge hug and whispered in her ear, 'You are a bloody knockout.'

Ellie saw that people from other tables were staring at them in an English kind of way, discreetly and perfectly, so she sat down quickly after introducing Wrigley. She noticed that the females at the table seemed to be lingering over the Wrigley introduction, nodding their heads, with extra large smiles. They all plied him with questions at once, but he, as charming as ever, managed to answer them with the skill of a graceful tennis pro.

Paresh and his strikingly beautiful wife Nira made quite an entrance. She wore a deep maroon and gold-trimmed sari and Paresh wore a dark navy suit and a turban in the same maroon colour as his wife's sari. Ellie was fiercely proud of her team tonight and Wrigley was happy to finally put faces to the names Ellie constantly threw at him.

Margaret arrived just before the starter was served. Breathless, she apologised, and introduced her boyfriend,

'Hello everyone, this is Bazza. Bazza's in sugar.'

There was a round of 'Oh's' and 'Pleasure'.

Daphne leaned over to Ellie and very quietly said, 'Of course he is, darling.'

Ellie turned to Daphne and said, 'Who does she remind you of?'

Daphne looked at Margaret for a moment, who was now explaining Bazza's mixed British and Venezuelan heritage.

'Horrors. It's me ten years ago. That's frightening.'

'Why? She's lovely and she'll be a good team member, wait and see,' Ellie said.

Wrigley was in a very complicated conversation with Paresh about a Sikh's diet. He was unaware that not all Sikhs were vegetarian and was fascinated with Paresh's explanation of all of the different sects of Sikhism. Oliver and Bazza discussed, what else, sugar, and Daphne had taken Margaret under her wing. Ellie looked at Floris whose normally olive complexion looked a little pale. Ellie excused herself and asked Floris to follow her.

Ellie and Floris found a corner of the room to stand in together.

'Floris, what's wrong?'

'Petrified. Absolutely petrified.'

'About your speech? Don't worry about it, Floris. Believe me, by the time you speak most of these people will have been plied with enough food and drink not to notice if you slip up. Do you have notes?'

'Yes, thank goodness.'

'Then you're fine. Really, Floris, don't worry about it. The tables are lovely too, you did a fantastic job.'

Just then Ellie eyed Jasper making his way to their table and they rushed back.

When Ellie approached Jasper she thought she recognised a glimmer of surprise in his eyes.

'Good evening, Ellie. Very nice venue.'

'Good evening, Jasper.' Ellie gestured towards Floris. 'Floris is responsible for many of tonight's arrangements.'

Jasper nodded towards Floris.

'Jasper, I'd like you to meet Wrigley Ainsworth.'

Wrigley stood up and shook hands with Jasper. Ellie soon found herself politely left out of the conversation. It seemed Jasper and Wrigley shared a sensibility to the history of the building and soon they were walking around the room commenting on the restored architecture.

Daphne lightly tapped Ellie's foot and nodded towards Corrine Baxter, who was walking towards their table.

'It's all right,' Ellie said to Daphne, 'I've spoken to her, she has a bit of a nasty problem in the boss department.'

Margaret, who was sitting across the round table from Ellie, caught Ellie's eye with a worried look on her face.

'It's all right, Margaret. It's all right.'

Ellie stood again and warmly greeted Corrine.

'I just wanted to say hello to you and tell you how happy I am that we had that coffee. You've been a big help to me.'

'Good, I'm glad we met,' Ellie said. Ellie introduced Corrine to the other people at the table.

Finally the elusive dinner was actually served. The whole table sat with bated breath as they waited for Wrigley's critique.

'It's lovely,' Wrigley said. 'The food is lovely. Please everyone, eat. *Bon appetit.*'

Floris and Ellie both were relieved that everyone looked as if they were enjoying themselves. After the main course, there was more mingling and tablehopping. Ellie took this opportunity for a quick loo break before the programme started.

As she opened the door to the ladies' the women descended upon her like a pack of hounds.

'Who is he?'

'You never told us he was so gorgeous.'

'Friends, Ellie? Are you sure that's all it is?'

'Where did he come from?'

'No wonder Preston's out.'

Daphne was there too. Leaning up against one of the basins with her arms folded she commanded the floor's attention.

'All right, Hart. Out with it. How long has he been mooning over you with those deadly attractive eyes?'

Ellie very calmly reached into her bag and took out her lipstick. As she was applying it she said, 'He's my best friend. We've known each other since I was a young girl. Our families have been friends for ages. That's all.'

'Right,' Floris said.

'Don't you have a speech to give?' Ellie asked her.

Panicked, Floris looked at her watch and rushed out of the loo. The group began to disperse until Daphne and Ellie were left alone.

Daphne said, 'My gosh, Ellie, can't you see that it's much more than "just friends" for him?'

'Maybe,' Ellie said. 'Wrigley and I have known each other for a long time, Daphne. What may look like something more than friendship to you might just be our regular kind of hanging-out style that we've actually perfected over the years.'

'Mm-hmm.' Daphne sounded unconvinced. 'We'll see.'

'We should get back,' Ellie said.

When Daphne and Ellie sat down again Wrigley passed her a pretty, tall-stemmed glass filled to the brim with trifle.

'I saved it for you. You ladies missed dessert. Everything all right?'

Ellie smiled at him. 'Yes, Wrigley everything is just fine.'

Floris was the first speaker of the evening. Ellie was pleased that Floris did actually use her idea of 'Gatecrashers' for her topic. However, Floris chose to take a humorous angle of the history of women at work. It was really very funny and a clever way of making the point of how far women had come in becoming a vital part of the workforce without rubbing the men's noses in it or denting their egos.

When Floris was duly applauded and came back to her seat, she looked immensely relieved.

'I have a new and reality-checked appreciation of presenters,' she said as she took a huge gulp of wine.

The evening's keynote speaker was an Englishwoman who had become the head of the European Women's Council. She had flown in from Switzerland to attend the dinner. Although she delivered the rah-rah speech that everyone expected, she spoke well and was even inspirational. Her words left the women feeling as though their contributions were of value and that they could be responsible for bringing about positive changes in the future.

When the dinner was over, the guests at Ellie's table lingered for a while enjoying each other's company. When it was time to go Daphne and Ellie took a few minutes to say goodbye to each other, while Wrigley, Ellie was happy to see, continued to mingle.

'I can't believe you're leaving tomorrow,' Ellie said to Daphne. 'It seems rather abrupt, for some reason.'

'It's been fun, hasn't it?'

'Yes, and surprising. Who would have thought it? Thank you again for all your help. I hope everything works out for you when you get back. I mean with Tyler and the new job.'

'I feel a little better about it now. It's sort of out of my control.'

'I'll see you soon. I'm planning to come to New York a few days earlier than the meeting. I want to have extra time to prepare.'

'That's a good idea. Are you staying at the company's regular hotel?'

'Yes, and you have my mobile number.'

'Let me know when you've got your flight details.'

'Will do. Take care.'

They gave each other a hug and then said their goodbyes to the rest of the group.

'That was a very interesting evening,' Wrigley said on the drive home.

'How so?'

'It was very revealing to see you in your environment. Don't forget, you always see me at work.'

'I hope it was good revealing.'

'But of course! I always knew that you know your stuff. But seeing you do your stuff is very different.'

Ellie laughed. 'My stuff?'

Wrigley laughed too. 'Your thing, your mojo, your stuff. Your staff really looks up to you. Your boss, what's his name – Jasper? I think he respects you more than you know.'

'That's very nice of you to say so, but now I need some tough New Yorkers to respect me too.'

'Ellie, look at me. They will. I have a good feeling about your project. I think it's great that your company has a conference for women and all that, but did you notice how Paresh stuck out like a sore thumb in that room? And he's a fantastic guy. I really enjoyed speaking to him. Your company needs your project. There's more diversity in my kitchen staff than there is the whole of your company.'

'Tell me about it.'

The Forager stopped in front of Ellie's house. There was a moment of silence between them before Wrigley spoke again.

'Ellie, the weekend after your trip to New York is the Chef's Table night. It's on the Saturday night after you return. It's my turn to host.'

'Is that the night where you snobby chefs get together and gourmet yourselves to death?'

'Thanks for being so delicate about it. Yes, there are ten of us this year and I wondered if ...'

'I know, a favour for a favour, you want me to ...'

'Ellie, shh. I'm not asking you to come as a favour. I'd really like it if you would be my date.'

'So.' Ellie looked down at her lap and said softly, 'How long has this been going on?'

He couldn't look at her either. 'I guess ever since you threw that apple at me in my family's garden when you were a wee thing.'

Ellie looked up. 'I forgot you had an apple tree in your garden! Did it have red apples?'

'I believe so. So what about it?'

'Would you allow me to say something painfully predictable?'

'As long as it's not a refusal,' Wrigley said.

'I would be crushed if anything were to ever interfere with our friendship.'

'Me too. But I think we ought to try this – you know, go slowly.'

Ellie leaned over, kissed him on the cheek and then opened the car door. She turned back to him and said, 'All right, it's a date, but if we fall out over this, I'll never speak to you again.'

Wrigley grabbed her wrist and pulled her back in the car. He gently leaned in to her and softly planted a sweet kiss on her very lovely lips. 'Thank you for tonight, Ellie, I've never enjoyed anything more.'

'Good night, Wrigley.'

Ellie fell into bed thinking about the events of the evening. 'Quite astonishing really,' she said out loud. 'One would think one's life was about to change.'

She wanted to indulge and replay the moment when Wrigley had firmly held her wrist and brought her back to him and into his kiss. But Ellie was a tired young woman and very soon she drifted off into a deep sleep.

The scent of a heady perfume woke Ellie up. For some reason, she could not open her eyes, but was able to continue to walk as she followed the scent. When the scent became faint, she turned and tried another path, when it became strong again she could open her eyes.

Mr Fairchild called out to her, 'Over here, Ellie. Follow your nose.'

Still she could not see him. The scent changed as she walked, it became sweeter, then more exotic, then again very subtle. In a moment, the haze that she walked in slowly lifted and she stood before Mr Fairchild. Once again, he stood at his work table with his heavy apron tied behind his back, and his great sleeves billowed in a gentle breeze and a mild afternoon sun.

Mr Fairchild was certainly very busy this afternoon. Upon his table were all types of gardening implements. There were wooden poles and strings and what looked to be several pairs of very old large scissors. He also had a large selection of knives in different sizes and shapes.

'Hello, Mr Fairchild.'

'Greetings, Ellie.'

'I'm always surprised to see you, Mr Fairchild. You do visit at the most unexpected times.'

'Ah yes, well such is the nature of these things.'

'What are you working on today?'

'I am continuing several very interesting experiments. I am interested in sap today.'

Ellie laughed. 'Sap?'

'Oh yes indeed. Discovering the nature and flow of the sap in each of these plants led to some very important discoveries in my day. In fact, I have failed miserably at many of my experiments with my little charges. However, once we know the particulars of the circulation of sap, then we are able to help those plants which seem, shall we say, a little more difficult than others. Some species are not so easy to graft. They take more concentration, more attention, if you will.'

'Oh,' Ellie said politely, not really understanding the sap lecture.

'But then, you would already know a great deal about this, would you not, Eloise?'

'I'm afraid not, Mr Fairchild. I hate to admit it to you because you would think by now I might have picked up a little more about your world, but you still stump me.'

Mr Fairchild laughed heartily. 'My goodness, you are terribly amusing.'

'Honestly, I really don't understand what is so funny,' Ellie said.

'My dear, please allow me to lift the veil once more. You have a natural gift for garden-tending, Ellie. Where others see difficulty and flee, you seek out the root of the problem. Please forgive the symbolism. Where others see trouble, you see solutions. Your method is much like mine. Where I retreat to the sap of the plant to understand its origins and potential, you also seek out the nature of the problem.'

Mr Fairchild paused to give Ellie's mind a chance to catch up.

He continued, 'For example, the woman at your place of business who spoke of you to her colleagues in a negative fashion, you made every effort to probe right into the root of her unhappiness. You could have easily and swiftly dealt with the symptom, but instead, you chose to take your very valuable time to seek her out and help her. That is one of your special talents, my dear. Wasn't it also relatively easy for you to help your good friend Paresh through a situation in which he was hesitant to confront?'

'Well yes, I suppose it was.'

'Those things that come to us in an easy manner are those we have a responsibility to teach to others. You do not shy away from confrontation, yet you do not use a bombastic approach. As you can see on this table, these are the tools I use to coax the difficult plants to health and bloom. You too have tools. These tools you use – collaboration, negotiation and the ability to neutralise heated situations – will be very valuable to you in the future. You must recognise them. Be alert to when you need them and know that when you need them they are yours for the asking. You have enough knowledge and expertise now to experiment. If one avenue becomes closed to you, choose another.'

'I think I understand what you're saying, Mr Fairchild.'

'Perhaps this will give you greater understanding of why you have chosen this particular path in your career. Your abilities to negotiate and collaborate lend themselves to your topic of passion.'

'You mean diversity?' Ellie asked.

'Exactly. There are not many people, who, when properly educated, would choose to create a monochromic garden. At times, a garden with a single colour can be quite tasteful, but it is rare, for there must always be green, and the songbird that lights upon a branch will insist upon being seen in all its blue glory. Even just a faint hint of another colour magnifies the dominant one. There are other reasons for choosing several different colours and plant species within the same garden. They begin to nurture one another, they have different uses; one plant may be useful for healing, another for its pure lovely scent, another for sustenance. One type of plant may keep the pests away, while another is able to attract the right kind of insect, quite like our lady beetles. Turn now, Eloise, look at you garden.'

Ellie had not realised that Mr Fairchild had so held her complete attention that she had not really seen her garden today. Mr Fairchild placed his small paring knife on the table and escorted Ellie around her garden.

'This is amazing!' Ellie exclaimed.

Indeed, upon first glance, Ellie's garden evoked the image of a happy mixture of bright flowers, herbs, greenery and potted plants without consideration of colour, coordination or arrangement.

But upon closer scrutiny, this initial impression of a charming haphazardness actually held strong elements of formality. The rows of potted plants created direct and functional paths; one led to the stone bench and apple tree, another to a group of large smooth stones, also for sitting and contemplation. The rose bushes, now in a neat circular formation, lent depth to the geography of the space.

This union of these two impressions – a romantic expression of abundant flowers and the underlying practical and disciplined order – made for a design that was perfect for Ellie. For she recognised the value and excitement of the synthesis of creativity and order and it was very comfortable for her.

'It's beautiful.' Ellie let out a long sigh as if she had been holding her breath for a very long time.

'I am very prejudiced of course, but yes, Ellie, it is beautiful.'

Sweet violets, Alpine poppies, foxgloves, blue forget-me-nots, Echinacea, granny's bonnets, black-eyed Susans, cream daffodils and roses, roses, and more roses filled Ellie's garden. The pots were filled with either Mr Fairchild's proud lilies or bushy angel's trumpets.

'However,' Mr Fairchild said as he stepped back to the work table, 'there is still work to be done.'

Ellie finally turned her attention back to Mr Fairchild and watched as he patiently coaxed a bending plant heavy with bloom to stand straight with the support of a wooden pole and string. It took him several efforts to get it just right, just the way he wanted it, but succeed he did.

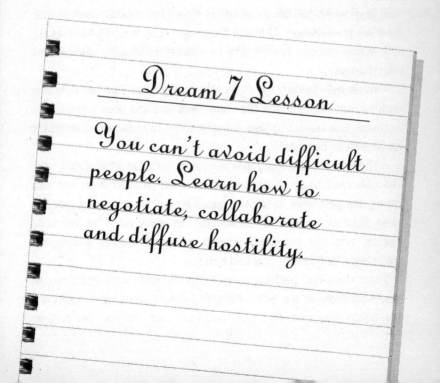

Dream 7 Lesson

You can't avoid difficult people. Learn how to negotiate, collaborate and diffuse hostility.

Bloomin' Ellie

Ms Hart ... Ms Hart. We're about to land, Ms Hart.' The flight attendant stood over Ellie, waiting for her to open her eyes.

'Thank you,' Ellie said. She flipped up the window shade and saw through the clouds the wondrous skyline of Manhattan.

She could scarcely believe that it was Saturday, a week since the conference dinner. Her presentation in New York had been postponed a few days, which had delighted her as it gave her another week to fine-tune her presentation. Although the presentation wasn't until Tuesday, Ellie wanted to give herself time to rest before Monday when Paresh would arrive.

When they landed, the flight attendant passed Ellie her new coat and her suit bag. For the first time since she had been travelling on business, Ellie needed to take a mental count to make sure she left the plane with all her extras.

The traffic into the city was fairly light for a Saturday. Ellie let her thoughts drift to all of the support she had received from everyone during the past week as the taxi glided across the bridge. Wrigley had been stupendous, insisting on keeping her away from the chocolate biscuits with his personally devised meals for energy and vigour. ('Whatever that means,' she told him.)

Her team had performed brilliantly all week with Floris almost single-handedly at the helm. Paresh's support had been a boon, and the bonus was that Ellie loved working with him on this project.

He had also managed to retrieve the elusive apology from Jeanette. At the Friday meeting Ellie bought them all lunch as a gesture of appreciation.

There were already two messages waiting for her when she checked into the hotel. Wrigley had called as well as Daphne. Waiting for her in her room was a huge basket of flowers. She opened the card, even though she could easily guess the name of the sender.

I'll be thinking of you. Just be yourself, Ellie. Can't wait for our first date. Love, Wrigley.

'Certainly too good to be true,' she said as the phone rang.

'Too tired for an early dinner?' Daphne asked.

'Hello, Daphne. Actually I am a bit peckish.'

'I know a great fish and chip shop,' Daphne said.

'You're kidding.'

'Yes, I am. How about a quiet dinner in the Village?'

'Sounds lovely.'

In another country, in another city, the two women once again sat across from each other and picked up right where they had left off a week ago.

'Any news with the Tyler episode?'

'You were right. They settled it. He leaves Alice alone and she doesn't press charges. It was simple in a way – he gets to run back to his fiancée, who still knows nothing of this, and Alice is left with the privilege of not being harassed. Mad.'

'Mad and predictable. What about the job?'

'That's his too.'

'No!'

'Oh yes.'

'I'm so sorry Daphne. You must be seriously disappointed.'

'I was crushed ... and angry. For a few days I could barely speak to anyone. I don't have to remind you that an out-of-country assignment usually means further advancement. Then I began to think that maybe it just wasn't meant to be. Well, obviously it wasn't, but I thought bloody hell, I'm not going to let them see me whine over this. So, maybe next time.'

'Quite right, Daphne, and you said you were happy in New York.'

'Yes, but I would have loved that job. Anyway,' Daphne straightened her back and sat tall in her chair in a gesture of moving on, 'I have something to tell you that may help you a bit. When you were here for our first meeting do you remember anything about Tyler that seemed a bit strange?'

'Hmm.' Ellie thought a moment. 'Yes, yes I do. When I first saw him I immediately noticed something, but couldn't put my finger on it. During the meeting he seemed almost comatose and then out of nowhere he pounced on me.'

'Botox,' Daphne said.

Ellie's mouth flew open. 'What?' Then she began to laugh, 'I do not believe you!'

'Oh yes.'

'But why? He's so young.'

'No, it's not for that, although I wouldn't put it past him. He gets injections to paralyse his expressions. He doesn't want to give himself away in meetings.'

'I've really heard it all now.'

'Oh, believe me, he's certainly not the first.'

'Did he tell you this?'

'Are you mad? Of course not, he doesn't know I know.'

'How *do* you know?' Ellie was highly entertained.

'I have a friend who's dating a dermatologist who hosts Botox parties. She invited me for a bit of entertainment and I almost ran right into him when he was leaving and I was arriving. I saw him and ducked. The party was on a Friday night, and believe me, I couldn't wait to run into him on Monday.'

'Did you succumb yourself?' Ellie asked.

'Not yet. Why ... do I need it?'

Ellie laughed, 'Of course you don't, silly. Did anyone at the office say anything about Tyler's wrinkle-free forehead?'

'At first they did, but they couldn't figure it out either. They've got used to it now and it's pretty much a non-issue. Certainly no one would ever guess he'd do that, although he's certainly not the first man to get Botoxed up solely for that reason. So when he stares at you completely expressionless on Tuesday you'll know why. Don't let it jar you.'

'Creepy. I still can't believe it. By the way, I have a little news myself.'

'Do tell.'

'I have a date with Wrigley.'

'Ellie, that is not news.'

'It is for me. It's a real date.'

'Look, I don't mean to ignore this momentous occasion, but really, you'll be planning your wedding by this time next year.'

'How could you possibly think that?'

'Oh please. I am so right here.'

'It's just a date,' Ellie mumbled but Daphne refused to be fooled.

By Monday morning the butterflies had arrived. There was nothing to do until later that day when the conference room would be free and Paresh had arrived. Ellie called her Mum and Wrigley, both of whom gave her enough encouraging words to see her through the rest of the day.

It was a relief when Paresh arrived; there was no time for a delayed flight. When he had checked in and freshened up he was full of energy and ready to go to work. Their taxi crept through the Midtown streets.

Ellie opened the door to the conference room and said to Paresh upon seeing the venue again, 'I think I'm going to throw up all over this place.'

'Think of this as a dress rehearsal, Ellie. Just try to use it to iron out any of the kinks before we head into next week's presentation.'

'Good idea. I'll faint tomorrow instead of next week.'

Paresh smiled. 'At least you still have your sense of humour.'

By early evening both Ellie and Paresh were satisfied with the set-up of the room. Everything was in place and ready to go for Tuesday morning's ten o'clock start.

After a quick dinner with Daphne and Paresh, Ellie retired to her hotel room. She felt that she was as ready as she could possibly be. When she went to bed, her earlier panic had subsided to dull little bunches of nervous spurts followed by moments of calm.

The next thing she knew her wake-up call was ringing in her ear. Ellie was surprised that she had slept so well. She made herself eat a light breakfast in the room, although she was not at all hungry, and then began to dress. She had chosen to bring the new made-to-measure trousersuit. It was made of a fine wool worsted fabric in a rich, not too dark, navy with a thin vanilla pinstripe. When she had slipped the jacket on during her final fitting, she could immediately feel the difference. It was unlike any other jacket she had ever worn; it was extremely comfortable and she felt her back straighten and her shoulders demanded to be held back as if they automatically respected the fine work. The trousers were so beautifully cut they appeared to make her legs look longer.

Because it was a very cold morning she chose to wear the new cream wool silk knit top she had bought with Daphne. It was an unusual choice. The close-knit top almost looked like a shirt, it had a collar and it buttoned through like a shirt, but had more texture and looked particularly sharp when worn under the suit. If the room was over-heated, and she felt most American offices were, she would then feel very comfortable taking off her jacket, knowing that she would still appear professional. She wore the top outside her trousers where it lay freely against her body.

The extra days she had gained by the trip's postponement had also given her a few more days to practise her makeup and hair. So when the knock on the door came at the appointed time, she was ready.

'Gosh!' Paresh said when she opened the door. 'You look like you mean business.'

'Thank you, Paresh, that was just the right thing to say. Are you ready?'

'Absolutely, let's get moving.'

Ellie's cell phone rang in the cab. Oh no, she thought. They've changed the meeting. But it was Wrigley wishing her luck one more time. She immediately chastised herself for thinking so negatively and felt her voice become calmer as she spoke to him.

They arrived half an hour early and took their time making a few more adjustments to the room. Ellie still felt a little nervous but the overwhelming feeling she was experiencing was excitement. She took a deep breath and gave a nod to Paresh, who was completely present and ready to go. One by one they trickled in. Daphne gave her hand an extra squeeze and leaned over to her and whispered, 'This set-up is quite a surprise. Go for it!'

The last to arrive was Jasper. He had just done four European cities in five days and had flown into New York last night. He could have been forgiven for being a bit ratty, but no, he was his usual alert and buoyant self.

There were a few new faces to whom Ellie immediately introduced herself. She walked over to Daphne and discreetly said, 'No Tyler?'

'Consider it a good omen. Don't worry about it.'

When all but one of the places were filled, Ellie stood before a large screen and gave her opening speech. She smiled at her audience and spoke slowly and clearly, but also with a tamed excitement. She introduced Paresh, who stood and nodded to the audience. The project that she and Paresh had been carefully planning was a multi-media presentation.

'The good news is that diversity has already travelled a long road.' Ellie began in a clear and poised manner. 'Our company will benefit from hindsight, problems solved, and issues addressed by others who have made this journey before us. There have been detours on the road and attempts from some to hinder the journey, but the journey continues. In an overwhelming number of cases, diversity has helped organisations keep a competitive advantage.'

Ellie paused just as Paresh dimmed the lights.

The group directed their attention to the large screen in front of them. Ellie stepped aside as images of men and women filled the screen. The people on the screen were representatives from another company; they were a focus group ironing out the issues of beginning a diversity initiative. The documentary-styled footage was compelling to watch as the participants defined what diversity actually meant for their company. It was clear to see that the definition was critical. The on-screen discussion faded as the lights were turned back on.

Ellie looked out over the audience to regain their attention. It didn't take long, they were all eager to hear what she had to say next.

'The biggest misconception and the most damaging thoughts to entertain regarding the definition of diversity is that it has only to do with race and gender – and that it is solely about recruitment. Lumping together men, women and people of colour shuns other aspects of diversity. People are not group members – they are individuals. There are other aspects of diversity including disability, religion, age and sexual orientation.

'The other mistake that some companies have made is that once they have made a large effort to recruit diverse employees, they then fail to follow through with giving them a reason to stay. Retention, keeping the employee, developing them to be successful, giving them reason and a means to stretch themselves – this would make for an outstanding diversity department. All employees have one thing in common. They want to be appreciated.'

Once again, Ellie stepped aside and Paresh coaxed the technology to cooperate. Ellie, with Paresh's help and expertise, had designed a mock website for the new diversity initiative for their company. The homepage opened with an artist's renderings of the silhouettes of many people. There were no faces, just various shapes, tall, short, round and thin. The shapes of the bodies had no gender and shapeless clothes draped them. Then, one by one, each shape, each body, slowly transformed, beginning with the figure's face. In a few moments, the screen gradually filled with smiling people representing a vast global community.

Each person on the screen then held out one of their hands and upon their palm was written one of the programmes Ellie had devised for the department. One hand said, 'mentoring', another, 'learning and development', another, 'affinity councils', until all the hands informed the surfer of their choices within the site.

Ellie sailed through each 'hand' and briefly described each programme. Paresh managed to keep up with her for the most part. The presentation was not flawless, but the slight pauses did not disrupt Ellie's flow or momentum.

The screen became blank again while Ellie discussed budgetary issues, time frame and launch incentives. She was so engaged in manoeuvering from one topic to the next that she did not have much time to gauge the audience's temperature except to feel that they were undoubtedly with her. Once or twice she glanced at Jasper and Daphne – both, to her surprise, displayed an intense interest.

'Diversity is a business issue. The workforce is changing and the customer market is changing and our world is changing. The people in it are very, very different. The world's people are now very savvy about what we, as a company, stand for. Companies are learning that diversity is not only good business practice, but it is the right thing to do. In fact, in the very near future our company will be so far behind that the word diversity will no longer create the buzz that it does now. The new word will be "inclusiveness".

'Ultimately, diversity is about improving creativity. An inclusive working environment improves creative thinking. When people are allowed to express ideas that might be considered somewhat different or controversial, we create an atmosphere that promotes and nurtures creativity and innovation.'

For the last time the lights were dimmed and Ellie stood by as the blank screen began to fill with the image of an empty patch of land. The land, a patch of green grass, was completely barren of anything other than the sky above it. Just as one might begin to wonder the purpose of such a scene, a white lily shot up from the earth and stood alone in what now appeared to be a field. White lilies began to pop up in numbers until the entire field was completely blanketed in white. The visual rested there for a few silent moments. The lilies were beautiful; they were large and healthy and aesthetically pleasing plants. At first it was pleasing to the eye to capture the field of lilies, but after a few moments Ellie heard the faintest sounds of a bored audience – which was just what she wanted. She glanced at Paresh, and in slow motion the image on the screen began to change.

A single very large, deep red dahlia appeared in the middle of the white lilies. It stood out so strikingly, that for a moment it held one's complete attention. But after a very few moments the dahlia seemed lost among the lilies. At just the right moment, another flower appeared. A voluptuous bearded iris stood proudly among the lilies, and then, one after the other, a variety of vibrant and intensely coloured flowers emerged from the ground until the field was covered in rich hues.

Ellie made no comment and allowed the scene to penetrate the minds of her audience. There was a palpable silence. When she signalled again to Paresh, he left the scene on the screen and turned the lights on again.

Ellie made her closing remarks by thanking them for their time and attention, and then offered to take any questions.

When she heard the applause, in addition to feeling startled, she felt a release within herself. She held back an overwhelming sense of relief in order to stay focused on the questions ahead.

But there were no questions; no challenges were thrown at her. She looked at Paresh who was beaming at her with no attempt at concealment. Daphne, who looked as if she wanted to jump out of her chair, gave her a less than discreet thumbs-up.

Almost everyone approached Ellie on their way out to wish her luck or congratulate her on the presentation. Jasper, who waited until the room had almost emptied, reached for her hand with both of his.

'Splendid, Ellie, splendid job. Great improvement. I'm pleased for you. Lunch next week.'

'Thank you, Jasper.'

'Excuse me, I've got to run now.'

When they were left alone in the room Daphne and Paresh approached Ellie and in a moment of pure energetic physical release hugged her, shook her, patted her and generally gave her everything short of a lift on their shoulders.

'Okay, okay, let's not get too carried away here. There's still next week to think about.' Ellie backed away from their exuberance.

'Bloody hell, Ellie, take a moment and enjoy this,' Daphne commanded. Come on, you two, I'm taking us all to lunch.'

On the way to the restaurant Daphne was full of questions; 'How did you two come up with the visuals? Where did you get that footage of the focus group? What company were they from?'

Paresh and Ellie looked at each other and a kind of hysterical laughter broke out.

'I don't know, I really don't know. We just did it,' Paresh said. Neither of them could look back at the long hours they both had spent bringing together the creative elements of Ellie's presentation without wondering how they had done it.

'I think Paresh was channelling some kind of high-tech sage from the future,' Ellie said.

As soon as Ellie turned on her phone it rang in her hands.

'Hello, Wriggers, yes, it's over. Well, I'm very relieved. Yes, I think it went pretty well.'

'Pretty well?' Daphne echoed.

She plucked the phone from Ellie's hand. 'Wrigley? Daphne here. Bloody marvellous, she was bloody marvellous. Absolutely fabulous, had them in the palm of her hand.'

Paresh laughed at both of them and he too grabbed the phone.

'Hello, Wrigley, I thought you'd like to hear the voice of reason. Stupendous, she was stupendous. No other word for it.'

Ellie took her phone back. 'Hi, it's me. They exaggerate. It went very well though. I felt good about it. All right then, speak to you later.'

The three entered the restaurant where they proceeded to have a very long, very delicious and very celebratory lunch.

◆

For the first time in months Ellie's attention was focused on something other than her work. The night of her date with Wrigley had arrived – her first date in two years. She was nervous about wearing her new dress and wondered what, if anything, she had to say to a room full of London's most interesting, and possibly best, restaurateurs.

When she stepped out of the taxi, Wrigley ran out of the restaurant to greet her.

'I'm sorry that I couldn't pick you up tonight. Not a very good showing for a first date, is it?'

'Hardly. I can't believe you didn't leave a restaurant full of customers to come all the way back to Chorleywood to fetch me. What a cad.'

When they entered the restaurant Ellie was amazed to see that all signs of a busy Saturday night had vanished. One long single table had been prepared for tonight's fussy visitors. The table itself was gorgeous. Traditional, overflowing cornucopias were placed along its length, and it was covered with long, draping white linen cloths. Heavy, slightly tarnished silver candelabra with wax already dripping down from them drenched the table in soft yellow light. The scene could have replicated the look and quality of an Old Dutch Master. Wrigley's special touch saved it from such a comparison.

'It's beautiful,' Ellie said. 'Wrigley's bountiful harvest.'

'Thank you. Let's have your coat.' Wrigley helped her to remove it. 'Golly, Ellie!'

'What? What's wrong?' Ellie looked around her.

For the moment they were still alone in the dining room. Jean-Louis and the rest of the staff were busy working away in the kitchen.

Wrigley stood before her and held her hands in his. 'You look beautiful.'

It had taken quite a while for Daphne to hammer into Ellie's head that the dress she was wearing tonight was perfect for her and perfect for an evening like this. It was a belted silk dress in a shade of rich lavender. This warm hue on Ellie was stunning. The colour so flattered the colour of her skin, hair and eyes that it was a wonder she had never chosen such a shade before. While the dress was not revealing, it was mildly provocative. The soft malleable jersey silk featured a deep V-shape neckline and back. It was sleeveless, straight-cut and a wide black leather belt, cinched at the waist, gave the impression of an hourglass figure. Ellie had argued with Daphne that the dress was meant for someone who belonged in the below-size-ten group. But Daphne told her she could not be more wrong.

Apparently Wrigley seemed to think she had made the right choice too.

Still unused to such heartfelt compliments, Ellie looked at her feet. But Wrigley would not let her off so easily tonight. He lifted her chin until her face tilted up and their eyes met. Just as he leaned in for the kiss, Jean-Louis came running out of the kitchen.

'Oops *pardon, pardon. Bonjour*, Ellie. *Pardon.'*

Ellie and Wrigley laughed and a flustered Jean-Louis ran back into the kitchen.

'I suppose I should see what he needs. But hold that pose.'

'Shall I come with you?' Ellie asked.

'No, you'll get splattered. I'll be right back.'

By the time Wrigley returned to the dining room his guests had begun to arrive. Ellie couldn't have been more wrong about the personalities that filled the room. The ten chefs and their husbands, wives, significant others and dates were warm and charming. As Wrigley had just recently experienced Ellie in her environment, Ellie now saw a different aspect of Wrigley's working life. Although she had always been aware that he was well respected in the restaurant community, it was touching to see how much these fellow chefs enjoyed his company.

It was no wonder they admired him. As host of the evening, Wrigley had taken great pains, as a theme for the evening, to find out each chef's favourite comfort food. He had phoned their families, combed the Internet for articles featuring the chefs, even disguised himself in a phone call to one chef as a journalist and performed a fake interview. His effort was well received that evening when each of the chefs were surprised by at least one of their favourite foods served à la Wrigley.

Ellie held her own as she sat among the food connoisseurs. She wasn't asked to talk too much about her work, but those who did question her seemed genuinely interested. Throughout the evening Wrigley always managed to direct his attention towards her in some way. He would whisper in her ear, or touch her shoulder or hand. She was pleased to see that he was enjoying himself.

'This is a very special first date, Wriggers. I don't know if you can top this.'

'Just you wait,' he said rather smugly as he poured her wine.

It was only the very late hour that broke up the party. No one was ready to leave, but there were nannies and children to think of and, for a few, Sunday brunch. And Wrigley's staff, who had performed brilliantly and more than deserved the overtime and bonuses they would receive, also deserved to go home.

When the last light had been turned off and the alarm had been set, Wrigley grabbed Ellie's arm and began to walk in the opposite direction to the Forager.

'Where are we going?' Ellie asked.

'I want to show you something.'

They walked around the square until they came to its far side. They could see Wrigley's restaurant from where they stood. Behind them stood a row of eighteenth-century buildings, some of which had been converted into shops.

Wrigley turned and led Ellie to one of the shop fronts, which was currently unoccupied.

'It's to let Ellie. Isn't it fantastic?'

'For what Wrigley?'

'I'm not sure yet.'

They had a peek inside through the large glass window.

'It was a bookshop, you can just make out the rows of shelving along the walls. I've been in already, there's another rather large-ish room in the back that you can't see from here. Come on,' he said, 'let's get going, it's freezing.'

'Do you want another restaurant, Wrigs?'

'Not exactly, not a replica of the one I have now. I'm ready to do something different.'

'You know what I've noticed? You spend as much of your free time as possible visiting local farmers. Can you in some way, help to develop them, maybe make them more commercial?'

'Yes, I've always been pretty interested in our small farmers, especially the organic farmers. I don't think as a community of restaurant owners we do enough to promote them. The same is true with the artisan food-makers.'

'Sounds like you want to do a bit of retailing, Wrigley.'

'I'm thinking of a speciality up-market food shop. Carefully selected, gorgeous produce, artisan cheeses, breads, that kind of thing, combined with a small breakfast-and-lunch room in the back – a more casual, quick version of the restaurant. London's welcomed these kinds of food shops over the last ten years or so. I'd like to add my interpretation.'

'What about your restaurant?' Ellie asked.

'The restaurant's well established and I think Jean-Louis can handle the dinner crowd now.'

They continued to talk about Wrigley's ideas as they made their way along the nearly deserted motorway.

'Have you spoken to your accountant?' Ellie asked.

'Not yet. I wanted to tell you about it first. It would be a big change and a bit of a risk.'

'Wouldn't this mean that you would have to give up your night-owl hours?'

'Give them up? I'll say. I'd like to see myself going home at a decent hour eventually. I suppose you could say I'd welcome the change in lifestyle. Some day I intend to get married and have a family – at least, that's what I want. I think my idea of expansion fits into that scenario quite well, don't you?' he asked pointedly.

'Uh-oh. There's an elephant in this car.'

Wrigley laughed. 'Sorry, did I scare you?'

'No, not really, just a little surprised, that's all.'

'I want to spend more time with you, Ellie, that's all I'm asking right now. We're both going to be very busy in the next few months, especially when you get your promotion and I begin my new venture.'

'*If* I get the promotion. Even if I've done the best job possible, if they don't want a diversity programme I can't make them change their minds.'

'Too right, if that's the case, we'll deal with it when the time comes.'

Ellie turned to him, 'I like the "we" bit.'

He smiled. 'Me too.'

It was very late when the Forager rolled up to Ellie's house. Both Ellie and Wrigley recognised that they were too knackered to have an awkward moment of 'What do we do now?' Wrigley walked her to the door and held her close to him.

'You have a nice long lie-in tomorrow, Miss Hart,' Wrigley said softly. 'And then how about a late breakfast so that we can continue this riveting discussion?'

'Lovely,' Ellie said, with a few stars in her eyes.

Wrigley gave her the kind of kiss that made her feel that the transition from best friend to boyfriend was not going to be as difficult as she might have thought.

Ellie and Paresh stood in the largest conference room in the building. She was minutes away from presenting to the leadership of the company. The room was prepared and they stood waiting for the executives to arrive. Ellie noticed that Paresh looked a little nervous and asked him to check a few cues just to keep him busy.

Ellie felt good. She also felt the nerves that were unavoidable at such an event, but she'd been there before and knew that she was ready. Her second made-to-measure suit was perfect for the occasion. A steel-grey jacket and skirt fitted her beautifully and the dark mauve blouse helped to make an overall strong and professional impression. She had made a trip to the hairdresser and the manicurist the previous day, so she could not have looked more polished.

She opened her bag to make sure she had turned off her phone, amazed that she would remember to do such a thing, and in it she saw a white handkerchief. Hmm, she thought. I don't remember putting this in my bag. She did not see the tiny long-stemmed red rose embroidered on one of the corners of the fine linen.

Soon the room was filled with the most important people of the company, the decision-makers and those who were responsible for its future.

'Good afternoon,' Ellie began. 'Thank you for being present today to hear my recommendation for a diversity initiative for the company.'

And Ellie was off like a young thoroughbred at the starting gate of an important race. This group did not need the Botox trick to appear poker-faced. Most of the men and women to whom Ellie presented were seasoned business executives who had risen from the old school of conservatism. But to Ellie's credit, they immediately became engaged in what they were hearing and seeing.

When the multicoloured flowers appeared again on the screen and Paresh had once more slowly turned the lights on for the last time, Ellie stood before the group with an overwhelming sense of accomplishment. No matter their decision she knew that she had done her best. She knew that her message had been heard and absorbed. If nothing else, she had awakened them.

❖

The following week Ellie was called into several offices of those who had heard her presentation. Jasper told her she could expect this. A private consult with each of the decision-makers challenged Ellie, and, to her satisfaction, in some cases turned into productive, collaborative meetings.

She did not know how long she would have to wait before she received their decision, so she tried to carry on as usual, going about the same day-to-day work that always begged her attention.

It seemed that all was quiet on the sixth floor. The frenzy of the Women's Conference, Ellie's presentation and various other projects had until recently kept a frantic pace in the very air of their offices. On a day when it seemed that a slower pace had finally been captured, the workers on the sixth floor heard a loud whooping noise. Those who were not in Ellie's Friday conference-room meeting were rocked by this noise, which emanated from behind the room's closed door. The whoops were followed by what sounded like a pounding on the table or walls, or both, and more yelps. It was the kind of noise that made people jump up to see what exactly was going on.

The conference-room door flew open and Ellie Hart could be seen sitting in her usual place at the table. It seemed that her staff had gone quite mad and Ellie herself looked a bit numb. For Ellie had received a call during her meeting, and when she put down the phone she had looked up at her staff and said in a very queer voice, 'Jasper says the word is out. A formal announcement is to be made on Monday, and I'm the director of the new diversity initiative.'

Noise explained.

◆

Ellie barely had time to let the news sink in before she was off to a business lunch. She wished she could have cancelled it, but the lunch was a special thank you to a young man who had been a bit of a technical whiz in helping her with her presentation. Paresh, after hearing about his talents, had tracked him down to his office in Hoxton.

Ellie sat back in the seat of the taxi and tried to relax. She looked out of the window as the taxi approached a new hip area of town that was close to her office. The Hoxton and Shoreditch area had been generating a huge amount of conversation these days, but she rarely ventured to this stone's throw from the City. She could see that this part of London seemed to have experienced a renaissance, even though rumours of Hoxton being uncool were already spreading through the media. Today the streets of Hoxton Square were lively. The tell-tale signs of converted warehouses, restaurants, bars and coffee shops begged to be seen as none other than a thriving place to be, hip or not.

She shook her head; she didn't entirely understand exactly what it was that made an area 'in' and then suddenly 'out'. She wished she did.

She thought that it might have something to do with having an ability to instinctively feel what was to come – to forecast. She tried to rely on her own instincts; instincts like the one that had led to her success today. Even though she had constantly questioned them, her instincts had told her that now was the right time for her company to move ahead with the creation of a diversity programme. And she was thrilled that the powers that be at the company thought so too.

Ellie breezed through a pleasant lunch. Robbie Poindexter was actually quite inspiring and urged Ellie to continue working towards creating a better than average website for her new department. After she left the restaurant she felt an incredible desire to walk. She desperately needed a few moments alone. She stopped in at a little supermarket and asked for directions to the nearest tube, thinking that a nice walk to the tube was exactly what would clear her mind.

She walked along Old Street and took in a few breaths of the crisp, cold air. She couldn't remember the last time she had strolled down a London street with no particular purpose except to walk.

Ellie had been walking for a few minutes before she realised that she really hadn't been paying that much attention to the directions she had received. She looked around for Old Street tube station, but it was not in sight. She walked a little further along when suddenly a strong odour of fish permeated the atmosphere. She looked at the shop fronts and discovered a Burmese fish and chip shop. She peered into the window and saw a bank of computers against the wall. Ellie laughed out loud. 'A fish shop with Internet access,' she thought. 'Definitely a sign of the times.'

She continued walking until she caught sight of a towering church spire that loomed into the sky. Ellie looked at her watch and saw that she had enough time to indulge herself in a little bit of exploring. She let the spire be her guide and she crossed the street towards it. She now found herself on Hackney Road.

She approached the church and was surprised that the ancient bell tower and tall standing columns, although very beautiful, seemed rather imposing. There was a large graveyard on one side of the church with numerous standing tombs, monuments and gravestones. But another area, about one hundred yards from the church's grounds, caught Ellie's eye. There was what looked to be a small city park or garden, hemmed in between Hackney's mix of new and old architecture.

As she drew closer to the garden, she came upon an old, but quite elegant, black iron railing. She ran her hand along the railing and slowly walked around the garden until she came to a gate. The gate, with its tall arched entryway, was open. She would not have normally stopped at such a place, but the gardens looked very peaceful and inviting.

She saw a well-worn wooden bench and felt compelled to sit for a moment. Immense London plane trees shot up from the grounds and Ellie's glance followed the line of the trees up to clouds that were beginning to form, threatening to shower down upon her. Across the street from where she was sitting she was slightly surprised to see a glaring orangey-red neon sign that read 'Strip Club'. Above and below the bold-as-brass words were two neon blue arrows pointing to the entrance. The sign was lit on the red brick wall of what used to be a pub. Two very hefty bouncers stood guarding the doorway.

Ellie could also see that London had increasingly become a city where old and new architecture were welded into liveable spaces. She noted that council flats, Peabody Trust properties and ultra-modern, super-luxury flats were coexisting and feeding off each other.

Again, Ellie tilted her head back and looked through the tall trees to check the progress of the dark clouds. It did look like it might rain, but Ellie, too comfortable to move, sat as if a powerful magnet held onto her coat. The news she had received today was just beginning to sink in and she relished this moment of complete peace.

Just as Ellie began to get that familiar slow, steady tug to head back to the office, she noticed what seemed to be a rather large stone situated near her in the garden. As she stood and walked over to the stone, the most peculiar feeling ran up her spine.

Ellie approached the grassy area where another large tree and a full green bush stood closely by a grey stone, covered in part by green fuzzy moss, a stone that looked much older than its surroundings. And it *was* a very large stone, it must have been at least eight feet long and four feet wide and it stood about three feet from the ground. Even though the stone was very old, someone still cared about the person whom the stone memorialised, for lying on the stone, right in the centre, was an exquisite wreath. The wreath's foliage had definitely dried at this point; for though it looked like a regal crown, it also looked fragile. The leaves, flowers and greenery had dried to autumnal colours of brown, bleached-out grey and beige.

Ellie leaned in closer to see who deserved such a memorial. She felt her face grow hot. Her heart was beating rapidly, and if it weren't for the cold air and a whipping breeze that had picked up, she might very well have fainted on the spot. For there, in front of her, written in plain English were words she could scarcely believe she was reading:

SACRED TO THE MEMORY OF MR THOMAS FAIRCHILD OF HOXTON (GARDENER) WHO DEPARTED THIS LIFE THE 10TH DAY OF OCTOBER 1729 IN THE 63RD YEAR OF HIS AGE. MR FAIRCHILD WAS A BENEFACTOR TO THE PAROCHIAL SCHOOLS AND FOUNDER OF A LECTURE ANNUALLY PREACHED IN SHOREDITCH CHURCH ON WHIT TUESDAY ON THE SUBJECT OF 'THE WONDERFUL WORLD OF GOD IN THE CREATION' OR 'THE CERTAINTY OF THE RESURRECTION OF THE DEAD PROVED BY THE CERTAIN CHANGES OF THE ANIMAL AND VEGETABLE PARTS OF THE CREATION.' THE STONE ORIGINALLY PLACED OVER HIS REMAINS HAVING GONE TO DECAY THE PRESENT MEMORIAL...

Ellie could not read the rest due to the worn small print that faded into unrecognisable letters.

'Mr Thomas Fairchild, gardener, Mr Thomas Fairchild, gardener,' Ellie kept repeating the words over and over, as she glanced back and forth from the words on the stone, to the church, and then the street, as if she were actively seeking some form of reality. She was definitely having a moment.

'Is this my Mr Fairchild?' she asked out loud.

There were for Ellie, myriad unanswered questions. She wracked her brains to remember if she had somehow, somewhere, stumbled upon the knowledge of the existence of this man some time before her dreams. But for the life of her, she could not remember having ever heard of him.

'Thomas,' she said, 'he has a first name.' How she wished she could lie down right now on one of the benches and dream him up. How she wanted to ask him if he was this Mr Fairchild, a real, live man who had existed hundreds of years earlier. A gardener no less! But Ellie knew that, even if she were at home in her bed right now, she could not dream of him on command. That was just not how it worked.

Ellie paused for a moment longer as she looked down at the memorial stone of Mr Thomas Fairchild. She looked around her at the little park, the strip club and the steeple of the church. She knew that she would never have discovered this stone by merely walking past. It was almost hidden: an oasis surrounded by an urban sprawl. She had only been to this area twice before and purely for business reasons when she ran in and out of Robbie's offices. And of course she knew that this discovery was no coincidence. But what exactly was it? What on earth did this mean?

It was time to listen to her instincts again, if she could find even one. She stood quietly and waited until she knew what to do. She tried to memorise the words on the stone and allowed herself to take in the atmosphere for one more moment.

Then, Ellie turned and walked towards the exit. After she had walked out of the gate and onto the street, she could now see that Mr Fairchild's stone was actually visible from the pavement, the stone lay very close to the black iron railing. However, she knew that, had she not entered the garden, she would have walked right past it without ever having known it was there.

She hailed a taxi and made her way back to the office. She would say and do nothing about this for the present. It was her secret, a special moment that she would not share with anyone right now, not her mother, not even Wrigley. She needed time to try to sort out what this meant.

When Ellie returned to the office she realised that she had yet to tell Wrigley the incredible news about her promotion and the launch of the diversity programme.

❖

When she reached him by phone and told him the news he insisted on an impromptu celebration at his restaurant. He would arrange for Poppy and Ellie's mother to join them too.

Ellie had previously planned to make a stop on her way home. She had a very important purchase to make and the shop just happened to be very conveniently located close to the restaurant. She had been there not too long ago on a very rainy evening.

Tonight the air was cold but the sky was only scattered with clouds and the sliver of a moon could be seen if one waited for a cloud to pass. Ellie rode in the taxi almost in a daze as she thought about the day's events. Touched by her staff's overwhelming support, she planned to treat them all to dinner soon. No doubt Wrigley would help her with that.

The taxi stopped in front of Dai Evans's shop in Holland Park. To Ellie's surprise it was still busy at the end of the day. Mr Evans greeted her warmly and assured her he would be with her shortly.

Ellie headed straight for the cabinet where she had last seen the posy ring. 'Surely this is where it was,' she said to herself. 'But I don't see it.' She panicked. 'Surely he hasn't sold it. Who would want that old ring?' But her spirits sank because she didn't see it and of course it was very possible that other customers would have appreciated its uniqueness.

'What a nice surprise,' Mr Evans said to Ellie. 'How lovely to see you again.'

'Hello, Mr Evans. My mother was ever so pleased with the mah-jongg set.'

'Yes, she rang to tell me. It was nice to hear from her. Is there something I can do for you, Ellie?'

'I had thought so, Mr Evans, but I see I'm too late. It looks like someone else admired your posy ring.'

'Oh yes, many have admired it since you were here.'

'Whoever the lucky person was I hope they're enjoying it.'

'Oh no, dear, it is still here. I just have it in the back. Giving it a good clean, you know.' He smiled at her.

'Do you mean to say it's still here?' Ellie became animated.

'Why yes, would you like to see it again?'

'See it? I want to buy it, Mr Evans!' Ellie was thrilled.

'Oh? Well of course, please excuse me while I get it.'

Ellie paced the floor waiting for Mr Evans to return. She had been thinking about this purchase for weeks now. This will make a lovely gift for Wrigley, she thought, but I won't give it to him just yet. I'll know when the moment is right.

Mr Evans returned with the ring and placed it in Ellie's hand.

'Mr Evans, you have made my day. It is as beautiful as I remembered it.'

'Well I don't mean to pry, but will you be wearing it yourself, perhaps on a chain? It would be very big on your finger, Ellie.'

Ellie beamed, 'No, Mr Evans. It's a very special ring for a very special man.'

'Ah, that is good to hear.'

◆

When Ellie arrived at the restaurant Wrigley looked so happy to see her. Or maybe it was that he was always happy to see her and she had just been too blind to see him. When he grabbed her and hugged her and kissed her face to congratulate her, Poppy and Georgie strained their necks to the maximum, trying to gauge whether love had finally hit its mark.

'We're very proud of you, Ellie,' Poppy said.

'Yes, we are. Aren't you a bit overwhelmed though, Eloise? This is such an important step,' Georgie asked.

'No, Mum, I'm not actually. I've got several weeks before we even get started. I've felt all along that this is the right direction for me to take. It is exciting though. Oh Wrigley, I almost forgot.' Ellie dug through her bag and handed him a thick folder. 'I've got something for you. These are copies of the business plans we were talking about a couple of weeks ago. I thought they might be helpful.'

'Thanks, Ellie, I'll read them on the train. I'm going to Manchester tomorrow for a few days to see my mother.'

'I didn't know you were going to see Meredith,' Poppy said. 'I would have come along, Wrigley, you should have told me.'

'Sorry, Aunt Poppy, need to do this one alone.' Wrigley glanced at Ellie.

'Oh?' Poppy raised her eyebrows. 'Do I sense some hidden import to this trip?'

'Poppy, let me pour you another glass of wine,' Wrigley insisted.

Ellie had not really had a quiet moment in which to assimilate the events of the day. She was as present as she could be at the dinner, but it wasn't until she was seated beside Wrigley in the Forager on the way home that the day really began to sink in.

'I hope you have a lovely time with your mother. When will you be back?'

'Monday night. I'll call you, though, over the weekend. I'd really like her to come back and spend a few days in London. Maybe take that outing with your mother that we talked about.'

'That would be nice.' Ellie's voice was showing signs of fatigue.

Wrigley gently applied the brakes and slowly pulled to a stop in front of Ellie's house. He got out of the car and very carefully opened the door. He put his hands on her shoulders and whispered to her, 'Ellie, Ellie, wake up, darling. You're home.'

Ellie opened her eyes not sure of her whereabouts, and looked up at Wrigley.

'Oh hello there, Wriggers, I think I fell asleep.'

Wrigley laughed softly. 'That you did. Let's get you inside.'

Wrigley took her inside and refused her invitation to stay for a cup of tea.

'You need to rest now, Ellie. I'll call you tomorrow. I think the day took more out of you than you know.'

Ellie leaned heavily on the banister as she climbed the stairs to her bedroom. Just as she had snuggled down underneath her duvet, she suddenly sat up, and with a renewed energy, jumped out of bed. She went back downstairs to where she had left her bag, opened it and retrieved the little leather box. She then went upstairs again and put the ring on the table next to her notebook and pen. Finally, she allowed herself the luxury of a long deep sleep.

The next thing she was aware of was that she was talking on the phone. She didn't remember it ringing or picking it up.

She heard Wrigley's voice: 'Ellie? Are you sleeping?'

'Mmm,' she said. 'Asleep.'

'Sorry to wake you, you must be napping.'

'No, I'm not napping. What time is it?' Ellie was confused.

'It's three o'clock.'

'In the morning?'

'No, Ellie, in the afternoon. Are you all right?'

'Oh my God, Wriggers, I think I've been asleep all day.'

'Are you sure you're all right, Ellie?'

'Yes, a bit tired. I don't know, maybe I'm coming down with something.'

'I hope not. I think you probably just need a good long rest. I'll call you later.'

Ellie went back to sleep again for a couple of hours. She woke famished and rushed to get to the Boverys' before they closed. The chilly early evening air woke her up a bit and by the time she returned home she was feeling better.

She phoned Daphne, not expecting her to be at home, but she was, and when she heard Ellie's news Daphne screamed into the phone so loudly that Ellie had to hold it away from her ear. Ellie made sure that Daphne knew how grateful she was to have had her help and support.

'Did you ever find out why Tyler didn't show up for the meeting?' Ellie asked.

'Botox infection.'

'You're kidding.'

'Yes, I am. He had to make an urgent trip to Singapore. He was gone for a week. It was bliss around here.'

'Well, soon there will be many more days of bliss when he's gone for good.'

'Yes, but will he return in the same form? That is the question.'

'I hope to see you again soon, Daphne.'

'You will, I'll be over next month.'

'Great. Bye for now.'

'Bye, Ellie, and congratulations.'

Ellie could not convince Wrigley not to cut short his trip and on Sunday evening he arrived at her doorstep with the makings for a huge pot of chicken soup and a maple walnut cake. She wasn't sure what the cake had to do with feeling a little tired, but who was she to argue with a man who baked her a cake.

He was undemanding of her this evening and she of him. They didn't speak of the future, or of work, or of anything that taxed either of their minds. They just sat by the fire and ate chicken soup and laughed at Chutney's lazy tail wagging in Wrigley's face.

Wrigley left early and once again Ellie fell into bed, still a bit more tired than usual but definitely on the mend.

She felt something gently tapping her shoulder. Had Wrigley come back? she wondered. But no, when she opened her eyes she found herself curled up on the stone bench. She saw Mr Fairchild standing above her.

'I do believe you have been napping again, Ellie.'

'Oh! Mr Fairchild? Okay, just a minute there, let me just ... okay.' She sat up and adjusted to her surroundings. It was late afternoon and the sun cast a soft light across the old man's face.

Ellie looked closely at Mr Fairchild. She was looking for an indication from him that he knew what she knew. If indeed she knew what she thought she knew.

Mr Fairchild looked into Ellie's eyes quite the same way he did when they had first met. Again, Ellie had the feeling of being quickly read, as if he knew each of her thoughts and her every intention. She met his gaze with expectation, waiting for a sign that they might discuss what she had discovered in the peaceful grounds near the church in Hoxton. She looked to him for a glimmer of an explanantion.

'Yes, Ellie, it is I.' Mr Fairchild paused.

Ellie felt her entire being become a little limp.

'Life can be extraordinary, at times,' he continued. 'Things have a way of coming to you when you are ready and willing to receive them. It is possible for assistance to wind its way to people in the most unorthodox fashion.' He sighed slightly. 'If only more people would listen.'

Mr Fairchild then looked upon her with his most endearing smile. Upon receiving the warmth from his smile, a smile that was as intense as it was pleasant, Ellie knew there would be no more discussion about this particular topic for the time being.

'Shall we take a turn then?' Mr Fairchild asked.

Ellie stood up and walked beside Mr Fairchild. As they walked, he stopped now and again to pull a weed.

'The garden is lovely to look at, is it not?' he asked Ellie.

'Yes, it is. It reminds me of the garden in my presentation. Oh my. I think I stole your garden plan, Mr Fairchild,' she said as they walked past the pots of white lilies.

'Impossible, my dear. Firstly, no two gardens are alike, and secondly, this *is* your garden. Now that you have won over this little plot of land, you must observe it carefully for signs of imbalance. Think balance and harmony rather than pure utility.

'Understanding and using balance will help lead to success in your garden. You must be patient, for finding balance may take some time and experimentation. And as your garden matures the balance may change. Listen and watch carefully, you will know what is needed to keep everything in balance.'

'Are you saying that I've been working too hard, Mr Fairchild?' Ellie asked.

'Gardeners should allow themselves the leisure to enjoy their hard work. You must learn balance in your work, Eloise. Striving for the stability that balance brings puts the mind at ease.

'Perhaps your energy was wisely used to reach this point, and one can never ignore the care that a garden needs; however, the gardener too must take great care. Knees and backs and fingers and hands can too easily become over-used. Just as the over-watered plant will wither, and the over-zealous pruner who cuts too deeply will destroy the ability of the plant's creative juices to flow, the gardener must know when to stop, to rest.

'Let us sit now before we lose the light.'

Ellie and Mr Fairchild sat for a while on the stone bench under the apple tree. Ellie watched him as he sat silently and surveyed the garden. She observed how his deep blue eyes with the grey flecks moved slowly from one part of the garden to another. When he held his gaze on one particular flower or plant, she too would look at the plant to see if there was something special to see.

Even in the quiet of the garden, with no words passing between them, he still sensed a slight restlessness within her. He focused on the beautiful white lilies until she too held herself still and silent.

'Gardens are not created or made, Eloise, they unfold. Your garden will always reveal your self.'

They sat together in the garden for a very long time while Ellie continued to study her garden – herself.

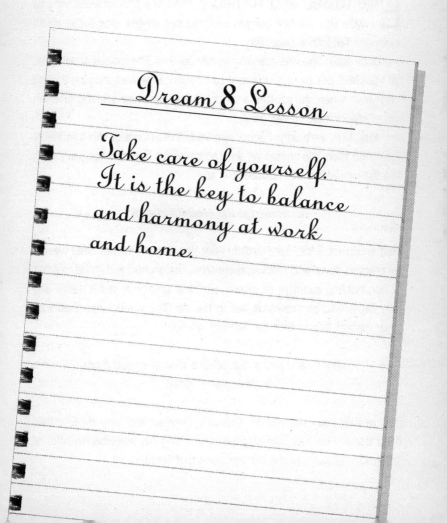

Dream 8 Lesson

Take care of yourself.
It is the key to balance
and harmony at work
and home.

Epilogue

Ellie tossed and turned a bit. She felt herself trying to wake up, but her body would just not let her. She became still again and fell into a deep sleep.

Once again she was standing in her garden. She looked around for Mr Fairchild, but he was nowhere to be seen. Ellie was enjoying a huge long yawn when she spotted a patch of dry, brownish-looking grass in one of the corners of her garden.

'Yuk, how very ugly. Funny,' she said, 'I didn't notice this a moment ago.' And then she smiled as she remembered that not too very long ago she wouldn't have noticed it at all.

Acknowledge the need for change.

That is correct, Ellie.' Mr Fairchild now stood by the tuft of dead weeds. He reached down and plucked them from the ground and stood in front of her, holding handfuls of weeds. He blew them out of his hands and they came whirling towards her in the air. The weeds separated into long, elegant letters that formed the words,

Identify and avoid distractions that keep you from attaining your goals.

Just as Ellie read the words, a slightly familiar, and very nasty odour filled the air. Mr Fairchild strolled by pushing his wheelbarrow full of dung. Ellie giggled as she remembered that awful night.

Preparedness is the hallmark of a professional.

Mr Fairchild disappeared for a moment and Ellie's garden quickly lost its light. Slowly a flame began to burn from a brass lantern that sat on the ground. Around the lantern danced the tiny red and black ladybirds that Mr Fairchild had brought into her garden in the middle of the night. One flew onto Ellie's hand, landed and fluttered its wings.

Learn how to delegate by letting go of fear.

Soon there were many lanterns in her garden, and the entire garden was glowing with light. Mr Fairchild was almost dancing around the plants and flowers. It looked as if he were stopping at each living thing in her garden and having a quick chat. In fact, that was exactly what he was doing. In the glow of the lanterns' light he bent down to this one and the next one and whispered to each flower, shrub, tree and plant. He glowed from the energy that emanated from his long lean body, and the garden, in turn, glowed from his care.

Never underestimate the power of communication.

Once again Ellie found herself seated upon the smooth stone bench. Her apple tree was laden with fruit and she could smell its sweet fragrance. Mr Fairchild walked by wearing one of his most elegant outfits. As he swirled around he now appeared in different clothes. He wore his sweeping, beautiful dressing gown, which reminded her of the evening she wore her tatty terrycloth bathrobe and shabby plimsoles. She glanced down at her perfectly manicured nails as she recalled the lesson.

The messages you send via your image can determine how you are perceived professionally.

Ellie rose from the bench and followed Mr Fairchild as he approached his work table. His brow was furrowed as he used a small knife to cut away at what seemed to be a very difficult piece of old vine. He was patient but firm as he pruned.

'That tough old vine reminds me of some of the people in my company,' Ellie said.

Mr Fairchild turned to look at her. They didn't need words at this point; both smiled.

You can't avoid difficult people. Learn how to negotiate, collaborate and diffuse hostility.

Ellie stirred in her sleep. She struggled a bit with the idea of waking up, but again, her body said no, it's not time yet. 'I deserve a lie-in,' she murmured. Time passed without any further interruptions, the soft rise and fall of Ellie's breath was the only thing that moved in the room.

Take care of yourself. It is the key to balance and harmony at work and at home.

Ellie opened her eyes and realised that it was Monday morning. She raised her arms in a long stretch and felt the refreshing results of having spent most of the weekend in bed. She looked at her clock and hopped out of bed.

It was time for Ellie Hart to go to work.

Also available from Vermilion

◇ The Gi Point Diet   0091900093   £7.99

◇ Intimate Solutions   0091891590   £9.99

◇ The Money Diet   0091894840   £7.99

◇ Stop Dreaming Start Living   0091894611   £8.99

◇ Weekend Life Coach   0091894689   £7.99

◇ Who Moved My Cheese? (paperback)   0091816971   £5.99
                                            (hardback)   0091883768   £9.99

FREE POSTAGE AND PACKING

Overseas customers allow £2.00 per paperback

BY PHONE: 01624 677237

BY POST: Random House Books
C/o Bookpost, PO Box 29, Douglas
Isle of Man, IM99 1BQ

BY FAX: 01624 670923

BY EMAIL: bookshop@enterprise.net

Cheques (payable to Bookpost) and credit cards accepted

Prices and availability subject to change without notice.
Allow 28 days for delivery.
When placing your order, please mention if you do not wish to
receive any additional information.

www.randomhouse.co.uk